Rayven's Keep

Kylie Wolfe

LYRICAL PRESS
Kensington Publishing Corp.
www.kensingtonbooks.com

Lyrical Press books are published by
Kensington Publishing Corp. 119 West 40th Street New York, NY 10018

First Electronic Edition: June 2013
eISBN-13: 978-1-61650-463-2
eISBN-10: 1-61650-229-0

First Print Edition: June 2013
ISBN-13: 978-1-61650-917-0
ISBN-10: 1-61650-917-1

Printed in the United States of America

Drugs, murder, conspiracy, and a headstrong heiress complicate his covert security mission.

Tru Creighton wants her wealthy and powerful family to take her seriously. Sneaking away to investigate bookkeeping discrepancies from one of their holdings seems the perfect opportunity to prove her worth. Stranded on a hostile planet with a price on her head, she seizes her one opportunity for survival.

Nick Rayven, determined to build his reputation and fledgling security company, doesn't flinch at difficult and dangerous missions. A former soldier and refugee from a war-demolished planet, he battles to create order and stifle his painful memories. His hard-won accomplishments are threatened when a spoiled heiress in danger awakens emotions he thought long gone.

Two people with plenty to prove risk everything to unravel their tangled missions. His sense of duty and vulnerable heart compel him to fight his growing attraction to her. Her heart demands she follow it straight into his arms. The people behind the conspiracy keeping them together and in harm's way have other ideas.

Books by Kylie Wolfe

Rayven's Keep

Published by Kensington Publishing Corporation

To my grandmother, Helen Brown
There are no words, only wonderful memories
I miss you

Acknowledgements

Every book starts with an idea, or in my case one sentence that sparks the story. Words tumble across the page giving life to the characters and their adventures until it reaches a satisfying conclusion. Writing is mostly a solitary activity, but a book is given added depth and made richer by those that help us along the way. Mine is no exception.

To Laurel Newberry, my critique partner and friend. Thank you for always being able to find the perfect word when I can't think of it, making sense of convoluted sentences and asking just the right questions to help me set the scene. I love Wednesday.

To Lisa, my sister and very first beta reader. I wasn't surprised by the fact you read my manuscript and never offered any criticism even though there was plenty of work left to do on my book. You are a wonderful sister who only sees the good!

To Julie Chaddock, thank you for taking the time to read my work and offer excellent feedback. I know this isn't a genre you usually embrace and the fact you did it for a complete stranger is incredible. Thank you! To Abby Rose, Thank you for aiding my recovery from adverb addiction and helping to make my story stronger.

To Penny Barber, Thank you for not giving up on me even when I was discouraged. Your editing has been extraordinary and I have learned how to be a better writer through your efforts.

To Louann, Kim, Sonny and Carol. Thank you for your genuine enthusiasm and letting me prattle on about my book – you rock!

And the biggest thank you to my incredible family for all the encouragement, tolerance when I got lost in my writing and being the best cheerleaders around. I love you guys!

Chapter 1

Nick Rayven hated Lodestone. The constant dust and fierce winds keeping it in semidarkness made his teeth itch. Hell, who was he kidding? He hated the whole damn planet. Whoever had come up with the name had a sick sense of humor and a distinct lack of imagination in calling both the port and planet the same. Far from a diamond in the rough, Lodestone was one miserable port of call on a thoroughly miserable world.

At least the hole-in-the-wall alehouse he found himself in had no such delusions of grandeur. He regarded the battered mug of local ale with distaste and slouched against the unforgiving metal of his chair. Hooking one arm across its back, he scrutinized the common room, noting the layout of every door and window, a habit that had saved his ass on more than one occasion. It was always good to know where the exits were just in case some idiot decided to start a fight.

Raised voices formed a raucous counterpoint to the hideous music piped through lousy speakers. The cacophony kept Nick irritated and on edge. He detested people, particularly in crowds, but his contact had insisted they meet here. Business was business and sometimes it required Nick to play nice and on someone else's turf.

He unclenched his jaw as he snagged his mug and took a long swallow. The sour taste burned all the way down, a caustic fire lacking any hint of civilization. So much for ordering the good stuff.

A furtive movement near the door caught his attention. The man entering the bar was average in height, with ordinary brown hair and nondescript brown clothes. Nick suspected his easy to forget appearance was deliberate, and his interest sharpened. Taking another sip of his ale, he watched the man inch closer, stopping a scant meter away.

"Nick Rayven?" The question was hesitant, the voice high pitched.

"Depends."

Nick studied the man in front of him and allowed a faint smile to curve his lips. Apparently, it was more predatory than friendly, and the other man flinched, eyes widening. Nick tried for non-threatening. Sweat broke out on the other man's forehead. Sighing, he gave up.

"Yeah, I'm Rayven. Who're you?"

"J—Jonas Spark." He cleared his throat and eased onto the seat across from Nick. "My employer, Axyl Hargrave, instructed me to deliver the package to you."

Straightening, Nick leaned his forearms on the metal table in front of him. "What of the payment arrangements? I assume the credits have been deposited into my account?"

Jonas nodded, his Adam's apple bobbing as he swallowed. "Half now, the...ah...balance when the package is delivered."

Nick swore viciously, the variety and virulence of the words demonstrating a fine command of the seedier side of several languages. Jonas shrank back in his chair. Some of the bar patrons glanced at them to see if a fight would break out but returned to their drinks when Nick did nothing more than glare.

"That was not the agreement," he ground out, when he trusted his voice.

"There has been a, ah, minor problem and a need to change the delivery destination. My b-boss is willing to double your fee for your trouble."

"What kind of minor problem?" Nick scowled.

Jonas opened and closed his mouth, but nothing came out. His eye twitched. It was obvious to Nick he would rather be anywhere but talking to him. Jonas took a deep breath before he plunged on, words tumbling over each other in his haste to deliver the message. "Our primary competitor suspects we have found something but doesn't know what we've discovered or where we found it. It is imperative we get this sample analyzed and our claim recorded before anyone else finds out what we have."

Jonas took a shaky breath and wiped sweat from his upper lip. He visibly wilted in his chair as Nick stared at him. "Mr. Hargrave wants this sample delivered to Dendera Labs on Kaydet within a standard-moon cycle." He pushed a small pouch across the table toward Nick.

Nick kept his eyes on Jonas rather than on the bag as he settled back in his seat to consider the offer. His company specialized in security, particularly escorting valuable or dangerous space cargo. Whatever the pouch contained must be valuable if Geotern Mining's owner, Axyl

Hargrave, wanted it delivered to one of Dendera's most remote labs. Obviously keeping their discovery secret was of primary concern.

This job represented his ticket to expand the business, move it from the fringes to a more lucrative prominence. Kaydet was a small, insignificant planet on the outer rim of the system and about as far from Lodestone as anyone could get. He would need to push hard to meet the deadline, but it wasn't impossible.

He nodded then drained his ale before he slammed the mug down. "Done." Amusement twitched at the corners of his mouth as Jonas yelped and jumped.

Nick lowered his voice to a gravelly menace. "You tell your boss this." Leaning forward, he pinned Jonas Spark with a look. "If he thinks to cheat me in any way I. Will. Hunt. Him. Down. All of the money in the universe won't be enough to protect him."

Nick released the seal of his jacket pocket and pulled out a small data drive. He keyed in a sequence of numbers and smiled at the influx of credits to his account. With skilled sleight-of-hand, he replaced the device and pocketed the small pouch.

Pushing back his chair, he stood and tilted his chin toward the empty container of ale. "Tell your boss thanks for the drink."

He didn't wait around for an answer.

As soon as he stepped outside, he knew it was time to go. Lodestone's weather was known to be volatile, restricting ship traffic with its violent and swift changing moods. Air transports crashed with alarming regularity, driven to ground by savage winds and poor visibility. Pilots demanded hazard pay whenever they landed here, which made for a profitable run that was almost worth the risks involved. Nick had built his business by taking calculated risks and the extra credits were a welcome bonus.

A severe dust storm warning had flashed to all pilots before Jonas Spark had arrived, and time was in short supply if Nick had a prayer of getting off this rock before being grounded for the storm's duration. Nothing was guaranteed to piss him off more.

With ground-eating strides, he hurried through the narrow streets toward the spaceport and his waiting ship. Squat buildings sat crowded shoulder-to-shoulder in the deserted industrial area he passed through. Dust devils wobbled drunkenly out of the narrow alleyways driven by the brutal winds that would soon be scouring the pitted surfaces of the buildings with gritty debris.

Glow lights powered up as he reached the last row of buildings, providing dim beacons against the encroaching gloom. The red orb passing for a sun on this world offered little warmth to the inhabitants mining the planet. Now, it was barely visible through the dust cloud. It was no accident most activity occurred underground. People only lived on the surface because it was necessary if they catered to ship traffic.

Nick was being followed and had been since he'd left the alehouse. It could be a coincidence they were going in the same direction through a derelict district at the same time, but Nick wasn't a big believer in coincidence. In addition to the unpredictable weather, Lodestone had a nasty reputation as a violent town. It was a safe bet the footsteps echoing behind him were more than another pilot with the same destination in mind. Robberies were common and transport pilots a favorite target, another reason most sane pilots avoided the place. Nick Rayven had no intention of becoming a Lodestone statistic.

Taking advantage of shadows between two buildings, he ducked out of sight, blending into the darkness. A gasp, barely audible over the wind gusts pinpointed his follower's position.

He didn't have long to wait before the huddled shape reached his hiding place. Nick threw a lightning-fast punch. The figure crumpled to the ground in a boneless heap. Shaking his knuckles he winced at the sting, glad he hadn't needed to use his blaster. He didn't need any more complications. Disgusted anyone would dare consider him a target, he contemplated the unconscious form and debated his options. Either desperation or stupidity had sent the youth after him. Regardless, Nick needed to deal with the situation and quickly. By his estimation, he only had a narrow window of time left if he wanted to get off this planet before the port was locked down.

Under normal conditions, he would prefer to tie up his stalker and leave him for the authorities to find, but the storm's momentum was building at a deadly pace. Grit boiled across Lodestone's surface, stabbing exposed skin and making it difficult to breathe. It would be certain death to leave anyone outside and unprotected during the planet-scouring devil screaming mercilessly across its surface.

"Damn it," he muttered. With aching fingers, he retrieved the narrow cord he kept in his utility belt. Squatting, he made short work of securing the slender wrists behind the other's back. Time enough, once on board, to get to the bottom of this without the worry of being grounded on Lodestone. If he didn't like the answers, it would be easy enough to toss the bastard out the airlock. A clean and speedy end to a problem. The idea had merit as a threat, if nothing else.

He grunted as he hauled the limp body over his shoulder. He sprinted toward his ship, grateful his burden didn't weigh much.

The *Messenger* was a small, ugly transport much like every other ship on the docking pad. He'd flown this one to his rendezvous counting on its very similarity to others to keep his presence concealed. Nick shifted his captive to sit a little more securely on his shoulder before pressing his palm against the security pad, begrudging the seconds it took to verify his identity. The door opened and a boarding ramp extended. Welcoming lights flickered on in the interior as he entered. He turned and hit the keypad, sealing the door behind him.

The cargo area to his left would hold his captive until he was off-world and had time to figure out why he'd been followed. Nick dumped his burden onto a pile of heavy covers behind a cargo net. He nudged the body with his booted foot. When there were no signs of returning consciousness, he shrugged. Not willing to waste any more time, he locked the cargo door behind him and loped toward the main cabin.

He skirted the small crew quarters and entered the bridge. Strapping in, he initiated the launch request to the port tower. He coughed metallic dust from his lungs as he tapped on the arm of his chair and waited for clearance. Every little delay and redundant launch protocol demanded by the tower increased his irritation. Powerful blasts of wind buffeted his ship, debris thumping against its exterior as he ran through another system check. How friggin' long would it take to gain clearance to leave Lodestone? He snapped his responses to the tower drone while he kept a wary eye on the storm.

Authorization lit the onboard computer screen. The ship's engines thrummed with building power readying for departure. Nick punched in the final coordinates and sank into his seat, braced for the bone-jarring force of liftoff. His ship bucked hard, fighting the planet's gravity and the turbulent storm doing its best to ground him. He adjusted his trajectory as the planet's atmosphere released the ship and reached the cold expanse of space. He relaxed into weightlessness and grinned when the artificial grav force kicked in.

Nick unbuckled his chair harness, leaned back in his seat and stretched. He rolled his shoulders and muscles popped as tension released. Fatigued, he rubbed grit from dry eyes and scratched the itchy, rough stubble along his jaw. He felt like hell and probably looked worse, but it was an unavoidable consequence of pushing himself so hard.

He levered himself out of his chair and headed toward the crew quarters. Once away from the helm, he brushed the worst of the dust from his clothing. He removed the small pouch from his pocket and stored it in a hidden compartment for safekeeping. Time to wake up his unwanted guest and get some answers.

* * * *

Tru Creighton regained consciousness slowly. She felt like she had been hit with a mining hammer. It was the only explanation for the ferocious headache pounding behind her tightly closed eyes. Her limbs felt heavy, weighted down by an unnatural pressure, and she frowned trying to figure out why. *Grav force.* Which could only mean she was on board a ship.

The odd thrumming of a powerful engine beneath her ear provided another clue she was off-world. While that sank in she struggled to put more pieces together. Her last clear memory was of trailing the large man moving like a shadow through the storm. She prayed she hadn't made a mistake because if he wasn't Nick Rayven, her chances for survival were close to nil. A shiver raced up her spine.

She tried to sit up, gasping as glass-sharp needles of pain shot through her abused skull and shoulders. Her hands were bound behind her back and no amount of struggle would release them. Tru panted through the pain and took stock of her surroundings. Information meant the difference between remaining alive and the alternative. She was all about surviving.

The soft whoosh of the door opening froze her in place. She closed her eyes to mere slits. Buying some time, she feigned unconsciousness.

Large, booted feet stopped in front of her and Tru's heart danced a spastic tango against her rib cage. If the size of the feet were any indication, her captor was a big man, and she was in serious trouble.

"I know you're awake. No use pretending." His voice was flat, cold.

A scarred, calloused hand grabbed her nearest arm and yanked her to her feet. Tru bit back a groan and tried to wrench her arm out of the implacable grip. Dizzy and fighting nausea from the foolhardy action, she prayed she wouldn't throw up. Sweat trickled from under her cap and stung her eyes. Perhaps it hadn't been the best idea to follow him after all. Maybe he wasn't the kind of man she'd imagined when searching through the data files. Reality painted a much different picture, one with wide brush strokes of barely-contained power and potential violence. He was much bigger up close than he had looked from her hiding place near the alehouse.

Much bigger. Angry. Too bad she hadn't considered that possibility when she'd hatched her desperate plan to escape Lodestone.

His silent regard stretched her nerves until she wanted to collapse into a whimpering heap on the floor. Deep-rooted determination locked her knees, but couldn't prevent the unsteady sway of her body. Mouth dry, unable to think, she kept her head lowered and waited. What else could she do?

"Give me one good reason why I shouldn't jettison you into space without a suit."

Horror snapped her head up. Chills sprinted along her skin, tightening muscles already trembling with too much adrenaline. Her lungs labored to draw her next breath. His eyes widened, then narrowed as he searched her face. Tru guessed her disguise was blown.

"Sonofabitch," he snarled. "Who the hell are you?"

"I c-can explain. G-give me a minute." She swallowed hard. The only thing keeping her upright was his iron grip on her arm

"Barf on my boots and I'll throw you out the nearest air lock."

Tru didn't doubt for a minute he would do as he threatened. She nodded and sucked in deep breaths, willing her stomach to settle. With her vision still blurred from the blow to her head, she fought to bring his face into focus, and then wished she hadn't succeeded.

"Well?" he demanded.

Words failed her. The dark cavern of her mind only echoed with the roar of the headache pummeling her brain like a punch-drunk miner. A quick, hard shake from Nick did little to help, nor did the potent curse he uttered when she lost her balance and fell against him.

A strong arm clamped around her back, giving her the opportunity to find her footing. Unable to do anything else, she rested her aching head against his hard chest and closed her eyes. Weariness dragged at her as the shock and fear from the past few days drained away. She trembled in his embrace and hated her weakness.

Nick Rayven had a reputation as a dangerous man to cross, but her careful inquiries had also shown him to be fair and well respected. She was betting her life on it. He was her best shot at getting out of the mess she'd found herself in. That is, if she could persuade him he needed to help her. A big if at the moment. Gathering herself, she straightened and pulled away.

It wasn't easy meeting his eyes. Somewhere in her mind it registered they were brown, but there was no warmth in their depths. Intense, missing nothing, his sharp regard made her squirm. When he pulled a knife from his boot, her luck might have just run out.

She opened her mouth to scream. Nothing came out but a mewling squeak. She jerked in his hold, but he tightened his grip until her shoulder felt as if it was being crushed. Heart racing, barely able to breathe through the panic constricting her throat, she shut her eyes and waited for the end. Awareness narrowed to a pinprick concentrated on the man in front of her. He stepped closer and she was surrounded by the heat of his body, heard his inhale and felt the brush of displaced air when his arm moved. She gulped a breath, drew in the taste of her own fear.

Time slowed and stretched each second into a lifetime. Nothing happened.

She peeked from one eye, wondering if her cowering posture had stopped him. "What are you waiting for? Go ahead and kill me. It isn't as if you're the only one trying."

"You aren't worth killing, little girl." Contempt spiked his voice and she cringed. "But if that was my intent, I wouldn't use a knife. I'd have to clean up the mess and that would just piss me off. If you want your hands free, it's faster to cut the ties." He shifted his grip on the knife and slashed the bindings around her wrists.

Her numb arms flopped to her sides and she sucked in a breath. Why was she still alive? Pathetically grateful, she turned, took a wobbling step and swayed.

"Now then. Who the hell are you?" Nick barked.

"Tru. Tru Creighton." Feeling began to return to her arms and razor-edged needles of agony shot from her shoulders to her fingertips, pulsing with the pounding in her head. She clenched and unclenched her fists, desperate for relief. Tears sprang to her eyes and she blinked rapidly to prevent them from falling.

"Okay, Tru Creighton." Nick enunciated her name as if he doubted she was who she claimed to be. "Why don't you explain why you followed me and we'll take it from there. I'm warning you, I'd better like the answers."

"No need to be snide. I'll get to it." She lifted her chin and scowled in his general direction, not quite daring to meet his eyes before looking away.

Silence stretched between them while she stalled. Intimidated and trying not to show it, Tru rubbed her wrists. Unable to stop herself, she stole a glance at him, stunned to see something perilously close to a grin and all coherent thought fled. Gathering her scattered wits, she tried again. "I...ah...need your help," she whispered.

He raised an eyebrow, his expression mocking.

Her spirits sank further. "I can pay."

Nick crossed his arms over his broad chest and snorted. "You don't look like you have two credits to rub together to me."

Her shoulders slumped. Nothing was going the way she planned. Licking dry lips, she stared into Nick's hard face. "Please."

Chapter 2

Nick rubbed his jaw and considered his unwanted passenger. The last thing he needed was to be saddled with another problem, and Tru Creighton had trouble written all over her. She also looked ready to collapse. He guessed sheer determination kept her on her feet. Weighing his options, he eyed his captive and blew out a breath.

"I'm guessing you have a hell of a headache," he said, careful to bury any sympathy deep enough she couldn't see it. Her bulky clothing had done a good job of hiding her gender, but it rankled that he hadn't suspected she was a woman right away. "Just be glad I decided you were too small a target to use the blaster on or the authorities on Lodestone would still be picking up pieces. You're damn lucky you got out of this with only a headache."

Nick watched her grapple with the ramifications, half expecting her to back down or apologize for her stupidity.

She raised her chin and said, "It's illegal to carry weapons in Lodestone. Off-worlders have to leave them at the spaceport before they can go into town. It is strictly enforced."

Instead, she'd seized on the one piece of information she must have thought would give her a moral high ground.

"You don't say," Nick drawled and relaxed back against the bulkhead, holding her gaze.

No point in telling her he was licensed on numerous worlds to carry weapons. He would hate to ruin the indignation sparking in her blue eyes, replacing the fear. Her fear bothered him. Hell, there was a lot about her bothering him, like how even dirty, bedraggled and swaying on her feet she managed to look cute. He didn't like the fact he noticed.

Nick shrugged, as if weapon laws mattered little to him, leaving no doubt he made his own rules. He watched her bite back any further comments and approved her caution in keeping her mouth shut.

"Wise move," he said as he turned and headed for the door. He stopped in the entrance and glanced over his shoulder. "Come on. I'll get you something for your headache, unless you plan to stay in the cargo hold."

Tru scurried out of the cargo bay. She gave him as wide a berth as the space allowed and waited while he closed the door. She winced with each step, and Nick remembered all too clearly the pain that battered a skull thanks to a concussion. She squinted through watering eyes as she entered the bright crew bay.

"Sit," he ordered. With a jerk of his thumb, he indicated the small table and chairs to his right. "I'll check the MedKit for something for your headache. Then we can talk, or rather, you can talk. I want to know what was worth risking your life to get my attention."

* * * *

Tru sank onto the chair, folded her arms on the tabletop and dropped her aching head onto her arms. Her wool cap itched, but she didn't have the energy to remove it. She'd been running scared for several days and didn't care if her stomach chose that moment to rumble with hunger. What was one more humiliation?

"Here." Nick's tone was rough, but not unkind, as he placed a metal cylinder of water and a 'gesic packet on the table. "I hear this stuff works quickly."

She eyed the offering for a moment, straightened and reached for the cup. The cold liquid soothed her parched throat and revived her spirits just a little. She tore open the packet, removed the 'gesic strip and placed it on her tongue to dissolve. Immediately her headache eased, and she sighed. Her eyes fluttered closed as she rolled the water cylinder against the throbbing bruise on her temple, appreciating the chill against her tender flesh. Opening her eyes, she murmured her thanks and offered a tentative smile.

Nick spun his chair around and straddled it. He looped his arms across its back. She couldn't help but notice the muscles in his thighs or the strength in his forearms where he pushed up his jacket sleeves. Her gaze wandered over his broad chest and shoulders and up to the scowling man looking back at her.

She wouldn't say he was classically handsome, but something about him drew her. Part of her interest stemmed from preliminary research she'd done a month ago on his business for her grandfather. If she were being honest about it she would have to admit to being fascinated with Nick ever since.

Studying his face, she wondered why she found him so appealing. He had high, flat cheekbones, a firm jaw and a hard mouth, with the bottom lip fuller than the top. It wasn't a mouth given much to smiling, but she would bet her last credit when he did smile it would be devastating. Thick lashes framed deep-set brown eyes and a small crescent-shaped scar cut through the corner of his left eyebrow. He had a strong face, world weary and harsh in its beauty.

Uncompromising. The reality of Nick Rayven was so much more than the image she'd studied. The sheer force of his personality weakened her knees.

"Looked your fill yet?"

The heat of a blush climbed her cheeks and she lowered her eyes. She placed the water cylinder back on the table, removed her cap and dropped it on the table. Running her fingers through sweat-dampened hair she tried to restore it to some order. His somber scrutiny was unnerving, and she dropped her hands to her lap, clutching them together to still the tremor in her fingers.

"I cut my hair to try to pass for a mining apprentice," she explained.

Normally she wasn't too concerned with her appearance, but Nick's cool regard made her nervous and aware of her present state. Feeling grubby and unattractive, she wished she'd kept her mouth shut when he flashed a ghost of a smile.

"I didn't have much time so I know it's cut badly. I had to use a knife of all things. I must look a fright. I rubbed dirt on my face to look like I'd just gotten off shift and I borrowed, um, stole these clothes, since mine were a dead giveaway."

Tru raised tear-drenched eyes to his and bit her bottom lip. "I didn't know what else to do," she whispered.

She wasn't making sense, didn't understand why her badly cut hair and ugly clothes seemed more important than anything else at the moment. They just were. Her emotions stayed too close to the surface, overriding everything else.

Reaching for the water to give herself something to do, she inadvertently knocked it over. Water cascaded across the tabletop, over the edge, and onto her lap. Jumping up from the chair proved a mistake as blood drained from her head. Black spots danced before her eyes and her knees gave way. She swayed, but before she collapsed, Nick caught her and lowered her to her seat. His large, strong hands gently pushed her head between her knees.

"Take slow breaths until you don't feel so lightheaded before you try to sit back up," he ordered, crouching beside her chair.

Embarrassed, she nodded, gripping the chair edge with shaking fingers. When the dizziness passed, she sat up, blinking to clear the grey tunneling her vision. He thrust the rescued container of water toward her and she automatically took it.

"Drink."

Tru brought the cylinder to her mouth and drank what remained.

"Feel better?" He rose, and went back to his seat.

Without looking at him, she nodded slowly, unwilling to make any sudden moves. She flinched, but held her ground when Nick lifted her chin. His calloused fingers warmed the skin along her jaw and she suppressed a shiver. This more compassionate side of Nick increased her growing attraction to him.

"When was the last time you ate or slept?" he asked.

Tru raised her eyes to meet his. Caught by his intense gaze, she couldn't look away until he dropped her chin and put a little distance between them. Rocking back in his chair, he crossed his arms and frowned. Whether he was irritated at himself or her, she didn't know.

"The day before yesterday...I think. I've been hiding, waiting for an opportunity to get away from Lodestone." Drained, she propped her elbows on the table and cradled the cylinder of water between them.

"And I was the opportunity. I could have proven worse than what you were running from, so what made you decide I was the best avenue for escape?" An unmistakable warning pervaded his tone. "Don't even think about lying either. I want the truth."

She bit her bottom lip. Nerves drove her heart rate up a notch. "I was desperate and trapped on Lodestone. I thought you looked like someone who might help, who could be trusted." She glanced at him. "I still don't know if I made the right choice."

Nick's mouth tightened.

Her simplistic answer wouldn't satisfy him for long. Whatever he thought was well hidden, but he didn't press for more. She was grateful.

"It must be your lucky day then. You're aboard my ship, the *Messenger*, and I'm Nick Rayven. Currently, we're headed to my home world of Alludra. Got a problem with that?"

"No, none at all. Thank you." She breathed her first easy breath in days.

He pushed out of his chair and rummaged in the food storage unit until he found a meal packet. He popped it into the heater, warmed it, then plopped it in front of Tru.

"Eat." He headed to the bridge, leaving her alone.

She waited, but he didn't return, so she relaxed enough to shrug off her outer coat and drape it over the back of her chair. It was a relief to remove the heavy garment. She would have liked to remove the work jacket she wore under it as well, but wasn't quite up to the task. Instead, she turned her attention to the foil packet in front of her and inhaled. It smelled like heaven, better than any gourmet meal she'd ever eaten.

She couldn't open it fast enough. She barely tasted the first few bites, but once her initial hunger eased, she slowed down and savored the food. She wouldn't turn her nose up at a prepackaged meal ever again. Finishing off the meal, she kept one eye out for the man who held her fate in his hands. Her gamble had paid off and she'd escaped Lodestone, but she might have just jumped from the fat to the fire.

* * * *

Nick listened to her quiet movements with half an ear. He wasn't without sympathy, although he did his best to hide it. Obviously, she was up to her pretty little neck in some kind of trouble. Whatever her problems, he had no intention of getting involved. He'd drop her off at the nearest city and let her fend for herself. What happened beyond that was of no interest to him. He had bigger problems to worry about.

The last minute change in delivery plans by Geotern Mining worried him. Why was it necessary to travel all the way to Kaydet instead of the original drop off on his home world? Dendera Labs had many outposts, but Kaydet lay way off the beaten path. If Geotern Mining was in such a hurry to register its find, then it made no sense to add so much travel time.

Nothing would be gained by brooding so Nick ambled back to the crew quarters to check on Tru. She slept at the table with her head pillowed on folded arms, the remnants of her meal pushed to one side. She looked vulnerable and young. Long lashes left crescent shadows against her cheek and the paleness of her skin highlighted the darkened bruise on her temple. It had not been one of his finer moments and guilt twisted his gut. He could do nothing about it now. Time would tell what trouble Tru Creighton was in and until she told him the whole of it, he would bide his time and reserve judgment.

He lifted her easily and carried her to one of the bunks bolted to the wall. She slept deeply without stirring when moved. Placing one knee on the pliant surface he shifted her against his chest one armed while he unbuttoned and removed her work jacket. He tossed it to the foot of the bunk and then removed her boots, letting them drop to the floor with a soft, metallic thud. He opted to leave the remainder of her clothing alone.

He got his MedKit and then did a quick scan using the portable MedScan. It showed her vitals were good, and her concussion nothing to worry about. She'd dropped into a restorative sleep. Some of the tension eased out of his shoulders as he put the device away.

Restless, he cleaned up the table then paced to the bridge to double check the coordinates. He settled into his chair and ran a long-range perimeter sweep to look for anything out of the ordinary, a habit ingrained from years in the military. Satisfied no one followed, he initiated a random scan program, and then pulled up a haloviz screen to do a little research on his sleeping guest.

His business relied on information and he was an expert at finding deep wells of it. All his ships were retrofitted with specialized, proprietary equipment, which interfaced with databanks scattered across the solar system. It gave him a competitive and personal edge, particularly since the technology was from his home world and not available on the open market. The beauty of it was even if someone did manage to steal it, it would be useless unless they understood the language of Tonlith. The likelihood was remote; few had escaped the planet's destruction.

Nick was no fool and always judicious in his use of his technology. He made sure he didn't trigger any warnings or leave a trace of his inquiries behind. It didn't take long to find the information he sought.

Her family had offered a reward for her safe return. Escaping family was common enough, but whatever had her fleeing seemed more complicated than family problems. His mouth tightened in a jaw-popping clench as he read about the reward offered for information on him. Tru Creighton had better have a good explanation. How in the hell had his name become linked with hers in the Alert Notice?

Scowling, he slumped back in his chair, going over the events of the day, scouring his memory for any detail he might have missed. He'd been careful, respecting his client's request for secrecy. The only one to follow him back to his ship had been Tru. He was certain of that. With no witness to their "interaction," there was no discernible reason for their names to be connected, no reason for anyone to think they might travel together. None. Nothing quite added up, and he didn't like loose ends.

The connection might have come from her, but there was another possibility. A firm believer in going to the source, Nick shifted into a more comfortable position and delved into the particulars of Lodestone

Mining Consortium, a fierce competitor of Geotern. He followed poorly hidden threads and traced the Alert to them.

Companies had been known to go to great lengths to undercut a competitor. Using a young woman to steal information or goods was nothing new. Having him arrested on a kidnapping charge would prevent him filing Geotern's claim and give Lodestone the opportunity to swoop in and stake their own. He didn't like the thought of being played, but there wasn't much he could do about it until he talked further with Tru.

His hand hovered over the keypad while he debated his next move. A grim smile curved his mouth, and he shifted his shoulders in response to the familiar visceral thrill of the chase. Leaning forward, Nick began the tedious job of opening a back door into Lodestone Mining's databanks. The reverberation of the ship's engine and creak of his leather chair faded into the background. Even the annoying blue backlight on the helm console was only a minor distraction.

The final sequence of code launched, taking with it the urgency that had kept him working. He'd be warned if anyone accessed the data he'd just manipulated. Input of his name or Tru's would start a catastrophic wipe of information. The "records" would download to his data storage for safekeeping, which afforded him a great deal of satisfaction. Two could play at this game and Nick always played for keeps.

He'd done all he could for the moment. It had been a hell of a day and he still wasn't sure what to do about Tru Creighton or Lodestone Mining. Relaxing his neck and shoulders, he slouched comfortably in his chair and gazed out the ship's viewscreen.

Space fascinated him, its vastness humbling and exciting. It was the reason he'd been an eager recruit for Tonlith's space military and had shot up through the ranks. There hadn't been a machine on Tonlith he couldn't fly. Nothing he couldn't push to its limits and make sing.

A decorated warrior, he'd been one of the best fighter pilots around, but in the end no amount of talent could have prevented what happened. He'd watched his world burn, helpless to do anything about it. It was something indelibly etched in his mind and heart.

His pleasant lethargy vanished, replaced by the all too familiar rigidity of muscles holding emotions at bay. Teeth gritted so hard his jaw ached was just punishment, in his mind, for allowing himself to think about Tonlith and the horrors of war. Nick didn't often let thoughts of his past intrude, preferring to keep that part of his life where it belonged. Shut away. His memories of the war buried deep. It was the only way he continued to move forward.

The crackle of the ship's communication frequency snapped his attention back to the present. Scooting upright, he hit the console to open the secured channel.

"Rayven here." His voice a rough growl, the gravel undertones pushed through his tight throat like granite cracking under brutal pressure.

"Whoa, what flew up your ass?" Seth Mandekor responded. "Is there a problem, boss?"

"Yeah, there's a slight change of plans. I'm headed back to base."

"The cargo?"

"On board, along with an unexpected guest. I'll explain when I get back." Nick rubbed the back of his neck, kneading knotted muscles.

"Do you want special accommodations for our guest?" Seth asked.

Nick frowned. Seth alluded to the secured rooms located below ground. "No. I don't think she's dangerous."

"She?"

The one word held plenty of interest and speculation, which Nick chose to ignore. "For now I need you to keep a tight rein on my recent whereabouts. If anyone gets curious make sure they hear I was somewhere other than Lodestone."

"Sure, no problem. Now what about your passenger?"

Nick severed the link.

In a black mood, he wandered to the crew quarters to check on his sleeping "guest". She hadn't moved, her slight form barely visible under the covering. He studied her for a moment. What had she gotten him into?

He crossed to the food unit, snagged a hot drink, and stood sipping it in brooding silence. Amazing, how his day had turned to shit when he landed on Lodestone. He would have some answers before he returned to base.

After draining his cup, Nick placed it in the scrubber and then headed to the tiny shower cleanser. He wanted to remove as much of Lodestone's pervasive dust as possible. The cleanser would do an adequate job, but he really wanted to spend time under the water spray at home, letting the bad memories and grime wash away in the warm slide of the water on his skin. He'd have to make do with the ship's accommodations for now.

Feeling better, he dressed in loose drawstring pants and considered putting on a loose shirt for the sake of modesty. "Screw it," he muttered under his breath, tossed the shirt aside and headed to his bunk. He stretched out, folded his arms behind his head and stared at the metal grillwork of the ceiling while he listened to the thrum of the ship's engines. He'd pushed hard to get to Lodestone to secure the job. This should have been an easy run with a healthy influx of credits to show for his time. Instead he was stuck with unwanted company and unanswered questions.

Grunting, disgusted with the events of the day and his black temper, he rolled onto his side, his back to Tru, and willed himself to sleep.

Chapter 3

A hand on his arm jerked Nick awake, heart pounding in his throat as screams echoed from the nightmare. Instinctively, he exploded off the bed, and shoved the figure bending over him against the bulkhead with enough force to expel a whoosh of air against his face. Adrenaline thundered through his veins, tightening muscles to steel. He rammed a forearm against a soft throat and leaned his full weight against the smaller body trying to buck him off. It took a moment for him to shake off the effects of his dream and recognize Tru making gurgling noises as she struggled to move his arm off her neck. Huge blue eyes, darkened almost to black, stared back at him.

Lightning fast, he released her, stepped back and ran a shaking hand through his short hair.

"What kind of fucking idiot sneaks up on a sleeping man?" he roared, more shaken than he cared to admit. He hadn't been in control of his actions. "I could have killed you. Sonofabitch!"

Needing physical release, he punched the steel locker compartment nearest him. He didn't feel the pain as his knuckles split.

It gave him little satisfaction when Tru jumped. He kept his distance as she rubbed her neck and slid as far away from him as possible in the confined space. Nick hadn't been gentle and she'd be sporting a new set of bruises by morning.

"I'm s-sorry," she croaked. Clearing her throat, she turned her head away, making him all too aware of the fury pouring off him in waves.

He fought for calm.

"You were moaning in your sleep. I thought only to wake you to see if you were ill."

He dropped his head, closed his eyes, and took several deep breaths to gain control of himself. Opening his eyes, he took a good look at Tru, huddled on the bunk, her back to the wall and her knees drawn up to her chest. She didn't meet his gaze, but her mouth was set in mutinous lines. He was surprised she wasn't crying. Obviously, she was made of sterner stuff.

He made an effort to gentle his voice. "I'm rarely ill."

No doubt about it, she was a mess. Not only did the right side of her face sport a nasty bruise, complete with a black eye, but now her throat showed marks of their most recent clash. He wasn't the kind of man who enjoyed hurting women. For the most part, he respected and liked them. He enjoyed intimacy with them. So, hurting her, even though it hadn't been deliberate, embarrassed and disturbed him. Dishonorable in his mind.

Crouching in front of the bunk brought them eye level, and he sought her gaze, holding it with the sheer power of his will. The skin around his eyes felt tight and he clenched his teeth until they hurt. A headache pounded behind his eyes.

"Don't...don't *ever* do that again. You're just lucky to escape with only a few bruises to add to your collection. You could be dead. Do I make myself clear?"

She might not like it, but she was smart enough to nod. Frustration, anger with himself and the residual echo of helplessness from his nightmare made him wonder what possessed her to believe she would be safer with him than taking her chances on Lodestone. At the moment, he felt like a very poor bargain.

Too many sickening memories crowded his mind, echoes from a past he tried to forget. He'd seen too much death and devastation during the war on Tonlith and the old, helpless rage burned like vitriol through his bloodstream, putting him on edge. It had been a mistake to think about the past earlier, and he had paid the expected price for his foolishness. Unfortunately, he hadn't been the only victim. He hadn't had a nightmare this bad in a long time.

Nick rose from his crouch and went to a cabinet to remove a compress. Twisting it released the gas inside and instantly cooled the slick material. He handed it to Tru and she pressed it against the tender skin on her throat.

He waited, giving her time to gather herself. No matter how she tried, she couldn't avoid him for long. If nothing else, curiosity would eventually get the best of her.

"What?" she snapped.

She seemed mad at herself for losing the silent battle of wills. He couldn't blame her for refusing to look at him, but when she raised her chin to glare at him, he knew she was a fighter. For some reason he felt the stirrings of perverse admiration in the face of her dogged determination.

"We have not gotten off to a good start, Tru Creighton, and I still do not know what you want from me or what you're running from," he said gruffly. "But, I swear I do not mean to hurt you and I regret you have been injured in my care."

For an apology, it wasn't bad. Stilted, but not bad. Threads of anger still wove their way through the words, but they were sincere. He wasn't much for apologizing at the best of times, but it was important to him she understood he didn't mean to hurt her.

Not knowing what to expect, it still caught him by surprise when the starch went out of her and she wilted against the wall behind her. She started to shake. He'd seen it often enough in battle to realize she'd reached an emotional overload and couldn't take much more. He experienced an uncomfortable flash of panic while his mind grappled with what he should do in the face of one small female falling apart. Men he could deal with; women were ever a mystery. In his limited experience, telling her to pull herself together would solve nothing and, quite possibly, make everything worse.

"I need your help. I'm in so much trouble and I...I don't know what to do. I'm so afraid." She dropped her forehead onto her raised knees and wrapped her arms around them. Deep shudders wracked her body. "Please," she begged in a whisper, "please."

She looked so small and defenseless curled in on herself, and he was so screwed. If he were honest with himself, he had been since their first meeting. He didn't want to bring trouble into his life but was helpless to turn her away.

Nick eased onto the bunk beside her and awkwardly patted her shoulder, offering rough comfort. He grunted when she threw herself into his arms. Instinctively, he wrapped them around her and cradled her close, his chin resting on the top of her head. Silky curls caught on the whiskers on his jaw and he sucked in a deep breath. He was surprised his body responded to the warm weight he held. It had been a while since he'd felt the stirrings of desire, and he shifted to ease his discomfort.

He held her while she wept on his shoulder. Held her until the tremors quit shaking her small frame and she finally leaned, spent, against him. As she stirred, he released her. Didn't comment when she placed a hand against the bare skin over his heart, although it shocked him nearly speechless. She looked up at him with tear-drenched eyes and Nick raised a finger to catch a drop as it slid down her cheek. What the hell had just happened? Off balance, he stood up and moved to the bunk across from her. It was unnerving to acknowledge he needed the distance between them, no matter how small.

"What are you running from, Tru?" he asked with a resigned sigh. He had some of the pieces, but he still hadn't figured out a lot. He saw her weighing her words, deciding just how much to trust him.

"Have you heard of Creighton Mutual?" She wiped wetness from her cheeks with the heels of her hands.

He froze at the name of the largest and most prestigious investment company on three worlds. Hell, he'd even put some of his hard-earned credits in the multiple businesses falling under Creighton's banner.

"Of course," he replied dryly. "Who hasn't?" There had been no mention of her connection to Creighton Mutual, not surprising if someone wanted to keep pertinent pieces of information buried. Regardless, he should have made the connection when doing his research. He must have been more tired than he'd thought, to have missed it.

She sniffed and cleared her throat. "My family owns Creighton. More specifically, my grandfather." Her voice was a little hoarse, but steady. "Most of my family is involved in the business one way or another and I'm no exception."

"If that's the case, then what were you doing in a backwater like Lodestone?" He watched her expression change and mentally ran down the information he'd discovered. "And," he continued, "I would think a family with the kind of associations yours has wouldn't allow one of their daughters to rub elbows with the kind of people blowing into a mining town. It is too dangerous. Hell, I would think the only thing required of you would be to marry the right person and further the aspirations of your family."

He knew he'd hit a nerve when she stiffened and shot him a resentful look.

"I have one of the best educations money can buy. I speak four languages fluently and have a mind of my own. A mind my family doesn't want me to use. I'm not like my sister. I want more from life than being an ornament on some man's arm. To be paraded about when it suits him. Or to be stuck in some corner office with a meaningless title while others do the work."

"So you ran off to Lodestone, of all places. Smart."

Two spots of color bloomed on her pale cheeks. "You don't understand!"

"Then enlighten me." Angry all over again, he stood and paced the small confines between the two bunks. "What in the four corners of hell were you doing in Lodestone? What kind of trouble are you in, little girl? Why would you think it wise to ask me for help?" Nick thumped his bare chest for emphasis and she jumped. "You don't know me. I might be worse than what you are running from. Did you stop to consider that?"

"I researched you," she answered in a small voice.

Nick stopped and turned to face her. She'd shocked him and not in a good way. Folding his arms over his chest, he braced his legs apart and scowled. A muscle jumped in his cheek. "You researched me?"

"Yes," she squeaked. Ducking her head, she plucked at a loose thread on her shirt. "You have to understand, I was desperate. I was trapped and I needed to get off Lodestone. I needed to get home. Everything I read indicated you could be trusted and when I saw you I chose to believe it."

"And, what pray tell, did you learn?" He was amazed he sounded so calm, almost conversational.

Tru scooted to the edge of the bed. She stood and slowly eased around him, away from the wall, her back to the open area. Maybe it hadn't occurred to her yet there was nowhere to run on the ship.

He raised an eyebrow and forced himself to keep his arms crossed over his chest. "I look like I can be trusted. Interesting. You got all that from a haloviz and a search on my name."

"N-no. I...ah...looked up your business records and noticed you have a good reputation for...um...being honest in your...in your business practices." She backed up another step.

He shook his head and huffed. He shouldn't have been surprised she would have access to some of his information, as he'd made a name for himself. He'd manipulated most of the available data on himself and the information was innocuous at best.

"I see. And how did you know I'd be on Lodestone? The trip was privately negotiated between Axyl Hargrave, the head of Geotern, and me. I didn't know what day I was going to be there. So how did you?" He stepped toward her and she stepped back.

"I d-didn't. Not really. I was looking for a way off-world and when I saw you I thought I'd found it," she said, staring at her feet.

"Warning. Warning. Captain report to bridge." The tinny sound of the ship's computer announced their approach to Alludra.

Needing to get to the controls, Nick grabbed Tru by her upper arms and moved her out of his way. He ignored her protests and strode to the helm console.

Sliding into his chair, he punched in landing coordinates to his private dock. He would have just enough time to dress before their final approach. He closed his eyes and pinched the bridge of his nose. He had a bad feeling about the situation he found himself in and his intuition was usually right on the money. Damn it.

Grimly, he opened a channel and let Seth know when to expect them. He kept the conversation brief, shut down the com, and returned to the crew quarters to dress for arrival. He wasn't paying attention to his surroundings as he grabbed his clothes and started to undo his sleeping pants. A small, sharp inhalation recalled Tru's presence. Swearing, he slammed into the cleanser room and banged elbows and knees trying to dress in the cramped space. His mood didn't improve when he emerged to see Tru once again wedged in a corner of her bunk.

"This conversation isn't finished, Tru. Not by a long shot. Lucky for you, I don't have time to continue verbally sparring with you." He searched her face, noting her mutinous expression. He took a slow, deep breath and let it out before he sat on the edge of his bunk to pull on his knee-high boots. "You will tell me what I want to know, make no mistake. Next time there won't be anything interrupting. In the meantime, you will be my guest while I figure out what I'm going to do with you."

Some of the tension left her shoulders, although her expression didn't change. He stood up and faced her, holding out a hand to help her move from her corner. She hesitated before she placed her hand in his, and he deliberately kept his clasp loose. Her cold fingers trembled against his palm. As soon as she gained her feet, he released her hand and stepped away.

"We'll land soon. I want you strapped in immediately."

Chapter 4

Tru leaned as far forward as the seat harness allowed, gaze glued to the ship's viewscreen showing Alludra's surface as they entered the atmosphere. She kept a wary eye on the man beside her as well.

They broke through the cloud cover, and Tru got her first glimpse of the white-capped mountains and deep forests spread panoramically below her. She tracked the winding path of an immense, slow moving river. Against one of its wide, gentle curves, a large city sprawled outward, its tall buildings gleaming in the morning light. The ship switched from the artificial grav needed in space to the gravitational pull of the planet below them.

"The city to our right is Glendoran." Nick adjusted their trajectory. "It's the biggest city on Alludra. The main spaceport has a great deal of traffic, but we won't land there. We're heading a bit farther west, toward a private landing pad."

"Yours, I suppose?"

He shrugged, leaving the interpretation to her. Nick slowed *Messenger's* descent, and the bottom of Tru's stomach dropped out with the sudden change in speed. The ship gave a great shudder in the clutch of Alludra's gravity and the reduction in engine power. Gripping the arms of her chair, she glanced at her companion. She'd never travelled on a ship as small as this one, where she felt everything. Unnerved, needing the distraction, she focused on the scene outside.

Sprawling cities populated her own world, Bretonne, a dense, multi-cultural planet with little green space. Her family's wealth guaranteed her home to be surrounded by beautifully landscaped gardens. Artificial and elaborate, they were designed to impress. She enjoyed the bubbling fountains, flowering plants and manicured pathways, but the verdant land below made her realize how pale those gardens appeared in comparison.

A staggering variety of giant trees grew on this world, gilded in colors she'd never seen before and hardly had names for. Even the color of the sky seemed brighter, with shades drifting from the palest of blues to deep indigo. Clouds buffeted by an unseen wind skittered across the clear sky, wispy trails of white blurring into the blue.

Nick banked sharply to the left, slowing their descent further and leveling off. Tru jerked and clutched the armrests of her chair tighter.

"Relax. I haven't crashed one of these babies yet, so stop worrying," he said testily, keeping his gaze on the navigation console. He moved his fingers over the keys, making small alterations to their course, inching the ship's nose up.

Closer to the ground, their airspeed was more noticeable. The land became less thickly wooded, giving way to gentle hills and valleys. Houses played peek-a-boo in the ever-changing landscape and farmland stretched like a brown scar through the brilliant colors of the trees.

Polished metal glinted in the sunlight. A handful of ships similar to *Messenger* occupied an immense landing pad and held little interest for Tru. The same couldn't be said for the sleek, small craft that attracted and held her attention. Narrow and clearly designed for only one occupant, they gleamed with predatory intent. They looked like weapons waiting to be fired. Why would he have such machines?

She turned to Nick to ask. The answer materialized right before her, reflected in the harsh beauty of his face. Here, barely contained, existed the same power and the same deadly potential. He was as much a weapon as the craft resting on the landing pad. A shiver rippled down her back.

His absolute concentration gave her the opportunity to admire the masculine grace and economical movements of his body as he prepared the ship for landing. Grateful the landing gear engaging camouflaged her soft sigh, Tru quickly turned her head and nibbled her bottom lip. She felt a powerful mix of uneasiness and attraction in his presence.

He set *Messenger* down with hardly a bump, engines hissing as they shut down and began to cool. With a flick of his wrist, he unbuckled the shoulder harness and rose while she fumbled with her own buckles. She stayed seated, because the tight confines of the bridge would bring their bodies uncomfortably close. She already struggled with her awareness of him and the idea of being near enough to feel the heat radiate from his big body sent a different kind of shiver down her spine.

He retreated a little and motioned for her to precede him to the back of the ship and the outside door. "We're just a short distance from my home. I maintain my business interests there."

She gave him as wide a berth as possible while rising from her chair and leading the way. His gaze drilled into the back of her neck, and her heartbeat kicked up a notch. She tried to keep her unease at his closeness hidden. Instead, she concentrated on keeping her pace languid and graceful while hampered by heavy clothing and clumsy boots. Who knew all the training in deportment she'd endured would prove useful? Remembering the lessons, she straightened her spine and raised her chin a bit more, finding courage enough to let a tiny smile tease the corners of her mouth.

When they reached the main hatch, Nick slapped a hand against the control panel and door seals hissed as they released. The panel opened and a ramp extended to the ground. Hot, humid air washed over her, redolent with the scent of growing things and the mingling overlay of machinery and fuel fumes. Squinting against the bright sunlight and even brighter flashes glinting off the metal surfaces, she fought a sneeze.

His hand at the base of her spine urged her forward. She swallowed a gasp as its heat danced seductive sparks up her back. Distracted she forced herself to watch her feet as she moved. Metal grillwork of the landing pad echoed as he hurried her toward the end of the tarmac. Stone stairs curved to a pathway bordered by flowering shrubs and unobtrusive lights. The juxtaposition between the harsh environment of the landing pad and the garden path before her was unexpected. Intrigued she glanced at Nick, but didn't have the nerve to ask questions.

By the time they reached the bottom, moisture prickled along her hairline and dotted her upper lip. Tru fumbled with the tabs on her heavy jacket and wished she dared stop long enough to remove it. Its weight suffocated her in the heat, but the impatience stamped on Nick's face convinced her otherwise. Instead, she contented herself with letting it flap open and catch any stray breeze coming her way. She refused to ask him to slow down, even though she trotted to keep up with his long strides. She had her pride, battered though it was.

They rounded a corner and before her, shimmering in the sunlight, was his home. She stopped dead in her tracks, trying to take it all in. He took a couple of steps and stopped. He half turned, an eyebrow raised in question. She shut her gaping mouth with a snap, ignoring the flare of satisfaction on his face. "Oh my."

The house spread before her wasn't large, at least not by her family's standards. And yet, it appeared nothing less than magnificent, designed to blend with its surroundings rather than draw attention. It was multileveled and built of a mellowed buff-colored stone with darker streaks running through it. Windows sparkled in the sunlight and flanked wide, deep stairs leading to the heavily carved front doors. Tall trees shaded the house and water splashed in a fountain encircled by flowers. A thick wall surrounded the house, looking impressive, rather than threatening, but she didn't doubt for a minute uninvited guests wouldn't make it very far.

Considered a masterpiece on her world, her family home seemed ostentatious and overblown compared to Nick's.

"Your home is stunning," Tru said. "It is not at all what I expected." She couldn't easily read his expression, but suspected her comment had annoyed him somehow.

He gave her a mocking bow and swept his arm out. "After you."

Unsure how to respond, she nodded and preceded him up the path.

The great hallway was cool and a welcome relief from the humidity outside. She blinked while her eyes adjusted from the exterior brightness to the relative dimness inside the house. Approaching footsteps echoed off the marble floor and a man made his appearance. A broad smile full of humor and mischief lit his handsome face, but interest flashed in his shrewd gaze before he turned to Nick.

She was caught off guard when the man stopped in front of Nick and saluted before punching him lightly on the shoulder. Nick grinned and punched him back. They launched into conversation in a language she'd never heard before. Smooth, musical words mesmerized as she listened to the ebb and flow of their deep voices. The language sounded complex, beautiful and utterly alien. Unable to follow the conversation, Tru settled for watching the men.

Nick might command a room with the sheer force of his presence, but certainly the other man would never go unnoticed either. Although he focused on the conversation, she sensed his awareness of her. The angle of his head and set of his shoulders made him seem watchful.

Another resident joined them, but didn't participate in the conversation. He listened intently, not paying much attention to her beyond the initial curious glance. Tru began to feel overwhelmed by so much testosterone in the room and it didn't help when the men darted speculative glances her way throughout their conversation with Nick.

He spoke a single, sharp word and all conversation ceased. The men turned their attention to her with military precision. She edged closer and stood slightly behind Nick.

He caught her arm and drew her beside him. "Tru, this is Seth Mandekor and Callen Bluestone, my partners." He'd indicated each of the men in front of her with a brisk nod. "And this is Tru Creighton." The subtle emphasis on her name confirmed she'd been the topic of conversation. Not a new circumstance, but one she'd never found comfortable.

Seth turned warm hazel eyes her way and winked. "Welcome, Tru Creighton."

His mischievous smile invited a response, and Tru relaxed enough to smile back. Seth Mandekor was as handsome as sin and she suspected not averse to using his looks to his advantage. Like Nick, he stood tall and broad-shouldered, with his sun-streaked brown hair, cut shorter than the current fashion. He exuded geniality, and the lines bracketing his mouth attested he smiled easily. He appeared a complete opposite to Nick's darker personality but the same shadows lurked in his eyes as in Nick's. She had no idea what had left such a mark on either man, and wasn't sure she wanted to know.

Callen nodded, but didn't say anything. He offered a brief smile, which for all its brevity still held enough charm to give her pause. His watchful winter gray eyes seemed reserved, too old for such a young face. He drifted away silent as a wraith, carrying himself like the others, shoulders square and movements bearing a lethal hunter's grace. He hadn't made her uncomfortable exactly, just very conscious of his presence.

"The boss man here says you're in a bit of trouble." Seth took her arm and led her deeper into the house. "I can't help but notice those nasty bruises you're sporting, darlin'. Just point me in the right direction and I will be happy to take care of the bast—ah, bully who did that to you."

Self-conscious, Tru lifted a hand to the bruising along her temple and brushed her hair forward, trying to hide the discoloration marring her skin.

"Ah. Thank you, but it won't be necessary," Tru assured him. She glanced over her shoulder at Nick frowning and pacing behind them.

"Now, you don't want to deprive me of a little fun do you? It wouldn't be right to let whoever did this get away with hurting a little thing like you, now would it?"

Tru ventured a quick peek at the handsome man holding onto her arm, unsure if he joked. His tone might have been light and teasing, but the tightness around his mouth told a different story.

"Let it be, Seth. I put the bruises on Tru," Nick growled from somewhere behind her.

Seth stopped and turned, drawing Tru along with him. "You?"

Nick nodded, holding his gaze. "Yes. Me."

The hand holding Tru's arm tightened as Seth's face darkened with confusion and something akin to anger. Responding instinctively to the rising tension between the two men, she jerked her arm out of Seth's grasp, a little surprised he released her so easily, and moved to stand in front of Nick.

"He didn't know I was a girl when he hit me. I shouldn't have been following him."

Seth took his eyes off Nick long enough to look at her. The tightness around his eyes lessened, replaced by a glint of amusement. She must look ridiculous, hovering between the two men. Her head barely reached Nick's shoulder, but there she stood, ready to defend him if necessary. Seth raised his hands in surrender and took a half step backward.

Some of the tension drained from Seth's shoulders and her own relaxed in response.

She glanced up at Nick. He seemed thrown by the turn of events and following impulse she moved closer to him. She felt the controlled strength in his hands as they cupped her shoulders. He rubbed them up and down her arms in a gesture of comfort. It was a side of him rarely seen, if the astonished look on Seth's face was anything to go by. She wondered if Nick was even aware of what he was doing.

"Sorry. I guess I overreacted a little."

"Easy to do, given the evidence," Nick replied.

Just like that it was over, and everything was back to normal.

Tru blinked a couple of times, wondering what had just happened. Deciding she would never understand men, she shrugged. Licking her bottom lip, she felt grit and grimaced. Hot and sticky with sweat, she slipped off her jacket and brushed at the streak of dirt on her right breast. Moisture trickled down her collarbone and her shirt clung to her back and chest, making it almost transparent in places. She undid the top buttons on her shirt, and wafted it to create a cooling breeze.

* * * *

Nick started to say something to Seth and completely lost his train of thought when he noticed what Tru was doing. The sudden silence must have alerted her and she looked up. Nick shut his mouth with a snap and could have sworn he heard Seth do the same. It was hard to hide his appreciation even when he noticed the blush climbing her cheeks as she realized he was watching her every move.

"The dust of Lodestone gets on everything," she muttered, while shifting her jacket in front. She frowned at the dirt on her shirtfront.

Nick raised an eyebrow and visually traced the new streak of dirt up to the pulse beating in her throat. Everything in him tightened and he wanted her with an urgency he hadn't felt in a long time. He started to step toward her but made himself stop. This wasn't the time or the place. Shaking his head to clear his mind, he tamped down on his desire.

"Let me show you to a room where you can clean up. I'm sure we'll be able find something for you to wear until more appropriate clothing is available." Even to his own ears his voice sounded rough, a little strained. "Seth, why don't you see what you can find?" he said over his shoulder as he guided Tru to the stairway sweeping in a wide curve to the upper floors.

It was difficult to ignore the slight tremor of her body beside him and his grip tightened, drawing her closer. He glanced at her averted profile and wondered what she thought. The fact it even occurred to him to wonder was a new and troubling experience. Rarely had he gotten far enough into a relationship to concern himself and he wasn't sure he liked it now. His lips compressed and he walked faster, only slowing down when her faint protest made him aware of what he was doing. It was not an edifying discovery to find himself acting like a damn fool kid who'd found himself alone with his crush for the first time.

He guided her down a long hallway before stopping outside a door at the end. Leaning around her to open it, he made sure their bodies did not touch. She stepped over the threshold and then turned to face him as he stood in the hallway. She continued to clutch her jacket like a shield.

"Thank you." Blue eyes rose to his and then were veiled behind lowered lashes. Her mouth opened as if she'd say something more, but Seth appeared beside him, and handed her a folded bundle of clothes.

"I think these will do for now." He offered her a roguish grin.

Tru nodded and took the clothes. She backed further into the room her eyes still on Nick. Seth took the hint and left as silently as he'd arrived.

"Get cleaned up, Tru," Nick ordered softly. "We'll talk later."

Unable to resist, he stepped over the threshold to brush a finger along the bruise darkening her temple and down to the marks on her throat. Her smooth, warm skin made it difficult to control the urge to slide his hand to the nape of her neck and urge her closer. He dropped his hand, fingers fisting against his thigh, and moved back. It took Tru closing the door to release him from the spell weaving between them. Even longer for him to walk away.

Chapter 5

Nick returned to the lower floor to seek Seth and Callen and entered the formal office designed for visiting clients. He'd richly appointed the room with a large barrow wood desk gleaming with the deep, russet grain of the native tree. Positioned in front of the window overlooking the gardens, it made a statement and drew the eye. Comfortable chairs flanked the desk and discreet art decorated the paneled walls. The elegant, masculine room represented the business face Nick liked to present his clients.

The real heart of the operation, on the other hand, lay hidden behind a section of wall to the left of his desk. Silently, the panel slid open and Nick stepped into the room. Callen worked at a haloviz console extrapolating data, while Seth made notes on a lightweight, flexible tablet. Both men stopped working when he walked in.

"Have we heard from Wulf?" Nick asked.

Burke Wulfric, the other member of the team, was on assignment escorting a dignitary from Paladin Minor to take her newly elected seat with the governing body of the Unified Alliance of Planets on Fionne. Raven Security hadn't protected individuals in the past, but when the company had been approached to offer discreet security for the new ambassador, Nick had agreed.

Nick assigned Wulf the job because he had a background with the diplomatic corps on Tonlith. Not that he'd been particularly forthcoming about his experience, but Nick used it as leverage when he'd needed an agent for the job. Wulf was also deadly in close-quarter fighting, if needed. He wasn't expected back for at least a standard moon cycle, but Nick required his agents to report.

"He checked in early this morning. He mentioned a few problems to take care of, but didn't go into detail. You know Wulf; he'll handle whatever gets in his way." Seth chuckled. "It seems Ambassador D'Kir is proving to be more of a challenge than anticipated and isn't following orders very well. That boy has picked up some very interesting language since he's been gone."

Nick snorted as he crossed the room.

"Callen, have you been able to find any information on the head of Lodestone Mining besides the usual drivel?"

"I've been doing some digging but don't have anything concrete yet. It looks like Malvin Sonne is a figurehead for the corporation. I haven't discovered the real power behind the man yet." Callen's voice was thoughtful and he frowned. "But you can be sure I'll find him, given a little time."

Nick nodded. Whoever had faked the advisory on him and Tru wouldn't stay hidden for long, not with Callen hot on his trail. The man was a genius with information.

"I liberated the pouch you brought home from its hidey hole on the *Messenger*." Seth put his tablet down and snagged the pouch from the console in front of him. He tossed it up and down, testing its weight. "This sure is a tiny package for something you tell me might revolutionize stardrive technology. Have you looked inside yet?"

"I was a bit busy," Nick answered, his tone dry. He pulled up a chair, sat down and crossed an ankle over the opposite knee. He slouched back and laced his fingers behind his head. "I'm not happy Axyl Hargrave changed the drop without consulting me first. I haven't quite made up my mind if Tru and the object you're holding are connected, but my gut tells me it's a distinct possibility. Regardless, I've taken the job of getting it to Dendera Labs for Geotern and I've plenty of credits riding on doing just that."

Seth stopped bouncing the pouch and set it back on the console. He leaned back, stretched out his long legs and grinned. "So, boss man, what do you plan on doing about Tru Creighton?"

"Damned if I know." Nick rubbed the back of his neck. "I guess it all depends on what she tells me. So far she hasn't been real forthcoming about what happened on Lodestone."

"She's in trouble, huh?" Callen didn't raise his eyes from the console pad on which he tapped. As usual, his focus remained on searching along another path of information.

"She was certainly running scared. Whatever she's involved with frightened her enough to follow me back to my ship in hopes of persuading me to take her with me." Nick scratched his whiskered jaw.

"It got her off-world though, didn't it?" Seth said.

"Yeah, I guess. The problem is, if she recognized me then someone else might have as well. It could explain how our names got connected. Damn it, the trip was supposed to be a quick in and out without any fanfare. Only the head of Geotern knew the day I planned to be there and he was invested in keeping it quiet. Hell, I even dressed like a friggin' transport pilot to blend in."

Seth snorted and shook his head. Even Callen stopped working to stare.

"What?" Nick snapped, daring either of them to say anything. When they suddenly became interested elsewhere, he grinned. Sometimes it was good to be the boss.

He stood, grabbed his chair and spun it back in place. He had too much to do to spend time in idle speculation about Tru. There was the small matter of the package delivery. It had priority above his own curiosity.

Idly, he scratched his jaw, felt the rough stubble on his face and grimaced at the dirt under his fingernails. His beard annoyed him and the grit left over from Lodestone irritated places it shouldn't have reached. Standing under a shower was just what he needed to wash away some of his annoyance from this trip.

As he sauntered out of the hidden room, he made sure the panel slid back into place behind him. He crossed through the front office and headed toward the stairs. He took them two at a time, and reached the top without being out of breath. Long strides took him to his suite of rooms at the opposite end of the hallway from Tru. Shutting his bedroom door, he took a deep breath and allowed some of the cares of the day to drop away.

A place to belong was important to him, as with the others. His home was his sanctuary. Losing everything that mattered to him after Tonlith's destruction had been a blow he'd never gotten over. After the disastrous final battle, he'd drifted from one world to the next, never satisfied, always restless. Angry. Disillusioned.

By sheer accident he'd discovered Seth in the middle of a bar fight, outnumbered, bloody and refusing to quit. Nick had been amazed the man had any fight left in him, but he had no interest in getting involved. About to turn away, he'd stopped dead in his tracks when he heard the man taunting his attackers in a language he never thought to hear again. It had snapped his attention back to the man.

Nick hadn't heard Tonlithian spoken in at least a year. A long, barren year. It was reason enough to wade into the brawl and help the other man. Maybe a good fight was just what he'd needed after all and hearing his native language soothed his battered soul. Introductions would wait.

After it was over, the two were barely standing. The same couldn't be said for their opponents.

A seedy bar, in a rough and tumble town on the world Euphonie, had been the last place Nick ever thought he'd find a fellow exile. For the first time he'd allowed himself to consider if they had survived impossible odds, then maybe others had too. It ignited a spark in both men and laid the groundwork for a strong friendship. Eventually, they found Wulf and then Callen. Theirs was a bond forged from the fires of war and the consequences, which had cast them adrift. Something none of them would ever forget.

When the idea for Rayven Security was born, they agreed on the planet Alludra as their base. The surrounding land was close enough to what they remembered of Tonlith to bring them all a measure of comfort. It was a start.

Shaking off his memories, Nick shed his clothing as he headed for the rain shower. The hot water was a welcome relief as it flowed over taut muscles and sloughed off the gritty dirt clinging to him. Closing his eyes, he placed his hands on the tiled wall in front of him and bowed his head, letting the water run in rivulets down his skin. His mind buzzed with unanswered questions and most of them seemed to lead back to Tru. Every time she got near, his body reacted, leaving him in a semi-aroused state, and it was playing hell with his nerves. The first time she raised those incredible blue eyes to his had been like a punch to his solar plexus and left him scrambling to form a coherent thought. That jolt, that sizzle of bone deep awareness hadn't stopped since, if anything it had gotten worse. He couldn't remember the last time he'd been so affected by a woman.

Growling, he slapped the wall and firmly pushed the images of Tru out of his mind. He had a job to do and he was not going to let hormones get in his way. What he needed was a quick trip to the pleasure houses in Glendoran to take care of his sexual needs. Maybe then, he could ignore the attraction heating his blood whenever she was around. A simple solution and one he needed to find time for.

The water had long since cooled before Nick shut it off. He grabbed a drying cloth draped it low on his hips and secured it with a quick fold. Moisture hung heavy in the air, and he wiped condensation off the sink mirror, getting a good look at himself in the process. Deciding there wasn't much he could do about his looks other than shave off the whiskers wasn't much comfort. His face looked lived-in, hard and unforgiving. The scar dissecting his eyebrow was a constant reminder of things he would rather forget. He'd been lucky the shrapnel hadn't cut his eye. He had learned to live with his past, had found a reason to keep living, but it had been hard won and it showed.

A droplet of water from his wet hair dripped onto his chest and traced a meandering path from his collarbone to the tattoo over his heart. Nick brushed the artistically scrolled letters, removing the water. The men in his unit had each sported the same tattoo design after a memorable shore leave. Reaching for his shaver, he ignored the flash of grief and concentrated on getting rid of the stubble on his face.

Chapter 6

Tru did her best not to tug at the hem of the large shirt she wore. To get a better fit, she fastened her wide leather belt loosely over her hips. It added some definition to the material, but the fact remained this was a man's clothing and dwarfed her smaller frame. She debated putting her jacket on over the shirt, but it was filthy and she couldn't bring herself to do it. The drawstring pants Seth supplied were impossible to keep up and too easy to trip over, even if she wore the scuffed and oversized boots she'd arrived in to give her added height. After a serious internal debate, Tru opted not to wear them and risk falling in an embarrassing heap when she walked.

Dressed in an acceptable manner, the shirt covering her from neck to knees, she still felt exposed and vulnerable. She shoved a long sleeve up past her elbow but it slid down to cover her hand again. Unsure of what to do next, she perched on a chair in the bedroom and tried to ignore the butterflies dancing in her stomach.

What did she know about Nick Rayven other than what she'd learned through research? If she were going to be being honest with herself, she would have to admit her imagination had cast Nick in the same mold as many of the men she knew. Urbane. Successful. Sophisticated.

After spending a brief time with him, she understood her naive assessment bore little resemblance to the man himself. He was tough, commanding and impatient, but he also made her knees go weak when he looked at her and had shown kindness when she was the most in need of it. He was everything she hadn't known she wanted, until she met him.

Still, she was stranded on an unfamiliar planet and in the company of a man she knew almost nothing about. Granted, he'd been polite and considerate of her well-being, but he could also have been plotting to hold her for ransom, for all she knew. Her family was well known for its wealth and payoff demands were not unheard of among the more affluent families on her world. It gave her pause. Attraction aside, she needed to be cautious.

An overactive imagination had led her into trouble more times than she could count, and once the idea of ransom demands took hold, she couldn't shake it. One horrible scenario after another whirled through her mind. Tying herself in knots, she took a steadying breath and stopped her train of thought. She jumped up and paced the bedroom telling herself nothing could be solved while she hid in the bedroom. She needed to see Nick. Firming her jaw, she straightened her makeshift outfit and marched out the door before her courage deserted her.

Barefoot, she glided down the stairs, keeping a sharp eye out for another person. It was quiet in the house. Where was everyone? She reached the bottom of the stairs and stood with one hand resting on the banister. Her bare feet curled against the cool tile and she bit her bottom lip. Maybe she should just go back to her room?

"Is everything all right?" Callen asked.

Tru let out a yelp, lost her balance and plopped on the bottom stair. Pressing a hand to her pounding heart, she stared wide-eyed at the man standing a few paces away.

"Don't do that," she squeaked. "You almost gave me a heart attack!"

He offered her a hand and pulled her to her feet. "My apologies. I didn't mean to startle you."

One lock of ash brown hair fell across his wide forehead. At first glance, he looked harmless, almost boyish, but the cool gray of his eyes held none of the amusement curving his lips.

"You're Callen, right?"

Thoughts she'd allowed to haunt her upstairs rushed back and it took effort to push them away. If she'd learned one thing from her grandfather, it was never to show fear.

"Yes."

"I must say you move very quietly. I didn't hear you at all."

"If you follow me I'll escort you to a sitting room where you can be comfortable while you wait for Nick."

He moved away, seeming confident she would follow. Tru debated staying where she was to see what he would do, but then decided it didn't matter. She watched his retreating back and had the distinct impression there was more to Callen Bluestone than met the eye. There was something about his enigmatic demeanor making her cautious, although she didn't feel threatened in any way. With a shrug, she followed him to a set of double doors just past the entry.

He held the door open and waited for her to pass, and she sailed through the doors with a regal tilt to her chin, ignoring the amusement crinkling the corners of his eyes. He followed her into the room. He may have startled her, but she refused to be intimidated. He indicated she should sit on a plush couch positioned against one wall.

Tru held his gaze and ignored the couch to sit in a chair flanking the stone fireplace. She sat on the edge, feet side by side on the floor with her hands folded on her lap. She lifted her chin and looked around, doing her best to look confident and self-assured. She could feel heat climbing her cheeks when she caught his knowing smile. She knew he saw right through her and it took some of the starch out of her. Subdued, she scooted back in the chair and lounged against the padded leather.

"Have you lived here long?" She asked.

"No, I haven't."

He wasn't being rude as far as she could tell, just uncommunicative. Not one to give up, she searched for another conversational gambit. "How long have you worked for Nick?"

"Not long."

He wasn't going to satisfy her curiosity. She'd been raised from the cradle to handle any social situation presented, but Callen was more of a challenge than she felt up to dealing with at the moment. She watched him move to one of the viewscreen windows beside the fireplace to gaze outside. Vexed by his reserve, she slumped further in her chair and twirled one of her curls around her finger.

"Not much of a talker, are you?"

"I've never seen the point of small talk," he remarked. "Please don't take it personally, but I would prefer we wait for Nick."

As soon as Nick entered the room, she felt immediate relief. If she hadn't been paying attention, she might have missed the almost imperceptible falter in his step before it smoothed out again. She had no idea why a stunned look had flashed across his face before he smoothed his features into a bland expression.

* * * *

Nick felt like all the air had been sucked out of his lungs. He was going to kill Seth when he saw him, slowly and with a great deal of pleasure. When he'd sent him to find something suitable for Tru to wear, he hadn't meant for it to be one of his shirts. His favorite shirt, no less. And, why were her legs bare? A man could only take so much, and the sight of those lovely, long legs made his mouth water. Swallowing hard, he crossed the room until he was standing in front of her.

"I see Seth found something for you to wear?" Nick's question sounded inane even to his own ears and he winced.

He tried not to notice the delicate lines of Tru's collarbone revealed by the too-large neck of the shirt, or the fact the fabric clung like a second skin to her small breasts. He jerked his gaze away from her and looked over her head toward Callen, who had the nerve to grin at him.

She shifted in her seat and the hem of his shirt rode up higher on her thigh. His blood pressure rose and his face felt frozen into a permanent scowl.

"Yes, thank you for the loan. There were trousers, but I couldn't keep them up and they were too long to walk in," she answered with a charming smile.

Callen choked on a laugh and Nick was ready to commit murder. Tru leaned around the chair and looked at Callen. She seemed surprised to hear him laugh.

'Damn it," Nick grumbled. "This isn't going to work."

He grabbed her hand, hauled her out of the chair and pulled her unresisting out of the room. She had trouble keeping up with his long stride and tried to jerk out of his grip. He didn't pause or slow down, just held her hand with bone-crushing force, leaving her to figure out how to keep up.

"Hey, boss..." Seth's words trailed after them but Nick didn't give him a chance to finish. He slammed the door to his office, cutting off the sound of Callen's amused chuckle and the bewildered look on Seth's face. He'd deal with the two of them later.

Nick dropped her hand as soon as they were alone and went behind the desk, motioning for her to remain where she was. He punched a series of buttons with more force than was necessary and a callscreen rose from its hidden place in the desk.

"Briella's," he barked to the automated inquiry, and then drummed his fingers on the desk while waiting for the connection to be made.

"Briella's, how may I help you?" The voice belonged to a striking young woman, elegantly dressed and smiling with just a hint of hauteur.

"I need clothing for my...er...client," he said. "I need it delivered immediately."

"I see. Is there any particular style you want?" The woman's smile was arch, implying Briella's catered to every type of need without unnecessary embarrassment to either of them.

Nick glared, and her smile slid away to be replaced by cool professionalism.

"She will need things suited for space travel, nothing frilly—utilitarian," he snapped, eyeing Tru. "Everything from the skin out. Dark colors."

He needed the clothing to be dull and sufficient to cool his growing sexual attraction to her. He gestured for Tru to join him behind the desk, positioning her so she could be seen by the salesperson on the callscreen.

"I don't like dark colors," Tru declared and raised her chin.

The sales woman looked from Tru to Nick and back again before she focused on Tru. Her smile warmed and she quirked an eyebrow. "Permission to scan?"

"Granted," Tru replied and then urged Nick to step out of the way. A small rainbow hued beam fanned out and scanned Tru from head to foot. Measurements, skin tone and other pertinent information was gathered and transmitted to the store.

"I will see appropriate garments are delivered right away. I'm sure you will be completely satisfied with the collection." She smiled serenely at Nick who inserted a data slip into a slot by the callscreen and authorized funds to be transferred. "It has been a pleasure doing business with you, Mr. Rayven." Her image blinked out and the screen slid into the desk.

Satisfied one immediate problem would soon be taken care of, Nick escorted Tru to a nearby seat. Too restless to stay in one spot, he paced the room.

"There was no need for you to order clothes for me, you know? I could have taken care of it myself."

"Really? How? If I'm not mistaken you are on the run right now without any credits to your name." Nick's voice sounded harsh, even to his own ears. He exhaled and forced a calmness he was far from feeling. "Speaking of running, it is time to tell me what is going on, Tru."

"I know."

Chapter 7

"Why were you on Lodestone? If I'm going to help you, I need to know the truth. Don't even think about lying to me."

Tru glared at him and then looked away.

"I don't have all day, Tru," he snapped.

"Fine! I worked in the department handling accounting for my grandfather's many interests. I'm good with numbers, but the job killed me with boredom. I wanted adventure and to travel, not sit in an office all day."

Nick crossed his arms over his chest and waited, his patience growing thin. Tru sat a little straighter in her chair and rushed to continue. "I was responsible for Lodestone Mining's account, and I began to suspect something wasn't right with the accounting. Money was being funneled into subsidiaries. It all looked good on the surface, but I kept running into walls when I tried to track it further. It was small things I couldn't explain and it made me take a second, deeper look." Her voice rose. "I tried to talk to my father about what I noticed, but he patted me on the head and told me not to be ridiculous. Lodestone Mining was a sound investment and I was letting my imagination run away with me."

"Go on," he encouraged, before relaxing enough to sit on the corner of his desk. He plucked a small, decorative glass disc from the desktop and tossed it from one hand to the other.

"I decided to take matters into my own hands and prove I was right."

Nick raised his eyebrows in mock alarm.

"I informed my family I was going to visit a friend. I didn't want them to worry, you see. I caught a transport to Lodestone under a false name so no one would know where I was and come after me. I informed the operations manager, Anto Geir, I was an auditor from Creighton Mutual doing a routine check. Everything was going as planned. I had even been able to discover the head of Lodestone Mining was not correctly accounting for the amount of mineral being shipped for sale—"

"How did you manage that?"

"I made friends with a shipping clerk. It wasn't hard to get him to talk about his job and fairly easy to figure out some of the shipments were conveniently going astray." Tru shrugged.

"Him? Just how, exactly, did you get him to talk, Tru?" Nick's voice was dark, dangerous as unwelcome jealousy stirred at the mention of another man. The emotion was so alien and so out of place, given the circumstances, it caught him off guard. He put the glass disc down with a little more force than necessary and curled his fingers under the edge of the desk, waiting for her answer.

Tru's shirt hem had ridden up her thigh again and she tugged it down. Nick almost groaned out loud.

"Oh, you know, we had drinks at his place a couple of times," she replied.

"Just drinks?" There it was again, a slight growl in his voice, and he winced. Damn it all, she was driving him crazy.

"Of course, just drinks. Good grief, Nick, what did you think was going on? He thought he impressed me with his importance. A few cups of the local ale and he prattled on without much encouragement. It was easy to cross-reference the dates he let drop on shipments against delivery. It wasn't until Anto Geir started questioning me that I got a little nervous."

"What kind of questions?"

"At first I didn't think much about it. He wanted to know how my audit was going, was everything in order, that kind of thing. He tried to make conversation about the people I spent time with. He started to really make me nervous."

She clasped her hands in her lap tight enough to turn the knuckles white then continued in a small, strained voice, "The next work cycle, the shipping clerk wasn't at his station. His body was found in one of the mines. Anto called it a tragic accident."

Expressions chased each other across her face, fear shadowed her eyes, and his long suppressed protective instincts chose that moment to make themselves known. Pushing himself off his desk, he crossed the short distance to her. Squatting, he took her small, clenched fists in his much larger hands, offering comfort as he rubbed his thumbs across their back.

"Tell me the rest, Tru," he ordered in a gentle tone.

"When I got back to my rooms someone had been there. Everything was tossed about. My clothes were in ruins. I knew whoever had been there was looking for information, but I never left my data drive in my rooms. It was always with me." Her voice trembled, and her pulse raced under his fingertips.

"I knew I had to get back home, but whenever I tried to contact anyone the channels were blocked. I couldn't even get a transport off-world. I wasn't sure what to do, whom I could trust. I was scared to death."

She raised fear-dilated eyes to his, the bruising on her temple dark against her pale skin. "I waited until it was full dark and managed to get out of my rooms unseen, and once the shift changed at the space port offices, I was able to sneak in and find an unoccupied room. They don't fully staff during the off hours and security is a little lax so it wasn't hard to do. I was able to gain access to an unblocked haloviz. I'd heard rumors you were coming to Lodestone when no one thought I was listening. It seemed to make people very nervous for some reason."

"It seems like Geotern Mining isn't as good at keeping secrets as they thought," he murmured. "What were the rumors you heard?"

"There weren't many really—rumors of a new mineral, speculation on why Rayven Security would be involved, but nothing concrete. Your name kept coming up. Even my grandfather had shown some interest in your company. I knew you were going to be my best chance to escape, so I waited and hid, praying the rumors were true and you would help me get home."

Nick released her hands and stood. He crossed to the window, his back to the room. "Finding me didn't prove to be such a bargain though, did it?" He glanced over his shoulder when he heard her leave her chair and cross the room to stand beside him. Her touch was hesitant against the rigid muscles of his back.

"If you hadn't arrived when you did, Nick, I would probably be dead," she said simply. "I owe you for saving me...and for helping me now."

"Do you still have the drive?" He turned enough to see her, but not enough to force her hand from touching him. Tru had been rubbing his shoulder in a soothing circular motion and he enjoyed the contact. He suspected she wasn't even aware she did it, but he would take what he could get.

With her free hand, she slid her fingers under a thin chain around her neck and pulled the end of it from under the shirt she wore. It looked like an ornamental piece of jewelry until he looked closer and realized it was a cleverly camouflaged data drive.

"May I?" He indicated the necklace with a lift of his chin.

She nodded and reached behind her to unfasten the dainty chain. He forestalled her by cupping her shoulders and spinning her around so her back was to him. He skimmed his palms along her tense shoulders until he reached the velvet skin of her neck and took his time tracing the fragile links of the chain with his fingertips, moving with the lightest of touches from her collarbone to the fastening at her nape. He slipped his fingers under the links and lifted the chain away from her warm, fragrant skin.

She caught her breath.

Slower than was necessary, he unlatched it, enjoying the softness of the curls clinging to her nape and wrapping themselves around his fingertips. Her breath trembled as she exhaled, and he struggled to keep himself from doing more than removing the necklace.

He cleared his throat to relieve the unexpected tightness. "I'll have Callen take a look at the data, if that's all right with you."

He didn't wait around for her answer. He left the room without a backward glance, needing to put some distance between them.

* * * *

Tru raised her hand and rested it against the pulse pounding in her throat as she watched Nick stride from the room in search of Callen.

She didn't move.

She couldn't even if she wanted to.

Nick's touch had been tender. Intimate. It left her yearning for...what? She wasn't sure, didn't want to name it, so she concentrated on calming her erratic heartbeat and bringing the fine trembling in her limbs under control.

He wasn't gone long, but it gave her enough time to regain her composure.

"What's next?" She asked, surprised and pleased her tone only held curiosity.

"We contact your grandfather and fill him in on what you've been up to."

"Do we have to? He's not an easy man to deal with and he's going to be furious with me."

"And so he should be. You put yourself in danger, lied about what you were doing and were lucky to get off Lodestone with your life." Nick's tone was implacable.

She flinched, but she set her jaw.

"He needs to know you are safe, and he needs to know about Anto Geir. He could very well be the one pulling the strings behind the scenes. Your grandfather needs to protect his investments and investors, because

I have a feeling Lodestone Mining is going to crash and burn before we're done here."

Her shoulders slumped. Nick was right. She knew it, but would rather walk across broken glass barefoot than deal with her grandfather when he was displeased with her. And he was going to be upset when he found out what she'd done. Very upset.

The front door opening and the sound of voices drew their attention. Footsteps headed their way. Nick stepped away from her and she tried not to be disappointed as they waited to see what the commotion was all about.

"Delivery for you Tru," Seth announced, coming into the room.

The sturdy pale pink travel locker he held would survive rough handling. Absurdly pleased by the color and graceful lines of the locker, she was willing to bet her last credit this was not what Nick expected if his expression was anything to go by. Stunned disbelief followed by outrage, and then weary acceptance. It was priceless.

"Don't tell me. The clothing from Briella's?"

Tru rushed to the locker, ignoring his pained look. She wasted no time in unbuckling the straps and opening the lid to reach the clothing inside.

"Yep." There was laughter in Seth's voice.

Beautiful jeweled tone fabrics spilled over the sides as Tru rummaged through, admiring the texture and cut of the clothing inside. They were made for hard travel all right, but fashionably simple and of the best quality. Everything she saw was as far from the utilitarian and dull items Nick wanted as day was from night.

"I need to change into something presentable if we're going to talk to my grandfather. Will one of you carry the trunk upstairs so I can get ready?"

Seth started to reach for the locker, but Nick nudged him aside. She exchanged a quick amused look with him as Nick hefted the locker and proceeded out the door. She couldn't suppress the delighted smile on her face and was glad he couldn't see it. Seth winked at her when she passed him and was whistling a merry tune as he followed them out the door.

Once in her room, she asked Nick for scissors. He didn't ask why, but his baffled expression said it all. As soon as he left her alone she set to work trimming her hair. She removed the ragged knife-cut edges and shaped it to lie in loose curls framing her face. She was happy with the results. The shorter hair drew attention to her large blue eyes and flattered her heart-shaped face. She looked less like a ragged urchin and more like the granddaughter of a successful businessman. The curls also camouflaged the bruising on the side of her face better than she'd anticipated. If she was careful how she turned her head, her grandfather might not even notice.

She rummaged through the clothing to find something she liked. She smoothed the material of the short, military-cut jacket, delighted in the feel of the supple fabric. She couldn't resist another peek in the mirror and grinned at her reflection.

Durable, lightweight black material encased her legs and fell in a straight line to her feet. Her new clothing was designed to handle travel well. The cut and fit of the garments was flattering without being confining. She slipped her feet into butter-soft boots and adjusted the narrow belt at her waist before she left the room. Stylish clothing bolstered her sagging ego, and would give her the courage she would need to talk to her grandfather. At least, she hoped so. Ignoring the nerves dampening her palms, she went in search of Nick.

Conversation stopped when she entered his office. The three men watched her move across the room with varying degrees of appreciation, but the flash of heat in Nick's eyes put a smile on her face. Feeling more confident, she met his eyes and held his gaze for one long moment before letting hers drop away.

Chapter 8

Damn it, was she flirting with him? Nick snapped his mouth shut and struggled to find the threads of the conversation he'd been having before she came into the room and turned his brain to mush. Surely, Tru wasn't aware of his attraction, not after he'd gone to such pains to keep it hidden. He shot a glance her way and wasn't sure if he was relieved or pissed when he realized she was laughing at something Seth said, her back to him. His fingers clenched and he forced them to relax until they rested against his thigh.

"Let's get this over with." Nick's voice was gruff, and he could have bitten his tongue out when the happy glow left her eyes. Mentally cursing, he kept his face impassive. Moving fast, he went to the callscreen and motioned for Tru to follow.

"We need to contact your grandfather privately," he said.

"I understand. He has a channel solely for family use. He'll stop whatever he's doing to answer it."

"Good." Nick drew in a deep breath and her delicate scent instantly assailed him.

The pulse in his head pounded and his control slipped another notch. He wanted to touch her, tempted beyond bearing by the silky curls waiting for him to run his hands through them. His mouth tightened into a thin line, and he took a small step away as he waited for her to open the channel to her grandfather. His gaze wandered around the room with his determination to keep his focus off her and his ability to think intact.

"Tru? Where are you? Are you all right?" The voice was deep and demanding, drawing Nick's reluctant attention back to Tru and the man on the viewscreen.

He couldn't help but notice the tears brightening her eyes once she saw her grandfather's face, and he fought the temptation to go to her. He was relieved when she straightened her shoulders and blinked the moisture away.

"I'm fine. I just got myself in a little trouble," she answered. Lifting her chin, she offered a serene smile. Nick glanced at her, wondering where the hell it came from. In their short acquaintance, he'd seen various sides to her, but serenity wasn't something he would ever associate with her.

"What kind of trouble? Where the hell are you?"

"She's with me for the moment." Nick moved to Tru's side so he was visible on the callscreen. "She's safe, but we have a situation and you need to be made aware of it."

"Who are you?" Maddox's voice was razor-edged, demanding. "And what the hell are you doing with my granddaughter?"

Maddox's bushy white eyebrows rose over his shrewd laser blue eyes. His frown was fierce, brooking no opposition, his authority clear in his unbowed posture. He exuded the energy of a much younger man and was not what Nick had expected at all. Revising his misconception, he realized it was what made Maddox Creighton rich and successful. He was a powerful man, used to having his own way, and it showed. Nick's respect for the man grew.

"Nick Rayven. Rayven Security," Nick answered. "Tru asked for my help when she ran into a problem on Lodestone."

"Lodestone? Are you insane? What kind of game of you playing here, Rayven?" His tone was sharp, his eyes flickering between Tru and Nick. "If this is a joke, I can assure you, I am not amused in the least."

"Grandfather, this isn't a joke. Nick is telling the truth. I...ah...went to Lodestone instead of going to Tuor to visit a friend like I told the family. I got into some serious trouble and Nick rescued me." Tru's eyes pleaded for understanding. "I'm sorry. I'm really sorry."

Maddox's face softened when he looked at her and Nick could see the strong bond between them. He looked away, giving them a moment to talk privately to each other, and to contend with the upsurge of longing he hadn't expected. It grabbed him by the throat making it hard to breathe.

Family. The word wrapped around him like a shroud, bringing with it the haunting ache that left him feeling as if his heart should cease to beat. Home. Connection. Irrevocably gone. He fought against the flood of memories crowding his mind, and by sheer force of will, pulled himself out of the abyss yawning under his feet. Therein lay madness. He clamped down on the past and pushed it away with iron control. Air expanded his lungs, his heart continued to beat, but the ache remained a constant presence nothing could heal.

"Tell me what happened, Rayven? Is it true what Tru said? Lodestone Mining is cheating its investors and falsifying its records?" Maddox's question was as close to a request as any man in his position was capable of making and brought Nick back to the present with a jolt.

He felt off balance and frustrated with himself. To lose his concentration like this and to dwell so much in his past was unsettling. He prided himself on his ability to cut to the heart of a matter and get a job done. Rayven Security was successful because of his focus, something he knew the other man understood. A company like Creighton Mutual took a tremendous amount of drive and determination to build, and its leader's strength reinforced its reputation. It was the same drive Nick poured into his own business. If he continued to lose his concentration like this, his company would suffer.

Tru must have sensed his turmoil because she put her hand on his arm, offering comfort. He stiffened, but then forced his muscles to relax. He looked down at her, perplexed by the sweetness of her smile, trying to gather his scattered thoughts. Delicate tendrils of awareness spun between them, reaching into the dark places he kept hidden, soothing the sorrow. It left him confused and yearning for things he long denied. Relief and regret shuddered through him when she removed her hand, breaking the tenuous connection.

"I had one of my men review the data Tru provided. He did some cross checking of his own and it looks like she was definitely on to something. I don't know how involved Malvin Sonne is with what is happening on Lodestone, but Anto Geir, the Operations Manager, is definitely dirty," Nick answered.

"Malvin Sonne? The President of Lodestone Mining? You think it has gone so high in the organization?" Maddox looked thoughtful for a moment, his mouth tightening. "I wondered why Malvin was here on Bretonne. He doesn't usually attend my annual investor meeting, preferring to send a subordinate." An arrested expression came into his eyes as he continued, "Come to think of it, he usually sends Anto Geir in his place. Damn it, I don't like this at all. Although it does make sense now as to why Sonne is nosing around and asking questions about Tru and the friends she was supposed to be visiting. He has seemed inordinately curious about her exact whereabouts."

Maddox frowned at Tru and she squirmed. "I've never even met the man."

"As far as he knows, you are still visiting friends. As far as I knew, that was the truth until this conversation."

"I think it would be best Sonne continues to believe she's in Tuor," Nick interjected, drawing Maddox's attention. "Until we know for sure what is going on it would be best if she remains with me. I get the impression Geir knew she wasn't who she claimed to be, but he couldn't get his hands on the data she has and needs to find her. It wouldn't be safe for her to return home until we get to the bottom of this."

"What makes you think she would be safer with you, Rayven?" Maddox barked, "I don't know you, don't trust you and I sure as hell don't like the idea of my granddaughter being in your company."

"Fair enough," he replied. "I'm sure I would feel the same way if I were in your position. I'm also sure you have already initiated a search of information on me and on my business. It won't tell you much."

"So I noticed." Her grandfather's smile was all teeth and sharp enough to cut metal as he studied Nick. Nick matched the smile, not giving an inch.

* * * *

Tru edged away from the callscreen. She hated being caught between two powerful, determined men. Even Callen and Seth watched intently, their stances showing they were alert to every nuance. It made the hair at the nape of her neck stand on end.

"I'm also sure you know my reputation and it means more to you than any official report, which can be easily manipulated. You also know I'm going to put a serious dent in your funds to protect Tru. I don't work for free. Let me do my job, Creighton. I'm very good at it."

Tru uttered a small, shocked protest before clamping her mouth shut. She glanced at Nick, but his attention was focused on her grandfather.

"It seems like we understand each other." The smile dropped from his face to be replaced with something more genuine. "I assume you have a plan for protecting my granddaughter and flushing out the bastards at Lodestone?"

Tru didn't stick around to hear the details, slipping unnoticed out of the room while all attention was on Nick. She resented being the topic of conversation without any consideration being given to her opinion. To think Nick thought of her as just another job to be done with a hefty payout at completion stung. The fact she'd intended to hire him herself didn't matter and was beside the point.

What she was feeling wasn't logical, but her emotions were in turmoil and logic was a distant memory. Confused and off balance, she sought a peaceful place to think and, if she were being honest with herself, to sulk.

Muttering unladylike imprecations under her breath about Nick, and men in general, she went outside to get some fresh air.

Sundown set the sky on fire with streaks of deep purple and scarlet. The humidity had lessened along with the oppressive heat of earlier in the day. Night creatures stirred, their rustling in the shrubbery drawing her attention and making her nervous. She wasn't familiar with the wildlife on Alludra and opted to remain close to the house. She wandered along the path she'd walked up earlier in the day surprised to realize it hadn't been that long ago. So much had changed in such a short time and she acknowledged her rash decisions had put her here. She couldn't blame Nick. He'd been direct and honest with her from the beginning.

Miserable, she clasped her arms around her waist and stared unseeing at the darkening landscape. She'd never met anyone quite like him before and the attraction she felt had been immediate. She didn't know why her heart insisted on skipping a beat whenever he was close, or why she found the scar near his eye charming. He didn't smile, ordered her about without compunction and treated her like a nuisance.

But, he'd also shown gentleness on the ship when she cried and offered gruff comfort when she told him what happened on Lodestone. His touch sent shivers down her spine, while warmth pooled low in her abdomen. She had no control over her reaction, didn't fully understand all it meant, but there was no denying what she felt.

Sighing, finding no solution to her mixed emotions, Tru turned to go back to the house and ran smack into an immovable, solid wall. Strong arms grabbed her and pulled her close, preventing her fall. It took a moment for her brain to catch up and recognize what her body already realized.

Nick. Warm, solid and holding her too close. Her heart stuttered once before settling into a steady rhythm and her forehead dropped against the hard wall of his chest. She relished the contact even though she knew she should move away.

"Are you all right?" he rumbled from somewhere above her. "I didn't scare you did I?"

He tilted his head to get a look at her face, but Tru kept it averted, afraid of what might be revealed to his perceptive gaze. She straightened and moved to take a step back. He released her, dropping his arms to his sides. She shivered in the cooling night air and wished his arms were still around her then got mad at herself for being foolish.

"I'm fine. I just needed some fresh air."

A whisper of a breeze skimmed along her body and teased her hair, blowing a curl into her eyes. She lifted an arm to move it out of her way, but Nick was there first. He caught the flyaway strand and watched it twine around his forefinger. She didn't move, afraid to even take a deep breath. His eyes darkened as he let his hand slide through the curls framing her face.

Her hand came up to rest against his chest and she could feel the heavy beat of his heart against her palm. She raised her face, leaning toward him. Inexorably drawn. Wanting. One minute she thought he was going to kiss her, and the next, he was several feet away. Bereft, embarrassed and confused by all she was feeling, she stood in the moonlight unsure of what to do.

"We're leaving early in the morning," he said without inflection. A muscle jumping in his lean cheek was the only indication he was not as unaffected by what had just happened as he wanted her to believe.

"All right," she answered, rubbing her hands up and down her crossed arms. She didn't bother to ask where they were going. What would be the point? It had been decided, and she was expected to follow.

"You're cold. Come back inside and I'll see you get something warm to drink. You must be hungry as well. Sorry, I hadn't considered that. My apologies. I'm certainly not doing a good job of taking care of you like I promised your grandfather."

"We certainly don't want to disappoint my grandfather, now do we?" Tru snarled, rattled by her strong reaction to him. She breezed past him and headed for the house. "It is important to keep me healthy long enough to collect your credits for a job well done."

* * * *

Open-mouthed, Nick watched her march to the house, her back stiff.

"Great...just great," he muttered under his breath. "You handled that well, didn't you Nick old boy?"

His head dropped back as he closed his eyes and took a deep, calming breath. He would never understand women if he lived to be a hundred. All they did was tangle up a man's insides until he couldn't think straight and then they taunted him by getting angry over nothing. Disgusted with himself, he trailed her into the house. He would get control of himself, see his job completed for Geotern Mining while keeping her with him and out of harm's way and return her safely to her family on Bretonne as quickly as he could. Why the thought of letting her go left him feeling hollowed out was something he refused to think about tonight.

"Tru has gone to her room for the night," Callen informed him when he entered the house.

Nick growled.

Seth lightly punched Callen's shoulder and chuckled. "Told you. The boss man has it real bad."

"Let's hope he survives it," Callen replied. "Hell, let's hope we survive it."

"Shut up, both of you. Instead of standing there and wasting time gossiping, you can get my ship ready for travel tomorrow. I'll be in my office. Don't bother me." He slammed the door, rattling the frame.

Chapter 9

Efficient in design, the starship *Dominion* was all business. Powerful. Maneuverable. Armed to the teeth. With an impression force shield for protection, it was also the fastest ship Nick owned, the crown jewel in his growing fleet, the design one of his own. Her technology pushed the limits, but her capabilities would never be known until it was too late.

He stood in front of his ship, hands on hips, and looked over the gleaming surface. This was going to be the best way to get the mineral sample to Dendera Labs in time. The only things giving him even a second's pause were the cramped quarters and knowing he and Tru would be sharing them for a long stretch of time. He wasn't sure she was going to appreciate the forced intimacy, but he wasn't going to give her a chance to argue. He intended to keep her safe and out of trouble while his team worked with Maddox Creighton to flush out those in Lodestone Mining after her. Simple. He hoped.

"She's ready when you are," Callen said as he came up to Nick. "We made sure you would have everything you need for an extended trip."

"Good. I want to leave before the sun is fully up. Less chance of our departure being noticed," Nick answered, distracted, still focused on the cramped accommodations and Tru.

"I did a quick diagnostic on the A.I. and she responded superbly. I have to say the voice you gave her is definitely interesting," Callen observed with enough dryness to catch Nick's attention. "It's enough to make a man sweat."

"Shit! I forgot about that." Nick ran a hand through his hair and shot a slightly alarmed look at Callen. "I should never have let Seth persuade me to program that voice for the ship. Damn it, what was I thinking?"

"Yep, Tru is going to love talking to Siren. I'm sure they will bond instantly." He smirked, enjoying Nick's sudden discomfort. "You are so screwed. It is too late to reprogram her now."

Nick grunted and knocked Callen's shoulder back with a friendly punch.

"It almost makes me sorry I'm not going with you." Callen laughed.

"Keep it up, laughing boy. Revenge is sweet and I'm not going to be gone too long," Nick threatened without heat, his attention again on the polished lines of the ship in front of him. Anticipation built as he contemplated taking *Dominion* out. This would be her maiden voyage and his fingers itched to put her through her paces.

The A.I. onboard was the first of its kind, the program refined and perfected from a prototype he'd been working on before Tonlith's war. Siren's voice was sultry, the dulcet tones guaranteed to get any red-blooded male's attention. She was programmed to learn preferences and to anticipate direction. In short, *Dominion*'s onboard A.I.'s voice was a wet dream waiting to happen and guaranteed to keep long, lonely trips interesting. The voice had seemed like a good idea at the time.

Nick patted the cool metal affectionately before he turned and jogged back to the house, intending to collect his things and roust Tru from her room. It was time to go. Time to get the mineral to Dendera Labs, collect the remaining credits owed and finish what she'd started on Lodestone. Time to decide if the simmering attraction he felt for her was more than just her sexual appeal.

He reached the house and ran up the stairs to his room. He didn't slow down as he passed Tru's shut door. He would deal with her once he geared up. He crossed his bedroom, went to an inset cabinet and punched in a code to open the heavy door. Behind it was an impressive array of weapons, and he removed a lethal-looking knife.

Bending down, he slid the sharp blade into the sheath cleverly concealed behind the buckles climbing the sides of his tall boots. He strapped his blaster to his right hip, fastened the holster straps around a thigh and then snapped a wide metal and leather cuff to his left forearm. An unobtrusive display lit up, and the readout showed he was connected to Siren.

He was ready and his impatience to start the journey ratcheted up a notch. He shrugged into a form fitting, short jacket and slung his utility belt over a shoulder. He grabbed his compact carryon and left his room. Tru's door was open when he reached it, and he stuck his head in. She wasn't there so he went downstairs.

She stood in the doorway, the rising sun haloing her in a red and gold blush. She turned her head and regarded him through solemn eyes as he slowed his descent and then crossed the foyer to stand beside her.

* * * *

Tru swallowed hard, her heartbeat fluttering as she raised her head to look at him. It just wasn't fair. All he had to do was look at her and her libido went into overdrive. She frowned, annoyed with him, with herself and the world in general.

"Are you ready?" Nick asked, with a hint of a smile.

"Yes," she replied, unreasonably irritated he could look so well rested and virile this early in the morning. She hadn't slept well and the bruising around her eye and temple looked worse than before. Choosing to travel in a black outfit probably wasn't helping her looks either, but it fit her mood.

His eyebrow quirked, and then his face smoothed into impassivity. Motioning with a free hand, he indicated she should precede him through the door. She flounced away, disgruntled and out of sorts. No one had seen fit to tell her where she was going, only that she would be traveling with Nick. On one hand, the idea appealed to her, but on the other, she resented any choice being removed. She was getting tired of the men in her life treating her like her opinion didn't matter.

First, her father had ignored her concerns about Lodestone Mining and even though she would concede her trip there had been disastrous, the information gathered proved her hunch had been right. Now, Nick and her grandfather shuffled her away for her own protection. She would have liked to at least be consulted before the decision was made. Immersed in her dark thoughts, she marched down the path to the landing area.

"Hey Tru," Seth greeted her with a lopsided grin. "Your stuff is loaded and secured. Man, I envy you getting to take *Dominion* out."

"Then maybe you should go instead of me," she snapped before she thought. "I'm sorry. I didn't mean it. I have a headache this morning." She laid her hand on Seth's arm. "Don't mind me."

Seth covered hers with one of his own, patting it before releasing it and stepping away. She pretended she didn't see the look he and Nick exchanged when they thought she wasn't looking.

The sun was almost up. Heat already had begun to crowd the coolness left from the night. Shadows danced over the ground where the light reached and the rustle and chatter of birds added music to the air. The sights and sounds lightened her mood, but she wasn't given the time to stop and enjoy the day's beginning. Nick's warm palm against her spine nudged her along. It burned through the material of her shirt, making her achingly aware of his tall presence behind her.

The pleasure of his touch was impossible to resist, so she didn't even try. They boarded *Dominion* without speaking, and she watched while he stowed his bag.

Tru stopped as someone spoke in honeyed tones. She had no idea what had just been said, but recognized the musical language right away as the same one Nick and the others used when she'd first arrived. She glanced around for the woman, but there was no one else onboard.

In the same language, Nick rattled off something she made no attempt to follow.

"Acknowledged,"

Tru's eyebrows rose, she understood what had just been said. "What just happened?"

"I've instructed Siren to use common speak in all communications so you can understand her."

"Siren? Who is Siren?"

"The *Dominion* is the first ship in my fleet to have an artificial intelligence onboard. We named her Siren," he explained. "This is her maiden voyage, and Siren has been programmed to learn as we go. She will be listening to voice patterns, learning preferences and adding to her knowledge. Tonlithian is her base language, with common speak secondary. She's learning other languages and will be able to translate as needed in the future."

Tru nodded, not sure she grasped the whole concept, but intrigued by the idea.

"Siren, secure the boarding ramp and seal the entry door," Nick ordered as he guided Tru forward so she could take a seat at the front of the ship. He took his seat and buckled in for takeoff. Her seat conformed to her body and she looked at Nick for an explanation.

"The ship will remember your shape and preferences," he said. "It is part of her design."

She nodded. Fascinated, she watched the flight console lights and readouts. She didn't understand what she was seeing, but wasn't concerned. Nick was at the helm.

"Captain, I have scanned communications and we are clear to leave. Weather conditions should guarantee a smooth lift off," Siren announced. "Would you like me to initiate final systems check?"

"Yes. Verbalize as well as display." Nick scanned the readouts and listened to the engines come online and hum with power.

"Manual helm control, Siren."

"Acknowledged, Captain."

Nick took over, and the ship lifted from the landing pad, hovering in position before rotating for takeoff. Anticipation and exhilaration sped through Tru's system, raising her heartbeat. She breathed through it, wondering how he could appear so unruffled by the force thrumming under her feet. The *Dominion* responded like a lover to his every touch, and he wasn't as unaffected as she'd first thought, if his wolfish grin was any indication.

One minute they were hovering and the next, the ship shot through the atmosphere like a bullet. Their speed blurred the landscape below and took them to space so smoothly the transition from the planet's gravity to space barely registered. The grav field came online without the usual hesitation and removed the standard stomach-churning weightlessness.

Tru abandoned her black mood of earlier and laughed. She thumped her chair arm. "This is incredible."

Nick glanced at her and grinned before turning his attention back to the helm.

"Siren, notify base we're safely away." He pulled up information on their destination and scanned it.

"Base acknowledges," Siren replied after a moment's silence.

"Excellent." He settled more comfortably in his chair before looking at Tru. "Siren has plotted a direct route to Kaydet, minimizing our journey time. At the speed this ship is capable of moving we should shave several standard days off the journey."

"Classification of human female, Captain?" Siren asked.

"Tru Creighton, passenger and guest," he replied. "Standard access required."

"Acknowledged. Welcome aboard Tru Creighton, guest of Captain Rayven."

"Ah, thank you, Siren," Tru said, looking at Nick for guidance. It felt odd to be addressing the disembodied speaker and even stranger to feel insecure because of the lilting, sensual voice addressing her.

"Please place your right palm on the sensor, Tru Creighton, for ship's designation and biological security scan."

A thin, flat panel slid out of the console beside Tru and the outline of a hand glowed. She looked at it and then at Nick. "What is a biological security scan?" She asked concerned.

"The scan allows Siren to recognize you. It gives you access to the ship with your palm print and limited access to other functions within Siren's control."

"Such as?"

"The meal server, databanks, communication protocols, med system. Heck, Siren even has games and books available to help us pass the time." Pride was evident in his voice, and Tru smiled. "She'll also analyze your voice patterns for verbal commands."

Satisfied, she placed her palm on the panel. Her palm tingled with energy and a slight prick of her finger made her jump. A tiny drop of blood showed on the panel before disappearing. She jerked her hand away.

Before she could get angry, Nick explained. "I should have warned you about the blood sample. The information is stored in case of a medical emergency. Siren will analyze and will have the data for treatment if needed."

"Female passenger, Tru Creighton, standard access granted," Siren crooned, distracting Tru. "Instructions, Captain Rayven?"

"Switching to auto, Siren. The helm is under your control until further notice. Initiate standard long range perimeter scans."

"Acknowledged. Auto engaged."

Nick unbuckled his seat straps and waited for Tru to do the same. "Let me give you a quick tour so you can familiarize yourself with the ship," he said. "Everything is designed to be stowed out of the way when not in use."

"Like what?"

He walked to the back of the ship and stopped in front of a wall panel. "Most of the crew amenities are accessed from this panel. The colors will determine what function. The blue touch screen will allow the beds to slide into place for sleeping."

He touched the screen and she watched, fascinated, as two beds opened and lowered into place from the walls. Until that moment, she hadn't even noticed them or thought about where she would sleep.

"The red section is for medical. The green is food service. You get the picture. I tried to keep the design simple to maximize space."

"Everything in its place and a place for everything," she quipped.

"Exactly." He studied her smiling face, his expression warning her she might not like what was to come next. "We need to talk."

Sitting on a bench nestled between the bulkheads, he motioned for her to join him. She sat and folded her hands on her lap wondering what the problem was now. She didn't look at him, only heard the stiffness in his voice when he spoke. "Your grandfather and I agree you will be safer with me for the time being. He'll keep Sonne occupied while we deliver the mineral sample to Dendera Labs on Kaydet."

Nick leaned forward and rested his forearms on his thighs, his hands clasped between his spread knees. "Geir is the wildcard here, Tru. I don't know if he'll come after you, but from what you told me I suspect he will. I would if it were me."

Nick stared hard at her willing her to look at him. She turned her head and met the intensity of his gaze.

"He has killed one person we know of and he won't hesitate to kill you if he can."

"But, why?" She asked in a small worried voice. "What would be the point?"

"Men like Geir operate in the shadows. He has to have partners to pull this off and I can guarantee they won't be happy to be put under any kind of scrutiny. If too much attention is drawn to their activities, they will take Geir out without any hesitation They will protect their identity. He has to find you. Anything short of stopping you is a death sentence."

She was frightened and trying hard not to show it. Her breathing was uneven and fine tremors wracked her body. She stood up, only to sit down because her legs were too shaky to support her.

"Captain, bio scans show passenger Tru Creighton to be in mild distress," Siren interrupted, her voice pitched to express concern. "Heart rate and respiration are accelerated, skin surface is clammy."

"Understood," he snapped. "Disregard."

"Acknowledged."

Tru dropped her head into her hands.

"There are still a few kinks to be worked out," he offered in way of apology. "Privacy being one of them."

She snorted a nervous laugh. Raising her head, she studied him desperate for reassurance.

"I'll keep you safe, Tru," he said simply, running the back of his fingers down her cheek. His touch was gentle, the barest whisper against her skin. She leaned into his touch, helpless to stop herself before he moved his hand away.

He leaned forward and dropped a light kiss against her jaw. Startled, she raised her eyes and locked onto his face, searching intently. With infinite slowness, he once again moved toward her, giving her time to turn away if she chose. She met him halfway and sighed when his mouth melded to hers. The kiss was a tender give-and-take and before it could evolve into more he broke it off. She felt dazed and off balance and regretted he'd ended the kiss, even while she acknowledged to herself it had been a mistake in the first place.

Kylie Wolfe

"Captain, scans indicate—" Siren intoned.

"Enough," Nick barked and pinched the bridge of his nose.

"Acknowledged." She sounded offended, and silence hung heavy.

"I seem to spend a great deal of time apologizing to you, Tru," Nick admitted, his voice low and tone clipped. "I should not have kissed you. You are under my protection. It will not happen again, I assure you."

"Whatever," she tossed back, proud her voice was steady. In reality, she wanted to groan out loud because she was confused and exhilarated at the same time. She wasn't sure why he'd kissed her in the first place but was annoyed he apologized and then told her it wouldn't happen again. Unsure of what to say next, she stood and crossed the small space to the wall panel.

"So, Nick, how do I get a drink?" She studied the readout with her back to him.

He swore under his breath and she glanced over her shoulder with a questioning smile. He scowled. She ran the tip of her tongue over her lower lip and his eyes narrowed following the movement. It was good to know he wasn't as unaffected by something which had just tilted her world as he would like her to believe. She turned away, mollified and infinitely more cheerful.

He helped her get the drink she wanted.

Chapter 10

Anto Geir fought the panic consuming him, tearing little pieces of his confidence away and spitting it out until all remaining was a jagged mess of raw nerves. Sweat beaded his upper lip, and he wiped it away with an unsteady hand. Too jumpy and angry to sit, he took another turn around his cramped office. Everything was falling apart, shot to hell because of one nosy bitch.

Slamming a fist into his opposite palm, Anto ground his teeth. He detested waiting and the fear gnawing his insides. Hated not knowing for sure where Tru Creighton hid. But, mostly he despised the bastards he did business with. Failure was unacceptable and if their little side venture was brought to light, he was as good as dead.

The callscreen chimed, and Anto jumped, his heart knocking hard against his ribs. Rounding his desk, he punched the button and waited impatiently for the channel to connect.

"What have you found out, Malvin?" he demanded upon seeing the other man's image fill the screen. "Have you located her?"

Malvin Sonne was the perfect figurehead for Lodestone Mining. Tall. Tanned. Debonair. And not a thought in his head beyond what was put there by Anto Geir. Right now, his handsome face was gray with strain. Running a hand through his hair, he left it uncharacteristically mussed.

"You have no idea how difficult this is," Malvin muttered, his eyes darting around the room. Leaning closer, his face filled the screen and Anto reared back startled. "Maddox Creighton is a hard man to question. I can't let him get suspicious. The only thing he has told me about his granddaughter is she's visiting a friend in a nearby town called Tuor."

"Are you positive? He doesn't know she was on Lodestone?" Anto shot back.

"Yes, I'm positive. He has no idea she was anywhere but where she said she would be and I don't dare push. He's already asking uncomfortable questions about Lodestone Mining. I swear he knows something, Anto. He's asked about you and is wondering why you didn't come to this meeting like you usually do."

"What did you tell him?"

"Nothing! Nothing, I swear. I just told him you were needed on Lodestone and I couldn't spare you for this event."

"Stupid! Stupid! We don't want him thinking there is something going on here, you idiot!"

"I was careful. I don't think he knows anything for sure. Why would he?"

Anto dropped onto his chair and leaned back. He steepled his fingers under his chin and looked at the ceiling, contemplating what had been said.

"You're right. There is no reason he would know about the shipments," he admitted. The more he thought his way through the problem the more his conviction grew. "If he thinks the Creighton bitch is in Tuor then it is to our advantage." Sitting up, Anto punched a finger at the callscreen and continued, "You keep Maddox Creighton happy. You hear me? Do what you do best, Sonne, and kiss everyone's ass. We don't want anyone looking too closely at Lodestone until I've cleaned up this mess."

"All right...all right." Malvin heard a noise and his head jerked around. "Someone's coming. I've got to go."

Anto stared at the callscreen in disbelief. No one ended a connection except him. No one. He jumped up and swiped his hand across the top of his desk, sending writing implements and hardware crashing to the floor. He resumed his agitated pacing.

It infuriated him the bitch had gotten off-world without him knowing. He'd spread the word no one was to give her passage without his consent, confident he would be obeyed. Yet, somehow, she'd managed it. Worrying his bottom lip between his teeth, he stopped his pacing to gaze out the window in his office. He'd been so sure he would have time to deal with her and destroy the information she'd discovered with her snooping.

He enjoyed playing with people, and seeing Tru's distress, particularly after he'd killed the idiotic shipping manager, had pleased him. Remembering the fear in her eyes when he'd approached her, the dropped hints about the dangers of meddling where she didn't belong and then ransacking her room to reinforce her fear, almost made him smile. He'd planned to run her to ground and have more fun, something a little more physical. She was attractive enough, for the mouthy type, and he could think of plenty of things to occupy that mouth of hers. But, she'd disappeared. Gone. No one had seen her leave or could give him the answers he wanted.

He couldn't believe his sheer dumb luck when he'd overheard a snippet of conversation in the alehouse. Geotern had contracted the upstart Nick Rayven to deliver the coveted mineral sample to Dendera Labs. Anto had nearly choked on his ale when Rayven's name was mentioned. He'd left before drawing too much attention to himself, the whole time cursing his bad luck.

He wanted the mineral for himself and his partners. He'd paid through the nose for information to that weasel, Jonas Spark. He'd needed an inside man since Geotern kept the location of the mineral secret and the only hope he had of getting his hands on it was by stealing the sample. Jonas was supposed to bring it to him so Lodestone would be the company staking a claim to the mineral rights. Instead, he'd given it to Rayven.

Acid burned in Anto's stomach, and he rubbed his sternum to relieve the pain. Another failure his partners wouldn't forgive if they ever found out. He consoled himself with the fact Jonas wouldn't betray him again or have a chance to rat him out. He'd made sure of it. By the time Anto was through with him, Jonas would have told him anything to stop the pain. Anto had thrown the body down the shaft of an old played-out mine.

He wasn't sure how she'd managed it, but he was positive Tru had somehow connected with Rayven to get off Lodestone. This posed a problem because Rayven had a reputation even Anto hesitated to cross. The man wasn't someone he wanted to mess with. Ever. But, he was desperate and if Rayven had Tru and the mineral sample, then Anto had no choice but to follow and try to get them back.

He was running out of time. His partners already wanted to know more about the mineral he'd told them about. They were also asking awkward and probing questions about why their profits were starting to fall from the normal shipments.

Anto swallowed hard. He'd gotten greedy and had been channeling some of the credits from the illicit sale of Lodestone Mining's mineral shipments to his own accounts. He was counting on the new mineral discovery and the promise of an even bigger payoff to placate his partners.

Pacing the office wasn't doing him any good. The walls closed in, making it hard to draw a deep breath, and his nerves jumped like bugs under a hot lamp. He debated going back to his rooms for the remainder of the day. He did it often enough and no one would question his whereabouts. Besides, he'd done all he could for the moment.

Locating a ship and crew operating in the shadows hadn't been too difficult to find. Pirates were a well-known risk and attacked craft unlucky enough to cross their paths with alarming frequency. There was no fear of reprisal since the normal shipping lanes in space were too vast for any type of law enforcement. Anto offered a sizeable reward to make sure Rayven's ship didn't reach its destination. He made it clear he wanted no survivors; he only wanted the mineral onboard the ship. Just in case that failed, he hedged his bets and hired a couple of mercs from Kaydet to stake out Dendera Labs. They'd take out Rayven before he delivered the mineral. Once in Anto's hands, it would be smooth sailing.

Running a hand through his sparse hair, he craved something to take the edge off and help him think clearly. He needed a hit of twist, the newest designer drug making its way across the galaxy with the help of Lodestone Mining. In his opinion, it had been sheer genius to hide the drug with the mineral shipments. No one would ever think to look for them there. Even Sonne didn't know. It made it easier to keep the profits from his side venture all to himself and his silent partners.

The temptation to try twist had been irresistible. The guarantee of an unlimited supply melted away any niggling doubts he might have had. The drug boosted his senses, making him feel as if he flew on the cusp of a breaking wave, alive and powerful. Invincible.

He'd started to increase his usage, ignoring the nerves jumping like live wires whenever he went too long without a dose. The craving for the drug worried him somewhat, but was a small price to pay for the euphoria he experienced.

Anto wiped his nose with the back of his fist then left his office. He announced he had business in the mines and would be gone for the remainder of the day. There was no response, but he didn't expect one knowing he was universally disliked. His presence served to dampen the somber mood of Lodestone's employees further. He enjoyed the effect he had on his office personnel.

Chapter 11

True picked at her food and Nick wondered what she was up to now. She kept her head bowed, but he was aware of her quick glances shot his way. It was playing merry hell with his concentration. Whatever she was thinking must have amused her because he caught the sly smile she tried to contain out the corner of his eye.

"Don't even think about it," he said matter-of-factly, not bothering to remove his attention from what he was doing. "It can only end badly."

Her head snapped up. She scowled at him through narrowed eyes while he continued to pretend he was reading information on the portable tablet in front of him.

"I have no idea what you mean," she replied stiffening.

He glanced her way and pinned her with his gaze. He raised an eyebrow, and watched her squirm in her chair.

"It doesn't take a genius to figure out what is going through your mind when you stab at your food and then glare at me." Pushing aside his tray, he relaxed against the back of his chair. Long fingers played with the tablet, slowly spinning it on the surface of the table.

"I was not glaring!"

He gave her a hint of a smile. "If you say so."

"Besides, how would you know what I was doing? You certainly don't pay attention to me." She shut her mouth with a snap as if she wished she could call back what she had just said. She sounded like a petulant child, which gave him pause. It wasn't how he wanted to view her.

Unable to stop herself, she continued, "We've been on this ship for days and we're still a long way from Kaydet. I'm bored, Nick. You have work to occupy your time. You get lost in it for ages and probably wouldn't notice if I decided to take a spacewalk until it was too late."

"I'd notice."

She jumped up from her seat frustration in every line of her body and took her half-eaten meal to the disposal unit. "That's not my point and you know it. You may find it easy to ignore me, but I find it uncomfortable to be trapped on this ship with someone who would rather I wasn't around."

"I want you around." Nick rose and disposed of his tray.

"You have a strange way of showing it."

"What do you want from me, Tru?" he shot back. "In case you have forgotten, this isn't a pleasure trip. I have to get the sample to Dendera Labs and keep you alive and out of Geir's hands. I'm not here to entertain you."

Hissing in a breath, she spun on her heel and stomped to her seat at the table. "I get it. Obviously, I was mistaken in thinking something as simple as conversation would be part of your job description."

He dropped his head and closed his eyes, praying for patience. "I will make more of an effort in future to include you, if it will make you happy."

"Don't do me any favors." Crossing her arms, she spun her chair so her back was to him. "I will be sure to stay out of your way from now on."

"Don't be foolish. I'm doing my best here."

He stared at the back of her head debating his next move. Part of him wanted to soothe the frustration and anger radiating from her and part of him wanted to keep a safe distance. Something much better for his peace of mind in the long run.

She was unlike anyone he'd ever met. He felt her unmistakable presence even if she didn't say a word. Something about the way she moved across a room made the space seem smaller and sucked the air right out of his lungs. He tried to treat her with distant courtesy, to keep her at arm's length, but the slow burn of desire he felt whenever she was near was like heat lightning, leaving him electrified and yearning. Nothing could have prepared him for his reaction to her. It kept him awake most nights.

His military training had taught him how to handle most situations in his life, something he did with ease under normal circumstances. There was nothing normal about the situation he faced now. He found himself watching her when he thought she wasn't looking. She smiled often, delighted in small things and made it difficult to concentrate on his self-imposed tasks. He wanted her to look at him, really look, even though he did everything he could to keep her at a distance. He wanted to see her blue eyes flash and know without any doubt she was aware of him as a man and not just someone hired to keep her safe. He bit back a curse.

"You know what? Never mind, just forget I even mentioned it," she said.

She spun around to face him and Nick let out a slow breath. "I can do that."

"Captain, scans show a ship coming up fast in our right quadrant." Siren's interruption broke the tense silence.

"Can you identify it?" He sprinted to the bridge and slid into his chair.

"Negative. All identifying insignia has been masked. Four life signs onboard."

"Hail the ship, Siren. Let's see what we have here."

"Affirmative. Channel open."

"This is Captain Rayven of the starship *Dominion*. Identify yourself."

"Well, well, well, Captain Rayven is it? Nice ship. I'm going to enjoy owning her."

The man speaking over the com sounded pleased with himself and Nick's hackles rose. "I wouldn't be too sure of myself if I were you."

"I've been searching for you. You have something onboard I want. Nice of you not to keep me waiting too long."

"And what might that be?"

"I believe you have a mineral my client is interested in, possibly even a passenger. Hand over the mineral and the girl and I might consider letting you live...or not." A deep chuckle came through the channel. "The girl might prove to be a little fun."

"I have no intention of letting you take my ship or what I carry onboard. Make this easy on yourself and scuttle away. I don't want to have to kill you."

"You feeling lucky, Rayven?"

Nick disconnected the channel, done with small talk. Sensors confirmed the other ship had closed the distance between them and was even now maneuvering into a better position.

"Siren, full shields. Bring weapons online." He buckled himself into his seat. "Tru, quit hovering and get your ass in your seat. I want you harnessed immediately."

"What's happening? Who was that?" She scrambled to her seat and fumbled with the straps.

Weapons fire rocked *Dominion*. Lights flickered.

"Status," he barked.

"Shield's holding, Captain."

"Bring us around, Siren. I want to see that bastard."

"Acknowledged."

Dominion banked left, hurling Tru against her seat. Gripping the chair arms, she braced her feet against the floor.

Nick eyed the viewscreen, not in the least intimidated by the bigger, battle-scarred warcraft. Battle, he understood.

The other ship came about, preparing to fire, but he was faster. Bright flashes of light hurtled through the black expanse of space, struck the other craft, exploding into a shower of sparks.

Return fire missed as Nick took evasive action and the shots streaked past. He loosed several rapid blasts to buckle the shields on the other ship. He scored a direct hit. The other craft listed to its side, maneuverability gone. He'd damaged them enough there would be no return fire.

Over almost before it began, the short battle did nothing to satisfy the violence thrumming in his veins, the brutal call of war demanding a kill. Fighting his training and every instinct he possessed, which dictated he destroy the enemy, he reached deep for control. He was no longer a soldier fighting a war where it was kill or be killed without reservation.

He sucked in a deep breath. "Status of the other ship, Siren."

"Shields down, left weapons port destroyed and unable to fire, engines at half power."

"Life signs?"

"I am still picking up four life signs, Captain."

"Good. Open a channel. I want to talk to the sonofabitch again."

"Acknowledged. Channel open."

"What? Want to gloat before you finish us off?" The voice rasped, fury dripping off each word like acid.

"Who hired you?" It was a demand more than a question. Nick's voice held no hesitation the other could use to his advantage.

The other man swore, promising retribution.

Unmoved, Nick waited.

"What's in it for me if I tell you?"

Nick could tell it had cost the other man to ask. He clenched a fist, his knuckles showing white, the only indication he gave of the savagery still riding him hard. "You get to live."

"Anto Geir."

"Looks like he has caused us both some trouble."

"So, what now, Rayven?" The words were bitter.

"I continue my journey."

"Look, no hard feelings. I was just doing a job. Maybe we can work something out here. You don't want to leave us like this. It will take months to get to the nearest planet for repairs."

Nick spared a look at Tru. All the blood had leached from her face. She clenched the chair arms so tightly the fine bones in her hand showed as fingers left indents in the soft leather. Her breaths hitched.

"Not my problem. The next time our paths cross I *will* kill you." He cut communication. It wouldn't take much to destroy the civilized veneer he wore and leave nothing but scattered pieces of the other ship floating in space. The temptation was almost too great. "Siren, take us out of here. Now."

"Acknowledged."

In a flash, Siren had pushed the ship to the upper edges of its capabilities. Adrenaline and fury still coursed through his body, making his heart thud in his chest. He rolled his shoulders to release some of the tension. He fought the impulse to touch Tru, knowing it would be unwise until he was more in control of himself. He pinched the bridge of his nose and concentrated on his breathing until he was sure he had the necessary restraint to take care of her.

He stroked her hand with a light touch until he felt some of her rigidity ease. He was gratified when she released the chair arm and allowed him to enfold her cold hand in his.

"I should never have left home." Her voice quavered like an old woman's, and he tightened his grip. "I should have left well enough alone. I could have gotten us killed because of my pride. Why did I go to Lodestone? I—Oh God, I could have gotten us killed!"

Nick unbuckled his harness and stood. He did the same for her before lifting her easily out of her seat and into his arms. In the crew quarters, he settled her in a chair, grabbed a blanket from one of the bunks and wrapped it around her trembling shoulders. He left her long enough to fix a strong mug of tayberry, a drink he'd been introduced to when he moved to Alludra. He'd developed a taste for the somewhat bitter beverage and made sure all his ships had it onboard. Down on one knee in front of her, he helped her wrap her hands around the warm mug and raise it to her lips.

"You need to drink this. It will help."

He kept his tone businesslike, unemotional, and was relieved to see some of the wildness leave her eyes as she focused on him and took a sip of the drink. When she looked a little steadier, he rose and took a seat opposite her.

He didn't know what to say, or how to reassure her. He'd been a warrior too long, had been trained to ignore the horrors and move through the fear. Everyone he'd served with had the same training. They all accepted the risks, knew the score. He still took chances every day; it was as much a part of his nature as breathing. This kind of violence was new to her and it was easy to forget she'd been raised in a civilized world far removed from the violence so familiar to him. The other ship hadn't stood a chance against *Dominion* and he'd known it from the beginning. His ship was faster, more maneuverable, and he understood what she was capable of doing.

"Will they come after us?" she asked in a small voice.

Her mug of tayberry wobbled and he removed it from her grasp to set it on the table beside them. He leaned forward, rested his forearms on his spread thighs and took her hands in his. He rubbed his thumbs across their backs as he searched her pale face.

"No. Their ship is too damaged to give chase."

"They would have killed us."

"Yes. Somehow, Anto Geir discovered we're together and where we're headed. I'll do my best to keep you safe, Tru, but you have to understand, there will be other attempts."

She took a deep, shuddering breath and nodded. He released her hands and she clutched the blanket a little closer around her shoulders.

"Thank you for being honest with me. I didn't mean to bring this kind of trouble to you. I hope you know that."

Before he could answer, she stood and crossed to her bunk. The lost look on her face was difficult to see, and it rocked him to know he would do anything within his power to prevent it from being on her face ever again.

Chapter 12

Bleary eyed and irritable, Nick rolled out of his bunk the next morning and headed to the cleanser. Nightmares had haunted his dreams every time he'd managed to fall asleep, giving him little peace through the long night. The dream never changed and he wondered if he would ever be able to escape the memory of being trapped in his disabled war ship and watching his home world go up in flames. The helplessness he'd felt and his screams of denial still echoed in his ears as he shut the cleanser door and turned on the water.

He felt like death warmed over. There was nothing he could do about it, and he was too weary to care. He only wanted to wash the dried sweat from his body and give himself time to clear his head before he faced Tru. After yesterday, he wasn't sure what he would have to deal with to help her.

The last thing he expected when he made an appearance was to be greeted by a hot mug of tayberry and Tru looking determined. He scanned her face to see if he'd disturbed her with his bad dreams, and noted with some guilt, dark smudges shadowing her eyes. He murmured his thanks for the drink and took a fortifying sip while he considered what he should say, if anything. To admit he suffered from nightmares was humiliating.

"I think it is time I made myself useful around here. I'm tired of having nothing to do. I want to learn more about this ship," she announced catching him off guard.

He lowered the mug and frowned, surprised by the resolve he saw on her face. "That isn't necessary. I don't expect you to become part of the crew."

"If you are worried it will affect the fee you collect from my grandfather, don't be. He'll honor the agreement."

"Money is the last thing I'm worried about." He straightened away from the table and placed his mug down with more force than necessary.

"Then what?"

"This isn't a game, Tru. You can't just decide between one day and the next to become part of a crew—my crew."

"I want to do this, Nick."

"Why? This isn't the life for you." He waved a hand to encompass the cramped utilitarian quarters they occupied. "Look around you. This is about as far from your normal life as it can get. There're no luxuries here. It is uncomfortable at the best of times and dangerous all of the time. The only reason you are onboard now is because of circumstances beyond your control."

She shrugged, her soft mouth set in mulish lines. "Believe me, I understand. I'm not a complete fool."

"Then give me one good reason why I should waste my time training you on even a basic level." In spite of himself, he was curious. He watched her glance around as if seeing their surroundings for the first time before squaring her shoulders and meeting his eyes.

"I always thought I could handle anything, thought I knew what was best. Going to Lodestone proved me wrong and from the very beginning, I was in over my head. I'm ashamed and embarrassed by my actions." She clasped her hands in front of her so tight her knuckles were white. "I might have been scared then, but yesterday terrified me. I had no idea what to do. I don't ever want to feel that way again. I need to be able to do something, no matter how small."

He picked up his mug and took a sip of his cooling drink in order to give himself time to think. They were going to be onboard *Dominion* for several more weeks and giving her something to occupy her time wasn't such a bad idea.

"Okay."

"Really?"

"I'm not guaranteeing anything here. This isn't something you can just decide you want to learn one day and then be able to handle a ship the next. I'll set up some learning programs for you. They'll take you through the basics. Siren will monitor your progress."

"Wait, Siren is going to instruct me? I thought you would."

"No. I've a ship to run, in case you've forgotten. Siren is more than capable of running you through the fundamentals. It will be good for both of you. Just think of what you can learn from each other." Nick hid a grin behind his mug then finished off his drink.

"Not exactly what I had in mind," she muttered.

"Did you say something?"

"Um...nope. So how is this going to work? You know, Siren teaching me and all." She tilted her head.

"Siren." Nick raised his voice and winked at Tru. "Implement level one ship introduction for Tru. Guide her through the basics and answer any questions she may have. Give her access through one of the portable tablets. I want daily updates on her progress."

"Acknowledged."

"Excellent. I will leave you two to get started then."

* * * *

Tru watched him saunter to the bridge, not sure what had happened. He never seemed to react the way she expected, and she'd been prepared to argue long and hard for what she wanted. The fact he gave in so quickly left her wondering if she'd missed something important in their exchange.

She was not lying when she told him she needed to feel she had some control and enough knowledge to help in a crisis. The attack the day before had nearly paralyzed her with fear, and it had taken a long time to quit shaking in the aftermath. Through the long hours of the night, she'd struggled with the truth of her precarious situation and her culpability in bringing it about.

She'd relived the events over and over, aware of Nick's quick actions and his absolute command at the helm. He was the reason they were still alive. Her guilt had only increased when she heard him thrashing around in his bunk and recognized he was in the grip of another nightmare. She'd wanted to offer comfort, but knew from her previous unpleasant experience not to touch him. She hated being nothing more than a millstone around his neck, helpless to do anything and relying on him for protection. She wanted to do something to show she wasn't incapable and weak.

Through her soul searching, she'd realized approaching him to learn more about the ship would not only mitigate some of her feelings of helplessness and ignorance, but would force him to give her the attention she craved.

Hands on her hips, she chewed her bottom lip. Her plan hadn't worked out the way she'd wanted. She was going to learn about the ship all right, but he was just as far out of reach as he had been. It wasn't fair.

"I have downloaded a beginning program for you," Siren said. "Shall we begin?"

Tru sighed and picked up the tablet on the table. "Why not."

"I can think of many reasons, if that is your wish and you care to explore them," Siren replied.

* * * *

Tru was immersed in her studies, one finger twirling a loose curl when she sensed Nick approach. She raised her head and watched his loose-limbed stride as he crossed the small space before stopping a short distance away to lean against a locker. She loved watching him move, loved the contained power and innate grace of his movements.

He had a razor-sharp mind, which challenged her. She enjoyed discussing her lessons over their evening meal, particularly when she had mastered a difficult concept and made excuses to seek him out during the day. The odd thing was he didn't seem to object to the interruptions, which pleased her. He was always on her mind, no matter what she was doing.

She looked up from her notes and caught his eye. "Do you have a minute, Nick? I want to run something by you."

He straightened from where he'd been leaning and took a seat across from her, slouching comfortably. Arms crossed over his chest, he waited. She was beginning to understand that look on his face, that gleam of anticipation in his eyes.

"I've been giving this a great deal of thought and you need to make Siren real," she said.

"What?" Dumbfounded, he sat up in his chair and looked at her like she'd lost her mind.

"Well, not real in the sense of a physical body 'real.'"

"I'm almost afraid to ask, but what kind of real are you talking about then?"

"Siren is a part of this crew, right? She interacts with us, is capable of handling this ship, follows orders and is developing opinions." She gestured expansively as she spoke and leaned forward in her seat, enthusiasm animating her face.

"It was the way she was designed, Tru. You know that."

"I know, but it is a little weird to be talking to a disembodied voice. Siren and I have been discussing this and we think you should give her a holographic presence."

"You discussed this with Siren? Are you kidding me?" He shook his head.

"Of course not. I wouldn't kid about something this important."

"Do you have any idea what you are suggesting here? Her design is complex. There're too many components, too much intricate programming involved to even consider that kind of change. It is impossible."

"Not for you," she replied, leaving him nothing more to say. "Just think about it, okay?"

"Captain, emergency imminent," Siren announced. "Solar storm approaching."

"Tru, get to the bridge and buckle in. Now. Siren, raise shields!" He ran to the front of the ship, jumped over the arm of his chair and slapped the shoulder harness on. "Hurry, Tru. Get the lead out."

"Shields raised."

"Siren, shut down all electrical unless required for life support. All power to shields."

The lights shut off, except those on the helm, casting eerie blue shadows on their faces. Tru's apprehension rose as she tested her shoulder harness and fidgeted in her seat. She looked to him, and drew strength from his rock-solid presence. She didn't know much about solar storms—only enough to be frightened. She clutched the armrest.

"Impact in three, two..." Siren intoned matter-of-factly.

The invisible wave hit them and electrical sparks flashed over the ship's nose, coming at them with terrifying swiftness. Blistering shocks pulsed along her skin and nerves felt as if they were on fire, burning her up from the inside out.

"Shields strong, life support holding," Siren continued.

The ship bucked and lurched, snapping Tru's head forward then back.

"Siren, how long until we're out of the storm?" Nick demanded, while he continued to monitor the power to the shields and make rapid adjustments only he understood.

The ship's engine groaned and metal screeched from the force of the storm. Lights flickered on the helm, sparks flying from wires affected by the solar pulses battering them.

"Hang on, Tru. We're almost through," he assured her while he swiftly rerouted connections.

"Storm end in five. Four. Three." Siren counted down and suddenly they were free.

The ship gave one more shudder and then all was quiet, except for the hiss of overheated engines and the crackle of static arcing from the wiring.

"Status," he commanded, his voice calm. A muscle jumped in his cheek from clenching his teeth.

"Fuel cells low. Shields on right quadrant compromised. Life support at eighty percent," Siren replied, the usual melodious tones of her voice absent.

Tru shivered and looked at Nick. "So that was a solar storm, huh?" Her voice cracked, and she cleared her throat. Slowly, she forced one finger at a time to release her death grip on the chair arms and tried to stop the audible hitch in her breathing. They were lucky the ship hadn't been torn apart by the storm.

He turned and looked at her. "Yes. That was a solar storm."

His lips twitched and then slid into a lopsided grin, revealing strong, white teeth. Mesmerized, she watched his eyes lighten to rich amber and the lines bracketing his eyes crinkle with the first signs of a real smile. It changed him, replacing the stern planes and angles of his face with an attractiveness she found hard to resist. He looked exhilarated, almost boyish. Handsome. Her heart kicked up a beat. Then he astounded her by throwing back his head and letting out a laughing whoop. It echoed through the dark cavern of the ship and drew a shaky laugh from her in response, even though she didn't feel like laughing.

"Captain, we will need to break flight plan and replace the damaged fuel cells," Siren said. "Scans show a space station one standard day away. Do you wish to contact?"

Nick unbuckled his harness then leaned over to unfasten Tru's. Not taking his eyes off her, he replied, "Contact the station and get permission to emergency dock. Arrange for the necessary fuel cell replacement, payment through Rayven Security."

"Acknowledged."

"Do a diagnostic on ship's functions and then report. Route required power to engines and shields—life support function to minimum."

"Acknowledged. Zeegret Station is prepared to assist and fuel cells will be ready when we arrive."

"Excellent. Good job, Siren," Nick said, a sincere note in his words.

She made a sound suspiciously like a purr, and Tru began to understand what a remarkable piece of design she was. Her lightning quick processing had gotten them through the storm with minimal damage.

Nick rose, and then helped Tru out of her seat. Her legs were wobbly, and she leaned against him, grateful for the strong arm he placed around her waist.

"I vote we indulge in a celebratory drink. We got through the storm in one piece and I, for one, could use it," he said, leading her through the dimly lit ship to the crew quarters. His voice still thrummed with the remnants of a battle fought and won.

"Drink? I don't drink." She was bewildered, still fighting the effects of an adrenaline rush and shaken by the full force of his smile. A drink was the last thing on her mind. What she desperately wanted to do was crawl into her bunk, pull the covers over her head and hide. Reaction hit her hard, and she started to shake, her muscles jumping in uncontrolled spasms.

"I want to go home," she whispered, head bowed.

All of a sudden, it was too much for her. She wanted to be surrounded by familiar things, safe from the dangers she'd landed herself in, and away from Nick. Learning about the ship hadn't helped. She'd still been scared spitless when the storm hit. She was no help at all, no matter what she told herself. She found it hard to understand the exhilaration she saw on his face from a storm that had left her petrified and lost.

He stopped and she knew he'd heard the tremor in her voice. His touch was gentle as he lifted her head so he could see her face. She could see the sympathy in his expression and looked away, biting her bottom lip to keep it from trembling. She knew it wouldn't take much to come completely undone and it was the last thing she wanted to do.

He widened his stance and drew her into his arms, resting his cheek on the top of her head. He held her close absorbing the tremors wracking her body, offering comfort. She burrowed into his warmth, feeling his strength surround her and was grateful.

"It will be okay. I will keep you safe," he murmured into her hair. "The storm is over."

"I wish I'd never gone to Lodestone," she whimpered, her voice muffled in the stretchy fabric of his shirt. "I don't think I'm cut out for adventure."

Nick chuckled. It rumbled under her ear and stopped her slide into self-pity. It was as effective as water dashed in her face.

"Tru Creighton, you amaze me." He dropped a quick kiss on the top of her head and hugged her harder. "You don't give yourself enough credit. You've stood up to everything thrown at you and come out fighting. Afraid of adventure? I don't think so."

His words had a bracing effect. He'd reminded her she wasn't a quitter. Creightons never gave in and she didn't intend to be the first. Standing in the shelter of his arms, listening to his heart beat steadily under her cheek helped push aside some of the terror. As tempting as the thought of wrapping him around her like a security blanket was, she gathered herself and stepped out of his arms. Her smile was a little unsteady, but genuine. With a tentative touch, she cupped the curve of his cheek, feeling the rasp of whiskers against her skin.

"Thank you," she said.

He searched her face for one long moment and then nodded. "You're welcome." His voice was a dark caress, its tone deep and with just enough gravel to send her nerve endings into overdrive. His expression might have returned to its familiar impassive mask, but his gaze was alive with things she desperately wanted to understand. She had trouble looking away from him, captured by the desire she thought she saw in the shadows of his dark eyes.

"I think I want to go to bed. To sleep. I need to sleep. Alone. Not that I don't usually, you understand." Scowling, she clamped her mouth shut to stop the flow of words. The urge to step back into his arms was almost overwhelming. What if she were wrong?

And there it was again, a devastating smile, starting in his eyes this time and moving slowly across his lips, tempting her.

"Sleep well, Tru," he murmured.

She fled, knowing he watched her from where he stood in the shadowed room. His absolute stillness heightened her awareness of him as she retreated to the sleeping quarters.

The slide of material over sensitized skin made her hyper-aware of cool silk and heated flesh as she undressed behind the privacy screen.

Confused by the emotional upheavals of the day, and her feelings for him, she crawled into her bunk and tried to ignore the heat pooling in her belly. She punched her pillow and searched for a comfortable position to sleep.

Chapter 13

Nick was no stranger to the tumult of feelings coursing through his body. He'd felt the punch-drunk assault of adrenaline many times in his career. He understood the heady rush of euphoria once the danger had passed and knew firsthand the reckless need for physical release in its aftermath. He recognized it a very human response to the need to reaffirm life continued.

All those feelings and needs made his hands shake and drawing breath into his oxygen-starved lungs difficult. He wanted to follow Tru to her bed and sink into her warmth with a painful intensity leaving his muscles taut and his emotions a tangled mess.

If the situation were different, he would have gone with his friends to a tavern and indulged in the usual male bonding ritual of congratulatory back-thumping and drinking until he was either too drunk to stand or had found a bed partner. A sobering thought. He'd been younger then, still idealistic and sure of his ability to survive what life threw at him. It seemed like a lifetime ago, and he'd learned surviving was sometimes almost too painful to be endured.

To let her walk away had cost him. The heavy thud of his heartbeat pulsed in his temple and restless energy held muscles rigid. He called himself ten kinds of a fool, even though he knew he did the right thing. He ran a hand across the back of his neck before he went in search of a canister of ale he knew was onboard. He didn't drink often, but tonight promised to be long and lonely.

After he snagged the chilled canister, he returned to the bridge. Slouching in his chair, he nursed the drink and stared moodily into space.

* * * *

Tru was freezing and woke from sleep curled in a tight ball. The temperature of the ship had dropped when life support functions were lowered. Shivering, she debated leaving the dubious warmth of her bed

Kylie Wolfe

and searching for another covering but it would take too much effort. Instead she tightened her grip on the blankets, bringing them closer to her cold nose. Her teeth chattered as her discomfort increased.

"Scoot over," Nick urged, his tone brusque, as he nudged her hip with a knee planted on the side of the bed. "It's too damn cold to sleep alone."

Shocked out of her drowsy misery, she reared up enough to look over her shoulder at the solid presence looming over her. "I have no intention of sharing this bed with you."

"You might enjoy keeping me awake with your chattering teeth, but I don't intend to suffer through a cold night when we can share our warmth. Now, move over."

His tone brooked no argument, and Tru moved before she thought. He lifted her blankets and slid in beside her. With a flick of his wrists, he spread his blankets over hers and then tried to settle himself without touching her. His broad shoulders took up most of the available space, making her hunch to keep an appropriate distance between them. She was uncomfortable, and the strangeness of having him so close rattled her. She'd never shared her bed with anyone. He muttered things she tried not to hear as he shifted, his elbow jabbing her in the back.

"Screw it," he said. Turning on his side he faced her back and hauled her against his chest, a heavy arm wrapped around her middle.

She let out a squeak of surprise, but the heat radiating from him felt delicious. Helpless to stop herself, she wiggled closer to settle into the curve of his body, desperate for the warmth. Ignoring the nagging little voice warning her she was asking for trouble, she relaxed, grateful for the heat he generated.

He hissed when her cold feet tangled with his legs. Surrounded by his clean male scent, she swallowed and tried to force her mind off the fact she was cradled in his arms.

The novelty of being this close to him, of feeling him pressed against her was an unexpected pleasure. She didn't let herself dwell on the fact he could easily have covered her with another blanket and remained in his bunk. She didn't want to speculate on his reasoning, just wanted to enjoy the moment of intimacy. Too tired to fight it any more or to think too deeply about his motivation, she slowly allowed the tension to leave and exhaustion to take over. A smile twitched on her lips when she heard his faint groan as she shifted to nestle her hips more comfortably against the firm length of his body. She dropped into a sound sleep.

She woke alone in the early hours and stretched muscles languid from sleep. Rolling over, she snuggled against the pillow, which still carried

Nick's scent. He hadn't been out of bed long because his side was still warm. Part of her wished he was with her, but another was very grateful she didn't have to deal with the awkwardness of waking up with him in her narrow bunk.

She flopped onto her back and stared at the ceiling, wondering what she should do. Would he say anything about their night together? Or would he continue to treat her with distant courtesy? She guessed he would treat her as if nothing significant had happened. She was a client and no matter how she might wish otherwise, he was very clear on the subject. When it came to Nick Rayven, he would lay down his life for her if needed, but he wasn't going to let her get too close emotionally.

She found it difficult to admit her awareness of him. The attraction keeping her off balance was one-sided. She was probably misreading the occasional touches and the emotions she saw move in his eyes. He was being kind—doing his job.

Demoralized by her musings, she got out of bed and headed for the cleanser. All of a sudden, she was desperate to remove his scent clinging to her skin. She knew she was in deep, and he already owned more of her heart than she could afford to give. She would get it broken before this was all over if she weren't careful.

* * * *

Nick slumped in his chair and sipped a cup of hot tayberry. He welcomed the bite of it this morning because his mind still felt sluggish from a bad night.

Idly looking over the ship schematics and working with Siren to shore up the damaged shields helped keep him somewhat occupied. His thoughts tended to wander back to Tru with a frequency preventing him from fully engaging in the task at hand. Concentration shot, he found it a little unnerving to realize he was staring at the computer tablet he held with no real idea what he was looking at yet again. He grimaced and put it down.

His resolve had been tested when he crawled out of bed and left the enchanting form who had slept so perfectly in his arms. Lying beside her without running his hands over the curves nestled so firmly against him had been almost unbearable, and he cursed the impulse that had driven him into her bunk. He'd been an idiot to give in to temptation, but he couldn't totally regret his actions, not if he were being honest with himself. It was becoming impossible to spend time with her and keep his hands to himself.

Annoyed, he tightened his grip on his mug as he wrenched his thoughts away from her and the question of what he intended to do about his tangled emotions.

A high-pitched wail from the back of the ship startled him into almost spilling hot liquid into his lap. He half rose from his seat before he realized what he was doing. He sank into his chair with a faint, rueful smile. Tru had just discovered the water in the cleanser was ice-cold. He lifted his cup to his mouth and took another sip of tayberry resigned to the inevitable explosion.

She stormed to the bridge, her hair dripping into her snapping blue eyes. Goose bumps pebbled her arms and her clothing clung in interesting places to her damp skin. She hadn't taken the time to dry off properly and it was impossible to ignore what was before his fascinated gaze.

"Why didn't you tell me there was no hot water?"

"You were sleeping the last time I saw you. I didn't think it was important enough to wake you." He tried without much success to keep his eyes off the sweet curve of her breasts and the puckered nipples brought on by the cold. He straightened in his chair enough to cross an ankle over his opposite knee and regarded her with wary interest over his mug. "How was I to know you would head for the cleanser first thing?"

"I do it every morning. How could you possibly not know? The water was freezing."

She glared at him before vigorously rubbing her hands through her wet hair, scattering droplets of icy moisture over him.

"Hey, what'd you do that for?" He lurched, sloshing his drink over his hand and onto his shirt. Scowling, he brushed at the mess with one hand while placing his mug in a holder with the other.

"Thanks for not warning me, jerk. You deserved it." Sinking into her own chair, she drew her knees up to her chest and wrapped her arms around them, matching his scowl with one of her own.

He studied the angry set of her jaw and felt a little guilty he hadn't thought to warn her. "You're right, I was thoughtless." Shifting sideways in his seat he reached for the jacket slung over the chair back. He leaned forward and carefully draped it over her hunched shoulders. "I wasn't thinking."

The jacket was heavy and swallowed her whole, but it would warm her up soon enough. She crossed her arms over her chest and pulled the edges of the coat closer. Then, she ducked her head into the fabric gathered under nose and took a breath. A tiny grin flashed and everything in him tightened.

"How long until we get to Zeegret Station?" It was an olive branch and he knew it.

"We're within a half standard day. I've been routing as much power as we can spare to the fuel cells to give us more speed. *Dominion* is fast, faster than any ship I've flown, and even with our current limitations she's making remarkable time."

"Will we be on the station long, do you think?" Idly, she traced a pattern on her raised knee with a fingertip.

"Depends." He watched her through hooded eyes. "It shouldn't take too long to remove the damaged cells and replace them with new, but you never know."

Her palm flat on her thigh, she languidly ran it over the smooth material of her pants up to her knee and back down again toward her hip. He figured she wasn't being deliberately provocative, but it didn't stop him from following the movement of her hand and thinking about what lay under it.

"I've never been on a space station before. Have you?"

He looked at her blankly. "What?"

"I asked if you have ever been on a space station before. Are you all right?"

"Fine. I'm fine. And, yes, I've been on a station before." He reached for his mug, and took a deep gulp of the now cold drink and forced himself to swallow. Sitting up, he dropped his booted foot back on the floor and swiveled his chair to face the console. Pretending an interest he was far from feeling, he checked the screens for status.

"What was it like?"

Her voice was soft, her tone curious and reached out to him like a silken web. His jaw clenched until his teeth hurt as he fought the irresistible lure she cast.

"Nick?"

"What? I'm busy here, Tru," he snapped, and then wished he could call the words back. Turning his head he glanced at his companion, his expression contrite. "Damn it, I didn't mean to snap at you." Irritated with her and with himself, he scrubbed a hand over his face.

She rose from her chair, removed his jacket from around her shoulders, and handed it to him with exaggerated care.

"Obviously, I'm in the way here." Careful not to touch him in any way, she stepped away and headed for the crew quarters.

All he could do was remain in his seat and not follow her. Unable to trust himself not to throttle her out of frustration, he stared out the viewscreen. He hardly recognized himself when he was around her. What the hell had happened to him? Where was his well-known control, his methodical approach to any situation? She only had to smile at him and he lost his train of thought. He handled explosive situations with aplomb, but found himself snapping and snarling at her with the least provocation. How damned humiliating to know one small female could tie him up in such knots.

"Captain, Zeegret Station is requesting an ETA." Siren's voice was clipped and held a note of censure that surprised Nick.

She'd been listening in again and heard his exchange with Tru. Conversational nuances still confused her, but she'd picked up the anger in his tone easy enough. Obviously, she disapproved.

"Thank you, Siren," he replied, pushing aside his thoughts of Tru. He was pleased with Siren's progress and noted on more than one occasion she tended to model her voice patterns after Tru's. He wasn't sure how he would deal with it once Tru returned to her family; the reminder of her would be hard to contend with. "Respond immediately to inquiry. Request docking instructions for arrival."

"Acknowledged."

"Call up electrical schematics for *Dominion*. I want to look at them again."

He forced himself to concentrate on the intricacies of his ship, what repairs were critical or could wait until they were back on Alludra. He refused to dwell on his attraction to his irritating passenger or to give in to the impulse to follow her and smooth over their most recent spat. He felt it best for her to keep her distance. At least, he kept telling himself it was.

Relief filled him when Siren announced Zeegret Station was on their approach. He watched the space station come into view and expertly guided Siren through the docking processes sent to them. She responded like a dream and he smoothly attached the ship to the designated docking arm with barely a bump.

"Siren, all commands to come through me for duration of our stay," Nick ordered, reverting to his native language. It was a security measure to prevent anyone from accessing the ship beyond necessary repairs. The odds of anyone speaking Tonlithian were astronomical.

"Acknowledged," Siren replied in the same language.

He exited the bridge and headed to the back of the ship. His steps checked for one heart-stopping moment when he saw Tru standing by the door. He felt the expected visceral punch, had even tried to prepare for it, but he couldn't anticipate the possessiveness hitting him from out of nowhere.

Mine.

Once the word entered his consciousness, it wouldn't leave. His heart beat heavily in his chest and he felt as if he were in freefall through space, unable to take his next breath. Astounded to realize his hands shook and confused by this unforeseen turn of events, he wondered what had happened in the brief time they had been apart to trigger the certainty revving his primal instincts to claim her as his own. He tried to shut it down, to ignore his body's response and the elemental recognition of a mate flooding his blood stream and leaving him burning. He didn't want this. Shouldn't want this.

He looked hard at her, seeking clues to the body blow he'd just taken, dazed by the internal shift unexpectedly throwing his world off kilter.

She'd changed out of her earlier outfit, which wasn't unusual. He'd been amused on more than one occasion by the mercurial mood shifts driving her to change her clothing to match her current mood. He didn't understand it, but a part of him enjoyed trying to guess what she would do next.

What she wore now was elegant in its cut and draped her body like a second skin. The short blue jacket nipped in at her tiny waist, emphasizing the gentle roundness of her hips and the length of her legs encased in slim trousers. The pants were tucked into tall, indigo-colored boots. She looked sleek, feminine, and the tentative smile on her generous mouth was guaranteed to drive him insane.

She'd made an effort to tame her curls with a headband, and he itched to release those soft curls from their confines, to see them frame the delicate lines of her face. Mine, he thought again, the word a persistent drumbeat in his head battering the wavering defenses he tried to shore. His mouth tightened into a thin line as he mentally kicked himself for letting this happen. He looked away and stared blindly at the ship's door while he fought for command of the powerful urges tearing at him.

Forcing a calmness he was far from feeling, Nick deactivated the environmental pressure seals between the ship's door and the docking tunnel. Once they were green-lighted, he opened the door and stepped through. He paused, turned back to Tru and offered her his arm. He waited for her to accept his unexpected gallantry. He wanted her touch, needed the connection even as he fought it.

He could see the uncertainty on her face. Knew her well enough by now to understand she'd been prepared to fight for the opportunity to visit the space station and had been caught off guard by his easy surrender. Hell, so was he, for that matter.

Seconds felt like an eternity as he waited for her to accept his wordless invitation. Her small hand came up to rest on his arm with only slight hesitation and his muscles tensed beneath her fingertips before they relaxed with a slight tremor. He hoped she hadn't noticed.

A warm smile bloomed on her lips and his mouth curved in answer. Entranced by the sparkle in her eyes and the excited flush on her cheeks he took a step closer, unable to help himself. Her delicate fragrance enveloped him and he breathed deeply feeling dizzy with the want and need clouding his mind. Her warmth against his side was both a pleasure and a torment, but he found he didn't care. He thought he heard her sigh, the barest expression of pleasure and fought the desire thrumming through his veins. This was not the time or place for his libido to go haywire. He would find a way to put a safe distance between them again, but not right now. Later. Much later.

"Ready?" he asked, his voice coming out as a deep rumble.

"Ready," she responded.

Chapter 14

Maddox Creighton was in his element. He thrived on the challenges in the business world and relished nothing more than overcoming resistance. It made him feel alive, on top of his game. Right now he focused on Lodestone Mining and Malvin Sonne. A slow, smile curved his mouth. He straightened his jacket to rest properly across his shoulders and then pulled his cuffs down before he turned and went in search of his quarry.

This was the final day of his annual meeting, and before he was through, Maddox intended to break Malvin Sonne. Then he was going to make sure Anto Geir understood going after one Creighton was the same as going after them all. By the time he was through, not much would be left of Lodestone Mining. No one messed with his family.

The day before, Callen Bluestone had arrived on Bretonne. The two of them had been closeted for the better portion of the day, going over the information Tru had unearthed. The more Maddox had seen, the angrier he'd become. He was a huge investor in Lodestone Mining and seeing proof he was systematically being robbed infuriated him.

Callen had proved to be a genius at following data trails and making connections that might not otherwise be obvious. The somber young man had impressed Maddox, which wasn't easy to do. He was both pleased and annoyed when Callen remained committed to Rayven Security and his boss even though he'd been offered work with Creighton Mutual and the prestige associated with it. Loyalty like his was hard to come by.

Everything was in place to take down at least one of the perpetrators of the Lodestone scam, and in so doing, Maddox intended to step in and take over what was left of the company. It was a challenge he looked forward to and sparked an interest he hadn't felt for a long time. His steps were brisk and energetic as he made his way to the day's planned events.

He met his son, Reid, at the doors leading into the gathering room. The resemblance between the two of them was uncanny but Reid lacked the drive that fed Maddox. Reid was an excellent administrator and handled the many arms of Creighton Mutual with ease, but he was content with the business as it was and felt no need to expand. It was a point of contention between them and Maddox knew it was the main cause of their emotional distance from one another. Tru was the other.

"Father," Reid said, with a curt nod.

"I assume you were briefed by Bluestone?" Maddox replied. He didn't bother to slow his steps expecting Reid to keep up and fall into step beside him.

"Naturally. Did you have any idea what Tru was up to?"

Maddox could hear the underlying suspicion in the question and the resentment his son tried hard to hide. Tru was closer to him than she was to her father, often approaching him to ask for advice and he knew Reid felt shut out. Although he had a great deal of sympathy for his son and encouraged Tru to seek out her father more, the strong bond they shared secretly pleased him.

"Don't be ridiculous. I was just as shocked as you were when I found out what that minx had been up to." He frowned, but couldn't suppress the note of pride in his voice. "I have to give her credit though. My granddaughter did a damn fine job of ferreting out what was going on. No one else caught it."

* * * *

Reid's gut churned with worry for his daughter and guilt for not paying enough attention to her concerns when she'd broached them with him. The thought of what could have happened to her would be enough to give him chills and sleepless nights for a long time.

Callen had filled him in on the details and put his mind at rest with assurances Tru would be well taken care of by Nick Rayven. Callen's calm, rational voice had been the anchor he'd listened to. Not his father, Maddox, but a complete stranger.

Reid put a fisted hand in his pocket, ruining the line of his tailored clothing, which would irritate his father. He admitted he was being petty, but he enjoyed a perverse sense of pleasure in the small childish rebellion. How was it possible to love someone and yet, resent them at the same time? A question he asked himself often.

"Ah, here comes Callen," Maddox announced, rubbing his hands together.

Callen's presence calmed the churning energy Reid felt whenever he was near his father, at least temporarily. He walked with unhurried grace toward them and stopped on Maddox's right side as his watchful gray eyes took everything in with a glance. There was something indefinable about Callen, a presence beyond his military posture and quiet air of competence. Reid respected the younger man's reticence even as he sometimes probed for answers. His questions were skillfully deflected without causing offense and Reid admired his skill. Chagrined, Reid found himself standing a little taller now that Callen had joined them. Out of the corner of his eye, he noticed his father do the same.

"Gentlemen." Callen nodded to each in turn.

In unspoken agreement, the three men entered the gathering room where the guests waited within.

Conversation paused as they crossed the threshold. Maddox smiled jovially and greeted many of his guests by name. Surrounded by powerful men and women in their own right, he still managed to set himself apart. He was treated with deference and only those paying attention would notice the occasional undercurrent of fear and resentment behind some of the social banter.

Reid noted with interest the various reactions from their guests as Callen was introduced by Maddox as a representative of Rayven Security. They were like sharks scenting new blood in the way they circled, in how they weighed and cataloged everything about him. Reid knew Rayven Security had just been given cachet within the business circles he and his father operated in. If Creighton Mutual considered a company worth a second look, then doors tended to open.

Callen blended with his surroundings. He said the right things, laughed in the right places and observed everything with dispassionate interest. When he walked away, he seemed to leave behind the impression of a savvy executive, but nothing else. As he circulated, he moved steadily closer to Malvin Sonne. Reid shook his head in admiration and moved away, confident Callen could handle himself.

* * * *

Callen snagged a drink from a passing waiter, raised the glass to his lips and sipped the fiery liquid while he considered his options. Maddox was across the room entertaining a small group of men, while Reid held court near a table laden with appetizers. Malvin was in a small alcove, partially hidden by a large cluster of plants. He looked worried and only ventured from his hideaway to snag additional drinks from a waiter. He looked as if he'd already imbibed one too many. Callen hid a grin behind his drink and bided his time.

"Mr. Bluestone, I presume." The voice was feminine, husky and as potent as the drink he held in his hand. Callen turned to view the owner of that fascinating voice. He wasn't disappointed; she was beautiful. Exotic. The signals she sent were intended to entice, and he recognized her efforts, even mentally applauded them.

"Yes." He offered her a faint smile.

"Forgive my presumption, but I overheard Maddox introducing you earlier. I'm Aislinn Thorpe." Her voice was pleasant as was her smile, but there was calculation in her brown eyes, and Callen's instincts told him to tread carefully. "It seems Creighton Mutual is interested in your company and if Maddox is interested, then so am I."

"And why would that be, Ms. Thorpe?" Callen sipped his drink and turned his attention back to the room at large.

She shifted beside him, drawing a little closer, and her perfume suddenly surrounded him. It was heady, sensual and his body reacted to the subtle message it sent. He knew her movement had been deliberate and clamped down ruthlessly on the unexpected sexual pull he felt.

"I'm always on the lookout for a company that guarantees confidentiality for their clients in handling pesky security problems." She turned slightly and her breast brushed his arm. He refused to move or to acknowledge her actions had any effect on him at all, even though he was uncomfortably warm.

He lowered his voice to a provocative growl, asking, "Would those pesky security problems have to do with you personally or are they of a business nature?" Her eyes widened before her full mouth compressed.

"Would it make a difference?"

He handed his empty glass to a passing waiter, and then turned to give Aislinn Thorpe his full attention. His smile was used to devastating effect and it broadened when he heard her breath catch. He cocked his head to one side and took his time looking her over. It was hard not to appreciate what he saw. Aislinn had curves in all the right places, and her clothing was designed to show off her assets to their best advantage.

"Darlin', I'm just trying to get a handle on what exactly we're talking about here." He drawled, his gaze lingering on her full, tempting mouth. He was being deliberately rude, but he didn't have time to play games no matter how tempting.

Wariness flashed in her eyes before she quickly looked away. She dropped the coy flirtation instantly and stepped back, putting space between the two of them.

"It seems we have a slight misunderstanding," she said stiffly, pretense gone.

"Quite possibly, Ms. Thorpe. If you need security then I would suggest you contact Rayven Security headquarters." Callen nodded and ambled away.

He didn't need eyes in the back of his head to know she glared daggers at him. If he hadn't other pressing matters to attend to, he would have been sorely tempted to see where her flirtation would take him. He knew she was up to something; he just didn't have time to find out what.

Callen searched the room until he spotted Maddox laughing with one the guests. He waited patiently for him to excuse himself, make his way to where Reid stood and then for the two of them to head his way. Of one accord, they approached Malvin Sonne.

"Hello, Malvin. You remember my son, Reid, don't you? And this is Callen Bluestone. He's an associate who works for Rayven Security," Maddox's said.

Malvin's face blanched when Rayven Security was mentioned. He looked everywhere but at Callen, his fingers beating a rhythmic tattoo against his thigh.

"We'd like to talk to you privately about a small matter. It shouldn't take long." Reid's voice was like steel as he clasped Malvin's upper arm. "Why don't you join us in the quiet conference room over there?"

They left Malvin no choice.

"W—what do you want to discuss? Can't this wait?" Sweat beaded his upper lip and, wild-eyed, he looked frantically around as if hoping someone would rescue him. No one paid attention and he wilted.

Callen closed the door behind them and leaned against it his arms crossed over his chest. Reid shoved Malvin into the nearest chair and then propped a hip on the table in front of him, letting his foot swing back and forth. Maddox frowned, his façade of false cheer dropping away once the door closed and he took the chair next to Malvin.

"It seems we have discovered a problem at Lodestone," Maddox said. "It has been brought to my attention there're mineral shipments going astray."

"What are you talking about? I don't know anything about this." Malvin wiped a hand across his mouth.

"How can that be? Aren't you the head of Lodestone?" Maddox leaned forward, pinning Malvin with an uncompromising stare.

"Yes, but I'm not in charge of shipments! I swear I don't know anything about this."

"Really? What about the sizable credits deposited to your hidden account? There is also the interesting fact of non-existent subsidiary companies being funded with a steady stream of credits." Callen's voice was soft, his tone even.

Malvin jerked. "How did you find out?"

"You made an effort to cover your tracks. It took a little digging to find what I needed. It's quite interesting what you can discover if you are patient enough."

"I hear the prison moon of Purgatory is pleasant this time of year. Of course, you will need a bio-suit to survive on the surface, but that shouldn't be much of a problem." Reid added.

Callen almost felt sorry for him.

Malvin's face was slick with sweat and his hands trembled as he ran them through his hair. "Look, I want to cut a deal. I'll tell you what I know and, in exchange, you protect me."

"Protect you from what exactly?" Callen pushed away from the door and strolled over to the table. He didn't bother finding a seat, just widened his stance and rocked back on his heels. He crossed his arms over his chest, stretching his jacket across his shoulders. There was nothing outwardly threatening about him, but Malvin shook so hard his chair rattled.

"From Anto. He'll come after me if he thinks I snitched on him." Words tumbled out in jerky bursts. "He got us involved in this. It's his fault. Now, there is no way out. I swear to you, I never thought it would go this far. It was only supposed to be a few shipments going astray. Anto found a buyer—he takes the shipments and sells them. We were supposed to split the profits equally. Only now, the buyer is demanding more and he's taking most of the split. Anto will do anything to keep the buyer happy and if he thinks I told you anything he'll kill me."

"Who's the buyer, Sonne?" Callen's voice cracked like a whip and Malvin huddled deeper in his chair.

"I—I don't know. Anto never told me." He was almost crying.

"What about Tru? Why are you interested in her?" Reid demanded. He stood and paced the small confines of the conference room. "What has my daughter have to do with any of this?"

"Anto knows she figured out what was going on. He wanted to stop her before you found out what we were doing. Too late...too late. He's going to kill me." Malvin sobbed into his hands.

"When is the next shipment supposed to be sold off?" Maddox interjected.

Malvin raised a tear-streaked face, stared at the furious visage of one of the most respected men in the solar system and hunched his shoulders. Callen could see no mercy in Maddox's face, just contempt.

"I don't know," he whispered. "Anto never tells me. I'm just supposed to alter the mineral reports to account for the difference between what is mined and what is shipped for processing."

Callen exchanged a look with Maddox and Reid over Malvin's bowed head. They would get nothing more out of Malvin until he was calmer. He felt sympathy for Reid, knowing his daughter was in trouble and being unable to get the information he desperately wanted.

"Shape up man, you're shaming yourself." Maddox jerked Malvin to his feet. "Callen is going to escort you to your rooms and post a guard until we can get you to the proper authorities. If you are smart, you will stay put."

Malvin nodded his understanding and glanced at Callen. He could tell the thought of going anywhere with him petrified Malvin. Callen raised an eyebrow and watched the other man's face blanch. He was almost disappointed he wouldn't get an argument out of him.

"When we pass through the outer rooms you will keep your head down and not speak to anyone. Am I clear?" Callen said. "If anyone asks why you are leaving, I will tell them you have taken ill and must return to your rooms. If you say anything to the contrary, I will make sure you are incapacitated immediately." He gripped Malvin's arm.

"One thing before you go." Reid said, stepping in front of Malvin. He threw a right hook, which snapped Malvin's head back and bloodied his nose. "That's for Tru. No one frightens my daughter and gets away with it."

Maddox slapped his son on the back. "I wish I'd thought of doing that."

Callen grinned and escorted Malvin out the door. No one stopped them as they crossed the room. Perhaps Malvin's white face and bloody nose telegraphed better than words he needed to leave the party.

* * * *

The next day Malvin Sonne was found dead in his room. There was no sign of forced entry, no visible signs on the body to point to cause of death. The guard posted at the door claimed to have seen nothing.

Tight-lipped, Callen surveyed the room for clues. Nothing was out of place. There were no signs of a struggle. Nothing. The only indication someone might have been in the room was the almost imperceptible trace of perfume lingering in the air. The familiar scent, the sensual notes, teased the edges of his memory. Provocative.

Aislinn Thorpe.

The image of the beauty from the previous evening burned, maddening him. What had she been doing in this room? What was the connection with Malvin Sonne? Clenching a fist, Callen vowed to find out. He strode from the room in search of her.

Gone. Sometime in the early hours, she'd disappeared. No one knew when or had witnessed her departure. He ground his teeth with frustration.

"What do you mean he's dead?" Maddox slapped his palms against his desk and surged to his feet when Callen finished telling the Creighton men what he'd discovered. "How is that possible?"

"I don't know. I assume you have security scans."

Maddox nodded and quickly punched them up showing the hallway in front of the guest quarters. "What the hell." he growled when a guard appeared asleep at his post while Aislinn slipped into Malvin's room. Mere minutes passed before she could be viewed hastily exiting, horror clearly showing on her face. She'd hurried away, one small hand covering her mouth as if she feared being sick.

Grimly, Callen watched the screen with single-minded intensity. Every recorded move she made burned into his retinas, fueling the mix of attraction and revulsion. He would find her. There wasn't a place she could hide he wouldn't be able to ferret her out. He would discover what had happened and soon.

"I'll have his head for this," Maddox snarled. "He'll never work another security detail if I have anything to say about it. Now we have to deal with damage control."

"I don't think his death is going to cause much of a problem." Reid leaned back in his chair, crossed his legs and propped an elbow on the chair arm. He rested his chin on a fisted hand.

"Eh? What do you mean?" Maddox demanded.

"Simple. We let it be known Malvin was ill yesterday. Everyone saw him being escorted out of the room, leaning heavily on Callen." Reid continued as if feeling his way as he spoke, "It will be easy enough to drop a hint here or there suggesting his death was a result of a sudden turn for the worse. No one is going to think to question what we say. We'll have him examined by our physicians to determine what actually happened. We can contain the flow of information for a while to buy some time while we figure out what we need to do next."

"Excellent suggestion. In the meantime, I'll find Aislinn Thorpe and try to discover what her involvement is in all of this," Callen said. The hunt was on and anticipation flowed through his blood, hot and heady.

Maddox nodded his approval before turning his attention to his son. "I have believed myself too old to be surprised by much, particularly when it comes to our differences in business. My mistake. Your idea is superb." A tiny smile played about his lips as he added feigned innocence. "It looks like I will need to call a shareholders' meeting about Lodestone Mining. I think it would be very wise if I were to step in to fill the gap so tragically left open by Malvin Sonne's death."

Reid choked out a laugh. "As if that wasn't your plan all along."

In perfect accord, if only for the moment, the two men exchanged amused glances.

Callen chose then to make his excuses. There was nothing more he needed to do on Bretonne. Maddox and Reid could take care of the cleanup, and he was eager to get back to Rayven Security. Nick and Seth would need updated on what had happened. He was itching to start a trace on Aislinn Thorpe. The few clothes he had arrived with were packed quickly and he boarded his ship for the trip home. He'd just broken through Bretonne's atmosphere, when Maddox's urgent voice crackled over the com system.

"We've got more problems, Bluestone. I've just been informed Anto Geir left Lodestone two days ago. It looks like he's going after Tru."

"Shit."

Chapter 15

Zeegret Station was a well-funded scientific research and observation lab. Poised midway between two large suns it was just off the main interplanetary travel grid.

Immense, and designed with the latest available technology, the station was occupied by some of the greatest scientific minds around. Tru was impressed and more than a little awed.

Engineering Chief Ardghal awaited them when they stepped through the final air lock to the main corridor. He was a barrel-chested man with a booming voice and an open heartiness she liked right away. She watched with interest as Nick and Ardghal sized each other up, apparently approved of what they saw and then launched into conversation about fuel cells. She lost track of the technical conversation between the two men and mentally checked out in favor of observing all the fascinating areas they passed.

From time-to-time, a door panel would slide open and she would catch a glimpse of its occupants busy with their appointed tasks. Voices drifted her way, tantalizing her with bits and pieces of conversation. Interspersed between connecting hallways were viewscreens overlooking the star-studded expanse of space surrounding them. Slowing her steps, Tru turned to watch a supply ship disengage from its docking arm and when she turned back found herself alone. Panicked, she hurried to the bisecting hallways hoping to see which way they had gone. Relief surged through her when Nick came striding toward her, a familiar frown drawing his dark brows together.

"Am I going to have to shackle you to my side to prevent you from getting lost?" He'd greeted her with mild irritation and something else she couldn't define in his voice.

"Of course not. I doubt there is any place I can go on this station you wouldn't be able to find me," she answered, falling into step beside him as he turned and led her down the correct hallway.

"Remember that for future reference. I will always find you, no matter where you are." His voice was a low, compelling rumble and she didn't doubt for a single minute what he said. Sparks of pleasure skittered up her spine as she considered his words and the subtle promise they held.

They caught up to Chief Ardghal and he guided them to the power lift, which took them down to the engineering section of the station. He caught the eye of one of the men standing to their right and motioned him over.

"Captain Rayven, Miss Creighton, I'd like you to meet Engineer First Class Kanta. He'll help replace the damaged fuel cells so you can continue your journey." Ardghal performed the introduction quickly. "Kanta, Captain Rayven's ship, *Dominion,* is docked at E37 while repairs are made. See that they're done without delay. We do not want to detain them longer than necessary."

Engineer Kanta nodded then shifted his gaze to Tru standing quietly beside Nick. Appreciation lit his eyes and his smile widened. He stared longer than was strictly polite, drawing a frown from Nick and a warning glance from his Chief. Nick placed an arm around Tru's small waist and drew her closer to his side. Kanta offered an apologetic smile before taking a half step back, putting more space between himself and Tru.

"Of course, Chief. I will see everything is taken care of promptly," Kanta replied. He focused on Nick. "Your shipmate, Siren, has filled us in on your needs and I have the necessary parts to complete repairs. Will she be joining us later?"

"No, Siren is a bit of a recluse and prefers to remain behind."

Tru jerk with surprise, but she held her tongue. She wasn't sure why Nick had misled Kanta about Siren.

"Too bad. I enjoyed communicating with her. You don't suppose she would make an exception, do you?"

"No."

Ardghal cleared his throat. "While the two of you take care of the fuel cells, why don't I escort your crew member for a short tour of the station?" He stepped into the small breach. "By the time we're done, your ship should be ready to leave."

Tru smiled and accepted the proffered arm from Chief Ardghal without hesitation. "Please, call me Tru."

"And you must call me Max," the Chief replied as he patted her hand. "Why don't I show you the main hub? We have shops and restaurants there to serve the families aboard the station."

"I'm not sure this is a good idea, Tru."

She glanced at Nick, surprised. He looked like he wanted to snatch her hand away from Ardghal and drag her back to his side.

"No need to be concerned, Captain Rayven. I won't let any harm come to your companion."

He and Ardghal exchanged a look she didn't understand.

"See that you don't. What are we waiting for, Kanta, let's get the ship repairs done. I don't have all day."

* * * *

Tru sighed with remembered pleasure as *Dominion* uncoupled from its docking arm and headed back to space. The tour of the station had been fascinating and Chief Ardghal a surprisingly interesting guide. The main hub was full of families shopping, enjoying the restaurants or meeting friends. Delightful smells from the restaurants tantalized her nose and made her mouth water, but the small shop she stumbled upon by accident piqued her interest and made her smile.

Browsing through the intricately carved metal and leather goods had been fun and she'd been unable to resist the purchase of the wrist cuff she now wore. She traced a fingertip along the scrollwork and debated whether she should give the matching one she bought for Nick to him now or hold on to it for a later time. It had been an impulse buy, the ship etched into the metal a reminder of their journey together.

Nick sat at the helm, granite-jawed and scowling. His conversation had been limited to grunts and terse one-word answers. She sighed and decided later would be best. His temper was too uncertain at the moment and she sensed he itched for a fight. Having no idea what had caused his present mood, she left the helm area and retreated to her bunk. After inserting a data strip into a portable tablet, she propped her pillows behind her back and soon lost herself in the book she'd chosen.

* * * *

Ship's systems were back online and Nick ran through one more diagnostic check to assess the shield strength. More a test of his own resolve than anything else, he used it as an excuse not to follow Tru. It hadn't taken near as long to remove and replace the damaged fuel cells, as it had to locate her whereabouts after it was done. Already on edge, he'd been ready to explode by the time he found her talking and laughing with a young ensign under the watchful eye of Chief Ardghal.

A red haze had clouded Nick's vision and it took all his self-control not to tear the other man apart when he had the audacity to take Tru's hand and wink at her. Adrenaline shot through his system and his muscles tightened ready to spring. The fact her face lit up when she caught sight of him and the speed with which she dropped the other's hand to join him had calmed the snarling beast inside enough he'd managed to be civil while they took their leave. When they were safely away from Zeegret Station, he had time to consider his irrational behavior when any man came near her. The realization was humbling that he didn't want anyone touching her except him. Ever.

He idled away his time, reluctant to give in to the bone-deep weariness dragging at him. His internal clock told him he'd been running on empty far too long and sleep was needed, but he continued to sit at the helm console, unwilling to seek his bunk. He scrubbed a hand over his face and blinked gritty eyes, knowing he was being idiotic. The trouble was, he didn't trust himself not to crawl into Tru's bunk and give in to the need slowly eating him alive. He knew he'd screwed up when he'd given in to temptation the night before, but he'd at least had an excuse, albeit a flimsy one. Life support had been restored and with it, any pretext of sharing sleeping accommodations had been removed.

Restless, he paced while he ran through complicated formulas to distract himself. Basic military drills were reviewed, every plane he'd ever flown was recalled in finite detail and every mission he'd flown was remembered. He realized he was wasting his time when he found himself standing beside Tru's bunk with no real memory of how he got there.

She was curled on her side, one hand hidden under her pillow, her other arm draped across her waist. She looked relaxed, peaceful and deeply asleep. He studied the faint bruising still marring her cheek and felt a little sick that he'd been the one to hurt her. He leaned over and skimmed his knuckles down her sleep-flushed cheek before he pulled her blankets up and covered her. Mine.

Tru sighed in her sleep, and Nick straightened, desire racing through his system faster than yesterday's solar storm. Forcing himself to step back, he grabbed a blanket off his bunk and went to the bridge. He didn't relish sleeping in his chair, but it wasn't the worst place he'd ever slept.

He would be damned before he would give in to his base nature and take advantage of someone in his care, no matter how much he wanted to. That was the crux of the matter. His job was to protect her until she could be safely returned to her family. He was bound by honor and ethics. After

Tonlith's destruction, his strong convictions kept him sane. They were the very foundation he'd built his business on and were inviolate.

More at peace with himself, Nick settled in his chair and propped his booted feet on the helm console. While he considered the ramifications of his situation he also faced up to the fact she had her hooks in him and he was caught, whether she realized it or even wanted it. He didn't find it particularly comforting to know she'd become so important to him, but he found he didn't mind as much as he'd thought he would. This job wouldn't last forever and then all bets were off. A smile curved his mouth. He knew he could wait, would wait to claim her.

He settled deeper into his chair, closed his eyes and allowed himself to drift off to sleep.

* * * *

Tru knew the strong aroma of tayberry wafting under Nick's nose would rouse him from sleep. Groaning he opened one eye to glare up at her. She grinned and held the mug just out of his reach, waiting. His sleepy gaze moved from her to the mug and back again before he moved like one of the ancients and scooted into an upright position. She watched him scratch the whiskers shadowing his chin, roll his neck until it cracked and then stretch like a big lazy cat. She couldn't look away, mesmerized in spite of herself. He snaked a hand out and snagged the mug of tayberry before she could react and then sipped the hot liquid while he regarded her over the mug's rim.

"You didn't come to bed last night," she said.

"Nope." He yawned until his jaw cracked.

"Is everything all right with the ship?"

"Everything is fine."

She bit her bottom lip and looked at him out of the corner of her eye. "The chair doesn't look like it would be a comfortable place to sleep."

He shifted in his seat and his lips twitched behind his mug. She suspected he was entertained by her questions and wasn't sure why.

"I've slept in worse places in my life. The chair isn't bad." He quirked a brow as if he waited for her next question.

"I'm just surprised you would choose to sleep on the bridge rather than your bunk." She flopped onto her chair and frowned at him, irked when he continued to sip his drink.

"It seemed like a good idea at the time."

Realizing she wasn't getting anywhere, she huffed out a frustrated breath and swiveled her chair until she faced the viewscreen.

"Whatever."

She shrugged and concentrated on the view of space in front of her. Silence stretched between them until she couldn't stand it any longer. She glanced his way. She wasn't sure how to react when he returned her look with amusement warming his brown eyes. He seemed more at ease than she'd ever seen him. The deep lines fanning his eyes smoothed out and the frown lines between his brows less noticeable. His mouth was softer, more tempting, and her lips parted in response. Nick always gave the impression he was carved from stone, but today he looked somehow different. Less care-worn and infinitely appealing.

He always managed to keep her off balance without any apparent effort on his part and it irritated her. Relaxed and sipping his tayberry was a side of him she didn't often see. Crossing her arms under her breasts, she tilted her head to consider this new version. She felt a thrill of excitement when he followed her movements with his gaze. When the material of her shirt tightened across her chest, his eyes gleamed. She felt feminine satisfaction to see he wasn't completely immune to her and was not bothering to hide it.

Giving in to curiosity, she asked, "So, why didn't you come to bed last night?"

"Are you asking why I didn't come to bed or why I didn't go to bed? They're two different things, Tru." His voice was languid and sensual.

"Oh." Heat flooded her face when it dawned on her just what he meant. "Oh."

Rising from his chair, he grinned wolfishly at her. He winked and then wandered off to the crew quarters leaving her staring open-mouthed at his retreating form.

Chapter 16

Freshly shaven and pleased with himself, Nick returned to the bridge. The planet Kaydet and Dendera Labs were hours away. Quick in, quick out was his plan and then he could concentrate on Lodestone Mining and Tru's problem. Simple.

"You have an incoming message, Captain," Siren announced.

"Put it on the com," Nick instructed. He stood beside his chair, one hand resting on its padded headrest, the thumb of his other hand hooked into a belt loop of his pants.

"How close are you to Kaydet?" Callen said.

"Close enough. What's up?"

"Malvin Sonne is dead. I left Maddox to take care of that complication, but I got word as I was leaving Bretonne Anto Geir had left Lodestone. I can only assume he's headed your way."

"Sonne is dead? What happened?"

"We're not sure. There seems to be some confusion about who or what killed him, and I'm tracking a lead. I'll find out, you can count on it."

Something in Callen's usually cool voice caught Nick's attention, but he let it go. Callen could take care of himself and if he said he had a lead then, guaranteed, he was on to something.

"What is the status of Lodestone Mining?"

"Maddox is in charge. He and Reid are launching a very public inquiry into the shipping discrepancies. They feel it is the only way to salvage what is left of the company and keep it under Creighton's banner."

"They think that will calm the investors?" He straightened, and then leaned forward, bracing himself with his palms on the helm console.

Callen's laugh held little mirth. "You've met Maddox, what do you think? He's like a force of nature. It's hard to argue with him."

"You sure Geir is headed our way?" Nick asked.

"He's in bed with some extremely bad people from what I can tell. Things are falling apart real fast for him and he's the type who needs someone to blame. Tru fits the bill. Yes, I think he's coming after her. Watch your back, Nick. He's dangerous."

"Thanks for the heads up, Callen. I'll be in touch when I've dropped the package at Dendera and we're headed back."

"See you do."

Nick disconnected the call and scrubbed a hand through his short hair. Frowning, he stared into space while he considered the information Callen had given him. If Geir had lifted off Lodestone, then he wasn't far behind them. The delay at Zeegret Station narrowed the time difference considerably. He would be lucky if they managed to complete the commission and get away before Geir caught up to them.

He wasn't surprised Geir was hard on his heels. After Nick had disabled the ship sent after them, Geir had to have known his hopes of a quick capture had failed. He would bet his last credit Geir had someone in place at Dendera Labs as a backup. Flexing his fingers, he thought about a confrontation with Geir, something he would relish if he didn't have to worry about Tru. To destroy the bastard if for no other reason than he'd threatened her would give him a great deal of pleasure. He'd make sure she was safe, and then he'd take Anto Geir apart.

Leaving the bridge, he sought Tru. He found her sitting at the small table in the crew quarters humming tunelessly while she brushed her hair. It had grown considerably in the days they had been travelling. Her impatient swipe when it fell into her eyes was cute. She was so absorbed in the task she didn't notice him. She put down the brush and twisted it into a knot at the back of her head, but the minute she pushed in the last clip and lowered her hands, it started to escape. She stopped humming.

She removed the clips, holding them between her lips while she pulled the sides back, and then shoved them in. He guessed she was hoping this would hold. It did, for all of two minutes. The clips slid out and curls fell into her eyes. Tight lipped, she slammed the clips onto the table and went in search of something else to keep her hair off her face.

Fascinated, Nick watched her, pushing aside the new danger facing them for a moment. He'd stopped midway to lean a shoulder against the bulwark so he could see what she would do next without intruding too much. She was back in an instant, flopped onto her chair and dumped several combs and strips of cloth on the table.

He wasn't sure he liked the idea of all those delicious strands being contained, but he recognized determination when he saw it.

He'd just decided to make a quiet retreat and talk to her later when he realized she knew he was watching her. Her hands tremble before she clasped them together atop the table, and he wondered if it was from nerves or something else. She glanced at him and her eyes were a fathomless blue drawing him in. She licked her lips and his insides knotted as if he'd taken a fist to the solar plexus. His lungs burned from lack of air and he drew in a deep breath. Nick pushed himself away from the wall and headed her way, unable to stop himself from drawing closer. "Need help, Tru?" He stopped just behind her.

She nodded and relaxed against the back of her chair as he slid his fingers through the thick masses. She shivered. Eyes half closed, she seemed to enjoy his fingers tangling in her hair as he massaged her scalp. Almost purring, she leaned her head forward giving him better access.

"I think it would be better to just keep your hair down." His voice sounded hoarse even to his own ears. "I like the curls as they are."

With infinite slowness, drawing out the action as much as he could, he forced his hands from the silken strands and to his sides. He took a step back and cleared his throat. He still itched to bury his palms in the soft, thick curls. He wasn't doing a good job of keeping his distance, but, damn, he would have to be a eunuch not to be tempted by those shining strands. Nick was no eunuch.

"We should be reaching Kaydet soon," he said. "Dendera Labs is located in the small town of Killjoy. It's close to the port, which makes it a little easier for me." He sat across from Tru and stretched out his legs. "This world is cold, mostly covered in snow and ice and fairly inhospitable. This kind of cold can be deadly. I'll have Siren contact the Labs so they know when to expect me. I don't plan to be on Kaydet any longer than necessary."

"Why in the world are we going there, then?" she asked. "Why didn't we go to one of the other labs on a more hospitable world?"

"The head of Geotern Mining wanted the mineral delivered here for testing. It wasn't my concern why. I was more interested in the amount of credits being offered to get it here." His smile was brief, before he sobered to continued, "Tru, there is something else we need to discuss before we land. Callen informed me Anto Geir is coming after you, and I have to assume he's somehow figured out where we're headed. My guess is there has been a leak in Geotern."

He watched the color drain from her face and clasped her hand to offer a small measure of comfort. "I won't let him harm you, you know that right? We will only be there long enough for me to take care of necessary business and then we will lift off as soon as I'm done. I doubt he has had time enough to get there before us, which is to our advantage."

Tru nodded.

"I want you to stay onboard *Dominion* while I make the delivery. You will be safer here."

"No!" Panic coated her words.

"This ship is secure. Geir will not be able to breach the defenses," he replied keeping his voice calm and reassuring.

"No. I want to be with you. What if something happens to you while I sit here? What if he figures out where I am? I won't stay here, Nick. I won't."

"Tru, you are being childish. It is far too dangerous for you to leave the ship," he said, beginning to get annoyed, his mouth firmed. "It is best you do as I say and stay onboard."

"No," she shot back. She slipped her hand from his and folded her arms across her chest. She lifted her chin. "You promised to protect me and you can't if you leave me on board alone."

Frustrated by her stubborn refusal, he narrowed his eyes. "You are being unreasonable. You will slow me down and get in the way of making this delivery."

"I will not stay on this ship while you go to Dendera Labs, Nick Rayven, and you can't make me. If you try to make me stay I will just follow after you."

Determination was in every line of her body, but the fear he saw in her face gave him pause. His instincts told him she should stay on the ship, but he found he couldn't force her when faced with the dread dilating her pupils and making her voice shake.

"This is a bad idea. I don't have a good feeling about it," he said with absolute conviction.

"Please, Nick." Her eyes pleaded, and she reached to clasp the hand she'd dropped earlier. He turned his hand in hers to link their fingers and gave a gentle squeeze.

"Fine, but you stick to me like we're attached at the hip. Is that clear?"

She nodded, and he saw the relief on her face

"I mean it, Tru. You do exactly what I say without question or hesitation. You understand?"

She nodded again, more vigorously this time.

"Shit. I know I'm going to regret this," he muttered, running his free hand across the back of his neck.

"Captain, we are on final approach to Kaydet," Siren announced. "Instructions?"

"You know the drill, Siren. Contact the port for permission to land. Inform Dendera Labs we will be there shortly and let them know I'm here to meet with the Administrator, Pol Dirn. He should be expecting us if Geotern did what it was supposed to." As he replied, he kept his gaze on Tru. He was going against his better judgment by giving in to her.

"Acknowledged."

"C'mon, Tru, let's suit up." Nick sighed, rose from his seat and pulled her up with a gentle tug. "I want off this world as quickly as we can manage it."

* * * *

The blast of icy wind was like a punch in the face, taking her breath away and stinging the tip of her nose where the protective hood of her coat had slipped down. She raised her gloved hands to tighten the fur-lined garment. Behind her tinted goggles, Tru scanned the desolate landscape awestruck by the designs etched in stark relief on drifts caused by the constant blowing snow. Visibility was poor beyond a few meters. Afraid she would lose him in the shifting light and near white out conditions, she clung to the back of Nick's jacket.

A few ships occupied the landing pad, dark hulking shapes adding to the surreal landscape. Drone vehicles crisscrossed the tarmac in a futile effort to keep it cleared of snow. The spaceport building looked like nothing more than a smudge on the landscape, but thankfully was not too far away.

Nick plowed through the snow, forging a path for her to walk in. His body blocked the worst of the wind and protected her from the icy shards kicked up by the storm. Kaydet was as different from Lodestone as night from day, but both places were equally hellish in her opinion. Her mood didn't improve with the comparison.

The entrance to the port building was a series of doors, each space adding a layer of insulation from the outside weather. The relief from the wind was instantaneous as were the slightly warmer conditions in the first entrance. Nick stomped snow off his boots and brushed it from his heavy outerwear. Removing his goggles and gloves, he turned to help her. He pushed her fur-covered hood back and smiled reassuringly once he'd swept most of the snow off her. Her cheeks stung from the cold and she dreaded to think what might have happened without her protective gear. The warmth of his fingers as he skimmed them over her chilled face felt odd, but she found herself leaning into the light pressure enjoying the brief contact.

"It will be easier going from here. There is a series of tunnels connecting the buildings, so we won't be out in the weather again until we leave," he said. "We just need to check in with the port authority with our plans and duration of stay."

"Whatever for?"

"Policy. It wouldn't be good for a visitor to get lost and end up dead from exposure." He shrugged as if the matter was of little import. She followed him to the next set of doors, trying not to think about the horror of dying in this unforgiving landscape.

The main offices of the port authority were much warmer, and she wished she could shed her jacket. Sweat trickled down her back and dampened her hairline. Nick didn't seem to be affected in the least and it was a small point of irritation keeping her focused on her growing misery. She barely paid attention to the woman manning the desk as their plans were logged and directions were given for the maze of tunnels connecting the various buildings and businesses. She was too busy feeling uncomfortable until she noticed the woman flirting with Nick.

Although she wouldn't call the woman beautiful, she was attractive and exuded confidence. Tru scowled at her and moved closer to Nick's side. The woman glanced at her dismissively and smiled at Nick, telegraphing her interest without subtlety. Tru's irritation ratcheted, but she was saved from making a fool of herself when he put an arm around her and pulled her closer. The other woman exchanged a wry glance with Tru and her posture straightened until she was no longer leaning close to Nick. Tru tried not to gloat.

"You are all set, Captain Rayven. Please check in before departure so we can account for your whereabouts," the clerk said, her tone brisk and businesslike now she knew he was off limits.

The well-traveled tunnels were brightly illuminated. Tru was surprised to realize there was a thriving community here, but couldn't imagine what drew them to this cold world. Nick wasn't inclined to talk and it took everything she had to keep up with his ground-eating stride. When he'd said he wanted business taken care of quickly, he wasn't joking. His urgency transmitted itself to her and made her heart beat just a little harder. Anxiety she tried very hard to hide made her stay close to his tall form.

* * * *

Dendera Labs was huge, well lit and sterile-looking. Pol Dirn, a small, thin man of indeterminate age, greeted them upon their arrival and then escorted them to a plush office to their right.

"I understand you have a mineral to be tested?" The question was directed at Nick as they took their seats. Pol Dirn settled behind his large desk and clasped his hands on the desktop. "Geotern thinks this could have potential as an alternative power source so I'm very interested in getting my hands on it to see if there is any basis for excitement."

Nick studied the man across from him. Warning signals were going off, but he couldn't put his finger on what exactly disturbed him. "I was told to deliver the package to you and no one else," he answered after a slight pause, "I just need you to sign off on the transfer for Geotern, acknowledging the delivery and then we're out of here."

"Of course, of course." Pol nodded and tapped information into his hand-held tablet. He gave a perfunctory smile before he scooted it across to Nick. "Look this over to verify its accuracy and then leave your thumb print in the lower right. It will be scanned and then an acknowledgement will be transmitted to Geotern's offices. That should take care of it."

"I want a copy transmitted to my offices on Alludra as well." Nick said, reading the contract in front of him. Everything looked in order and he pressed his thumb where indicated.

"Excellent!" Pol's smile looked more genuine as he rubbed his hands together. "Now if you will just hand over the package."

Nick reached inside his heavy coat and unfastened the tab to his lighter flight jacket underneath. He pulled out the pouch containing the mineral and handed it to Pol. He watched the other man, noting his hands held a slight tremor and his gaze skittered away, avoiding direct eye contact. His certainty grew something was off.

"A most satisfactory conclusion to our business, Captain Rayven. I will turn the mineral over to the lab techs right away and get started with our testing." Pol started to stand, but Nick held up a hand stopping him. Pol sank onto his chair and regarded him warily.

"The documentation acknowledges the transfer of the mineral from me to Dendera Labs." Nick raised an eyebrow and pinned Pol with a stare. "But I do not see documentation registering the mineral to Geotern Mining. I was contracted to make sure there is no mix up in the process."

"I don't understand." Pol frowned and ran a forefinger along his eyebrow, looking more worried than the question warranted.

"Let me clarify this for you then so there is no misunderstanding. I'm not leaving this office until Geotern Mining is registered as the owner of all mineral rights associated with this sample." Nick lifted a brow. "If you have trouble with this request, then we have a problem and I don't like problems. Does that clear it up enough for you?"

Pol Dirn looked like a small animal caught in a predator's stare. Nick leaned forward in his chair and Pol shrank back.

"Y-yes. Perfectly clear. Must have slipped my mind. So sorry," he stammered, and reached for the hand-held tablet on his desktop. He scrolled through documentation until he found what he looked for. "Here it is. Ah, I just need your thumbprint as before."

Nick read over the document, making sure the mineral rights were correctly registered, and once he was satisfied, placed his thumb on the screen. "I think we will wait until the documents have been transmitted and acknowledged. It shouldn't take long." He stretched his mouth into a mirthless smile, making sure he showed a lot of teeth, and settled more comfortably in his chair.

Pol gnawed at his bottom lip while he transmitted the documentation. It was obvious he was afraid of something, but faced with Nick's large, implacable presence he did what he was told.

Satisfied everything was now in order, Nick rose. "It's been a real pleasure doing business with you. I will be sure to report our interaction to Geotern and to the proper individuals within Dendera Labs." He dropped the pretense of a smile from his face and raised an eyebrow. "If I find there has been a problem with ownership of the mineral or the results from its testing go astray I will be sure to look you up. Count on it."

Wide eyed, Pol nodded and rubbed his palms on his pant legs. Nick rose to leave, followed closely by Tru. He was satisfied he'd secured Geotern's rights.

Nick ushered Tru from the offices and moved quickly down the tunnel headed to the Port Authority offices. Every instinct he had screamed danger, but he had no clear indication of where or what it was. He always trusted his instincts; it had saved his ass on more than one occasion.

Tru trotted to keep up, her face flushed from exertion and a worried frown marring her smooth forehead. He appreciated she wasn't asking questions and distracting him as she usually did.

The corridor forked ahead and he slowed, motioning for her to stay behind him. It was unnaturally quiet in the corridor, the absence of people disturbing. He scanned the area ahead for the threat he could sense but not see.

To get back to the ship, they needed to stay to the left. That corridor led them through the lively business section and to the Port exit. If memory served, the right corridor ended in storage units and was off limits. He moved forward with caution while reaching into his jacket to remove the blaster he'd tucked into a shoulder holster. Thumbing the safety off, he pointed the barrel down and held it pressed against his thigh out of immediate sight in case he'd misjudged the situation.

Lights flickered ahead and then went out where the two corridors bisected, throwing the area into darkness. Cursing under his breath, he stopped and pressed Tru against the wall, sheltering her behind his much larger frame. Her small start of surprise seemed overly loud in the sudden silence.

Adrenaline pumped hard and fast through his system, as he debated retracing their steps to Dendera Labs or taking their chances by pressing ahead. The lights behind them flickered off. Straining for the slightest sound, he waited until he heard the barest whisper of noise coming in their direction.

"Whatever you do, stay behind me and stay low," he ordered, barely above a whisper. She nodded, her fear almost palpable.

"Now isn't this interesting, Crowder. Looks like we captured ourselves a little tattletale and her bodyguard," someone taunted, but he couldn't see anyone. The sound bounced eerily off the smoothly curved walls making the speaker hard to pinpoint.

Nick listened intently and raised his blaster, waiting for the next hint of movement to give him a fix on the owner of the voice.

"Don't that just beat all," another man with a rasping voice replied conversationally. "Must be our lucky day."

"I wouldn't be too sure," Nick answered.

"You're outnumbered and last I checked it doesn't look good for you," the first man scoffed.

The scrape of a boot across the floor was all it took, and Nick fired. A shocked, painful grunt let him know he'd hit his target, but not taken him out.

"Friggin' hell, Crowder...I'm hit."

"Shut up, you fool," the man called Crowder hissed angrily. "Stick to the plan or you'll get us all killed."

Before he could react, Nick was struck from the side by a heavy weight, which took him down and knocked his blaster out of his hand. He landed hard, hitting his head as the force of his attacker skidded them both across the rough floor. Fighting for leverage, Nick freed an arm and delivered a powerful punch to his assailant's jaw. The man's head snapped back and his grip loosened. Nick rose to one knee and gained his feet.

Fighting dizziness from the blow to his head, he blocked the punches thrown his way and managed a roundhouse kick connecting with a satisfying thud. He followed the kick with lightning fast fists, driving his attacker back. Tru screamed from somewhere behind him as he broke the nose of his opponent, dropping him like a stone. He spun toward her. Lights suddenly lit the corridor like the midday sun, temporarily blinding him, making him blink rapidly.

Fists raised, he crouched, ready to defend her, only to be brought up short when he realized she was held immobile by a beefy arm across her throat and a blaster pointed at her head. Frightened blue eyes were wide in her colorless face, and his gut twisted with helpless rage because he hadn't protected her after all.

"If you don't want to see this cute little thing get hurt, you will keep your hands where I can see them."

He recognized the voice as belonging to the one called Crowder. Nick judged him to be hired muscle, the kind who had few scruples and a violent nature. He wouldn't hesitate to inflict pain on his unlucky victims.

Breathing hard from the fight, Nick straightened and raised his hands to shoulder level. A glance located the man he'd shot, his left arm cradled against his chest. Pale and sweating, he glowered at Nick. He heard the third man stirring behind him and braced for what he knew was coming.

Chapter 17

Consciousness returned slowly, painfully. Nick heard Tru crying above him and felt her ice-cold fingers flutter over his face. He forced one eye open between swollen eyelids and attempted to bring her pale face into focus. He hurt everywhere; the simple act of drawing a breath was agonizing because of his bruised and cracked ribs. He'd survived the beating, and was thankful his heavy jacket had prevented too much damage from being inflicted by his infuriated captors. Small consolation now he was awake and aware of every ache and pain in his abused body.

He couldn't prevent a groan from escaping between his cracked and bloody lips when she leaned too heavily against his chest.

"I'm sorry...so sorry," she crooned. A warm tear trickled down her cheek and plopped against the corner of his injured mouth. He felt her brush it away with careful tenderness.

"Where are we?" he croaked, tasting blood from his split lip. He tried to sit up and bit back a moan. Resting on one elbow, he cradled his ribs with his other arm and breathed shallowly through the burning pain and cold sweat coating his body.

"We're in a storage unit off the main corridor. Are you all right?" Tru's voice hitched with suppressed tears. "How badly are you hurt?"

"Help me sit up, will you?" His voice lacked its usual strength, but he injected enough steel in his tone to have her hasten to obey.

Moving so she was better positioned, she helped as much as she could while he struggled to prop himself against the smooth wall of their cell. Both were panting from the effort by the time he was settled. Nick rested his head against the wall and took inventory of his injuries. None were life threatening just painful. His ribs would cause some problems, but he'd worked through worse while in Tonlith's military. Nothing was broken and he was grateful.

"There is a small pouch attached to my utility belt with med supplies," he said, his breathing more normal now he wasn't moving. "There are some 'gesic strips and a spray to seal the cuts on my hands and face. I don't think I can manage to get them, Tru. You need to do it, okay?"

She wiped the tears from her face with the heel of her hands and bit her bottom lip. She took a deep breath and then moved aside his heavy coat. He knew she was making every effort to be gentle as she skimmed her hands along the woven belt around his waist until she found the small pouch attached near his right hip. She slid her fingers under the tab, opened it and dug out the items he requested. She also pulled out bandages and a small tube of antibacterial cream.

She tore open the 'gesic packet and waited for him to open his mouth before she dropped the strip on his tongue. While it dissolved, she cleaned up the dried blood on his face. He hissed in a breath when she dabbed at the corner of his mouth, but remained stoic from then on. She lifted one of his large, scarred hands to smooth the cream over his knuckles before sealing the cuts with the spray. He was surprised when she laid a tender kiss on his palm before placing it back on his thigh.

"Is the 'gesic helping?" she asked.

"Mmm. I'll be good as new before you know it," he lied, offering a ghost of a smile. Searching her face, he noted her huge, dilated eyes and the spasmodic jerks of muscles reacting to extreme stress. "How are you, sweetheart? Did they hurt you?"

"No. No, I'm fine." Her gaze skittered away from his, and she smoothed a hand over his jacket.

"Tru?" He captured her fluttering hand in one of his own and brought it to his chest. "Tell me what happened." It was a gentle demand.

"I was just threatened, Nick. It was nothing," she insisted. "Nothing I can't handle."

Nick had a fairly good idea of what the threats had been and white-hot rage boiled through his system blinding him to his surroundings for an instant. He was sure they had been vile and delivered in graphic detail. The last clear memory he had before he'd lost consciousness was Tru struggling in Crowder's grip. One beefy arm had been around her neck while his other hand wandered under her jacket. Crowder's leering and triumphant smile had been focused on him, knowing he was helpless to stop what happened.

Nick's breath shuddered as he struggled for control. He knew it wouldn't do either of them any good if he gave in to his anger, and he fought to rein in the fury. Retribution would have to wait, because right now he needed to think clearly. Stuffing his emotions into a cold hard knot, he focused on the problem of getting them out of this mess alive.

Wanting to offer comfort, he urged Tru closer and wrapped an arm around her shoulder. She didn't protest or pull away, but came into his arms with a quiet sigh. Relieved, he held her close, ignoring the fire in his ribs. He made a silent promise to himself that before he was done, Crowder would regret ever laying a hand on her.

He rubbed his hand up and down her arm while he considered their options. He was still wearing the leather and metal cuff around his wrist, which connected him to his ship and to Siren. He wasn't surprised Crowder and his men hadn't bothered to search him thoroughly. They were big on brawn, not so much on brains and probably assumed his blaster was the only weapon he carried. Big mistake.

Nick suspected they were going to be left alone until Geir showed up. He was sure Crowder had been acting under orders, and being locked in this room meant Geir was not on the planet yet. Obviously, he required them to be stowed away until his arrival, which bought Nick some time, although he couldn't be sure how much.

Thinking quickly he ran through scenarios until he had a rudimentary plan. It relied too much on luck for Nick's peace of mind, but he didn't have a lot of options. Geir could not be allowed to escape and the only way to be sure was to remain where they were until he could get the authorities to show up. He knew it was risky and dangerous, but he was certain Geir would keep coming after Tru until he got what he wanted unless he was neutralized. This would be their best opportunity to see that happen

Nick contacted Siren and succinctly laid out what he wanted done.

"Are you sure this will work?" Tru asked.

"We don't have much choice here, Tru. There is no way out of this room other than through the door and I would bet my last credit Crowder and his men are guarding it."

"But can Siren handle this? What if she can't get the authorities here in time? What will happen then?" Her voice shook and she pulled away from him to sit up.

"I admit a lot is riding on Siren here, but she has already proven herself to be very capable, right? Remember she has already interacted successfully with Zeegret Station. They never knew she was a computer and accepted her requests without question. There is no reason to doubt she'll be able to do the same here. I'm going to do everything in my power to make sure you are safe. I won't allow Crowder to get his hands on you again."

She looked at him, her eyes large and haunted with shadows, and he reached up to brush a curl away from her cheek.

"Okay."

Her complete trust in him was humbling, and he struggled with his decision even though he knew it was their best option.

He had no idea how long they'd been held in the storage unit. There were no windows and only a dim glow bulb overhead. Time ceased to have any real meaning. Tru dozed by his side, jerking awake at every slight sound, but Nick stayed alert knowing it was too dangerous to let his guard down enough to give in to the pain and weariness pummeling him. Instead, he concentrated on the feel of her beside him and the way her hand rested soft and warm on his chest.

Once she'd drifted into a deeper sleep, he shifted enough to slip his knife from its sheath in his boot and hide it within easy reach.

* * * *

Anto Geir's angry voice carried through the walls and warned of his presence long before the doors were unlocked and shoved open. Nick had just enough time to struggle to his feet and make sure Tru hid, protected behind storage containers in the far corner.

"Where's the little slut? Come out, come out wherever you are," Geir sneered in a singsong voice.

A snide smile plastered on his sweating face, he strutted into the room. He was followed closely by Crowder and his two cohorts, who were heavily armed and doing their best to exude menace in spite of their injuries. Nick leaned a shoulder against the wall as if he didn't have a care in the world. It brought Geir up short.

"Anto Geir, I presume?" Nick straightened, forcing his aching body to move with a fluid grace he was far from feeling. He let the smile drop from his face. His gaze flickered dismissively over Crowder and his men, and he was satisfied to see the shock that crossed their faces when they found him standing instead of insensible on the floor.

"You must be Rayven," Geir stated, keeping his distance and glancing quickly around as if to make sure Crowder's men protected him.

"Right on the first guess."

"You don't look so tough. My boys gave you quite a beating by all appearances. Ruined that pretty face of yours."

Nick shrugged. "Appearances can be deceiving. You, on the other hand, look exactly like I pictured you."

"What's that supposed to mean?" He took a threatening step forward, but then a hasty step back when Nick crossed his arms over his broad chest, raised an eyebrow and turned his expression mocking. Geir bristled, his outrage almost palpable, but he didn't move.

"Just shoot him and let's be done with this," Crowder snarled. His gaze darted around the room, his unease unmistakable

"Shut up. Shut up!" Geir yelled, rounding on Crowder. Spittle flew from his mouth and he wiped it away with the back of his hand. Obviously struggling for control, he added in a calmer voice. "I'm in charge here. No one is shooting anyone until I say so."

Geir seemed agitated, his movements jerky. Sweat slicked his face and his fingers drummed against his thigh without any discernible rhythm. Nick was surprised to see the telltale signs of a serious drug addiction and hoped he could somehow use it to his advantage. He wondered if Geir was somehow mixed up in the ring distributing the latest designer drug. Geir didn't strike him as having the intelligence to mastermind the complexity of a drug ring, but it was a possibility albeit a remote one. A more likely scenario was Geir was just a convenient cog in the wheel being manipulated by someone more powerful. Geir was foolish enough to get addicted to the product he was handling. From there it was an easy jump to assume Lodestone Mining was involved somehow and Nick cursed, believing the problem was much greater than he originally thought.

"I want the bitch, Tru Creighton," Geir demanded, snapping everyone's attention back to him. "Bring her to me."

Crowder started to move toward Tru crouched by the storage containers, but paused when Nick moved to intercept him.

"I wouldn't do that if I were you," he cautioned, his voice hard.

"You plan to stop me?" Crowder said. "You and who else? Last, I checked you lost your weapon and I don't see anyone else here except that sniveling bitch shivering in the corner. Get out of my way or I will finish what I started and kill you."

"Call off your bully, Geir, before I do something you will live to regret," Nick ordered, keeping an eye on Crowder. "You don't want to push me."

"Push you! What are you talking about? Push you? Are you crazy?" Geir's laughter sounded insane. "I'm in charge here and I give the orders. In case you have forgotten, Rayven, I have the weapons and you have nothing. I want Tru. She's going to pay for what she did and you can't stop me."

"Don't be too sure," Nick answered, pinning Crowder with a look, watching closely for any sudden move he might make. Shoulders square, hands loosely at his sides and balancing on the balls of his feet, Nick was ready to move if Crowder so much as twitched in Tru's direction.

Tight-lipped, he pushed away the grinding pain in his ribs and the ache of bruised muscles, not allowing them to divert his focus. His knife blade was hidden in his hand, ready to use, and he didn't doubt for a second his first target would be the thug in front of him.

"I don't think your boss is going to appreciate you harming the granddaughter of Maddox Creighton, do you? I'd bet my last credit whoever he is, he likes doing business in the shadows and harming her is guaranteed to cause him all kinds of problems," he continued in a conversational tone, risking a shot in the dark he was right about Geir. "You and I both know Creighton is a powerful man and will stop at nothing when it comes to protecting his family. He's dangerous to mess with, but not nearly as dangerous as I am. I will hunt you to the ends of this universe if you hurt her, and I will destroy whomever you are working for just for the hell of it. Mark my words."

"Hey, you didn't tell us she's that kind of Creighton," one of the men flanking Geir complained, frowning. "I ain't messing with him. You're not paying me enough for that!"

His companion nodded in agreement, and dropped the muzzle of his blaster.

"Shut up!" Geir's eyes bulged. "You'll do what I tell you, or else."

"Or else what?" Crowder demanded, keeping an eye on Nick. "This was supposed to be a simple grab, no complications. If I'd known who she was, I would never have agreed to this job. No one in their right mind messes with her family."

"I paid you good credits to get her, now bring her to me," Anto ordered. He shifted from one foot to the other, his movements more and more uncoordinated.

"I don't think so. I didn't sign on for this," Crowder snarled. He backed away, his men doing the same. "We're outta here."

"I'm sure I'll be seeing you around, Crowder." Nick's smile was full of promise. "You can count on it."

Anto tore at his sparse hair. "Come back here! I didn't say you could leave!"

"Well, now. Things have certainly gotten more interesting, haven't they?" Nick said with no small amount of satisfaction when Geir paused for breath. His grin broadened; security awaited the three men ready to take them into custody.

He'd contacted Siren earlier through the com system imbedded in his wrist cuff and given her their location and instructions to alert the authorities when she heard Geir enter the room. She'd kept the com open to record everything that had transpired. It would guarantee Geir and his men would spend some quality time on the prison moon, Purgatory. They would be gone for a long time if he had anything to say about it.

Tru left the protection of the storage containers and hurried to his side. Nick spared her a glance to make sure she was all right. Through the soft skin of her throat, her pulse beat like a wild thing, but she seemed steady enough. He wanted to grab her hand and pull her closer, but didn't dare. He needed to keep his focus on Geir. The effort to remain standing was making his head swim and cold sweat popped out along his hairline. All he had to do was stay on his feet long enough for security to arrive.

Tru stepped nearer and he stiffened. She stopped instantly when he shook his head. He didn't want her too close in case things went south in a hurry.

"This isn't how it was supposed to happen," Anto said without inflection, "I was going to have a little fun with you before I killed you, you know? I had it all planned out. Once you were out of the way no one would find out about the shipments and what they contained." He sneered at Tru. "I'll let you in on a little secret, my dear. You think this is all about the minerals and the paltry profits from their sale, don't you? You're wrong. The minerals were a convenient means to an end. No one would ever suspect there were drugs transported along with the minerals. That's where the money was—not in a few loads of rock going missing."

Tru gasped, and he waved a hand in dismissal. "It was so easy. The played-out mine shafts hid the drugs smuggled in by a transport and from there, I made sure it was dispersed to our clients on other worlds. Simple."

"Until you started sampling the product," Nick added.

Anto rounded on him, rage twisting his features. "Why shouldn't I enjoy a little of what we're selling? People were paying a fortune for twist and I got as much as I wanted for free. How was I to know how addictive it was?"

His mood did a lightning swift change and he quieted. Calmly, he ran his fingers through his mussed hair and smoothed out the lines of his jacket with a sharp tug. "Unfortunately, my superiors in the organization began to get a little suspicious of me and I had to find some way to fix that. Geotern's discovery was my ticket out of the difficulty I found myself in. I would be invaluable to them if I could deliver that prize." He turned to face Tru and his mouth twisted into a cruel line as he continued, "But you came along and ruined everything with your snooping. I thought I had it all figured out, had blocked all your exits and it was only a matter of time before you were mine. It was inconceivable you would find a way off world, that you would hook up with Rayven and leave with him. You ruined everything. All my careful plans wrecked."

"Who do you work for, Geir?" Nick asked, watching for any sudden moves.

The man was coming undone before their eyes and there was no way to predict what he would do next. If he were lucky, Nick would get a few more answers before the security force arrived.

"I can't tell you. They have a long reach and will kill me if they think I talked to anyone," Geir murmured, more to himself than to Nick. "I must keep quiet about what I know. Shh. Can't tell anyone. They will kill me."

"They?" Nick prodded.

Geir shot a pitying look at Tru, who hovered beside Nick. "You don't know what you have unleashed, do you? So sure of yourself, waltzing in like you owned the place. So disdainful of me and my position within Lodestone Mining. You didn't think I noticed, but I did. I have to kill you. It is the only way."

He reached under his jacket, pulled out a small, palm-sized blaster and aimed it at Tru. Reacting instinctively, Nick shoved her away just as Geir fired. Agony shrieked across his shoulder, igniting nerve endings and leaving him struggling to breathe through the excruciating pain. The force of the shot spun him to the floor, and he dropped his knife.

Fighting to stay conscious, he wobbled to one knee, trying to gain his feet as the room swam before his eyes. Desperate to locate Tru, he blinked to clear his vision while struggling with uncharacteristic clumsiness to reach his knife. It slipped, his blood-covered hand making it difficult to hold.

From what seemed like a great distance, he heard shouts as uniformed men burst into the room and forced Geir to the ground, ordering him to stay down and put his hands behind his head. Chaos reigned as Anto was removed, screaming he had to kill Tru at the top of his lungs.

The knife clattered to the ground, let loose by his nerveless fingers, when Nick realized help had arrived and his strength gave out. He managed to grab Tru's hand and held it to keep her near, while medical personnel swarmed over him and stripped off his outerwear to expose his wound. Faces swam in and out of focus, and he bit back curses as hands explored his injuries. A groan wrenched through his tightly clenched lips when pressure was applied to his bleeding shoulder. The world went gray and sound receded to a distorted echo in his head as he endured this new assault pushing him to the edge of his control.

Nick sagged with relief when he was given something to shut off the waves of agony pounding his abused body. Marginally aware of what was going on around him, he clung to the small, warm hand anchoring him to the world. He refused to let go even when he was lifted onto a MedTransport to be taken to the medical facility.

Drifting in a pleasant haze, he closed his eyes and felt a goofy smile spread across his face. He couldn't seem to control it and felt laughter bubble just below the surface. He tried to open his eyes to share this problem with Tru, but they refused to cooperate and it suddenly seemed unimportant in the grand scheme of things.

He gave in and accepted the swirling multicolored world behind his closed eyelids and decided to let someone else worry about the drug-induced smile, which wouldn't go away.

Chapter 18

The astringent smell universal to all medical facilities tickled Nick's nose and irritated his dry throat. He licked dry lips, aware of a raging thirst making it difficult to swallow. His thoughts were sluggish as he debated with himself if it was enough to make him want to leave the half-dream world he currently inhabited to ask for water or if he should just let himself drift away again. His body felt heavy, the effort to move impossible to contemplate. The drugs given to him earlier were keeping him pain free, but experience warned him any sudden movement would bring the waves of pain crashing back without mercy, so he lay still.

Thinking took too much effort, and he could grow to appreciate the medicinal smell surrounding him. It meant he could keep the world at bay for a while longer, so he drifted off, seeking the dark cocoon of sleep to give him its comfort. Time had no meaning there, dreams didn't harry him with regrets and despair, and Anto Geir was no longer a threat.

Anto Geir.

Nick frowned and his mouth tightened, stopping him from fully sinking into the welcome oblivion he sought. There was something he needed to do, something about the name swimming in his thoughts, causing his heartbeat to increase and making him shift uneasily in his bed. Pain lanced through his shoulder. He stifled a groan.

The soothing darkness behind his closed eyes began to lighten and swirl with gray, gradually resolving itself into colors. Lashes, which felt glued together, parted reluctantly and the blinding light revealed through barely cracked eyelids shot shards of pain through his brain and shocked him back to full lucidity with cruel suddenness.

"Sonofabitch," Nick croaked. He squinted against the brightness and tried to focus. The sound of his voice, weak and barely a whisper, was an unpleasant surprise.

At the rustling of fabric to his left, he turned his head in time to watch Tru launch herself out of her chair to reach his bed. She looked disheveled. Her curls were a riotous halo surrounding her head and her eyes large and bruised-looking in her worried face. Raising his hand off the bedcovers took tremendous effort, but it was worth it when she slipped her hand into his and held on tight. She knelt beside his bed and pressed her forehead against the back of his hand. The wetness of unchecked tears dashed against his bruised knuckles. He raised his other hand to let his fingers slide through her hair before tracing down her wet cheek and lifting her chin so he could see her face.

"Hey," he whispered. "No tears, okay?"

Tru nodded as he wiped away the wetness with his thumb. Mouth quivering, she gave him a shaky smile and nuzzled her cheek against his palm. The effort to hold his hand against her face proved too difficult and he allowed it to sink weakly to his side.

"Hey, yourself," she replied, her voice raspy. "How are you feeling?"

Rising from her knees, she perched on the edge of the bed beside his hip. She turned her palm against the hand she held and linked her fingers through his. Nick was surprised by the comfort her ordinary gesture gave him and squeezed her hand in return. She looked him over carefully, and he suspected she was searching his injuries, cataloging each and every one of them. He tried not to squirm, but it was making him uncomfortable.

He grimaced, feeling the pull of bruised and torn flesh. "I've felt better," he replied without a trace of self-pity. "I probably look worse than I feel."

"I hear you are going to make a complete recovery and nothing vital was hit," she said. "You might be left with a small scar on your chin and one on your shoulder, but I'm told they can be taken care of later if you want." Tracing the old crescent scar near his eye with a finger, she wiggled her eyebrows suggestively. "If you ask me, I think another scar will just add to your rakish good looks."

Nick snorted and then immediately regretted it when his shoulder began to throb. Careful to keep his discomfort off his face, he attempted a wry grin. "I've never been accused of having good looks, so I don't think one more scar is going to do much damage, do you?"

"I thought you were one of the most handsome men I'd ever met when I first saw you. Nothing has happened since to change my opinion, nor will it."

She leaned forward to brush her mouth across his, a move that seemed to surprise her as much as him. She started to draw back but he was having none of that. He released her hand, and reached up cupping the back of her head. Her face was inches from his, the gentle pressure preventing her from moving away. By the look in her eyes when she met his gaze, he knew she was unsure. For one timeless moment they regarded each other. Then, as he pulled her mouth to his and nibbled along her lips in a series of feathery kisses, her eyelids drifted closed.

Her hand flattened on the bed kept her balanced above his prone body. He absorbed the delight of having her mouth pressed against his and knew the instant her lips softened to allow more. The burn of desire kindled, racing through his system and the fire consumed him. The pain of his injuries receded, his whole focus on Tru. Taking command, he explored the warm depths of her mouth.

His heart hammered in his chest, driving the last remnants of the drugs in his system away. He kissed her as a man kisses the woman he wants above all else, his mouth claiming, taking everything, giving no quarter and then demanding more. He swept his tongue into the dark recesses of her mouth, enthralled by her taste, mindless to his surroundings, blind to everything but the woman he was kissing as if his very life depended on it.

The sound of a throat cleared jerked him back to reality and broke their kiss as effectively as being physically pried apart. Nick rested his forehead against hers for a moment and suppressed a groan, his heart beating a painful rhythm against his cracked ribs. As he dragged air into his starved lungs, he dropped his hand from the back of her head and released her.

Tru scuttled back, her cheeks reddening. He regretted her obvious discomfort at being discovered in a compromising position, but didn't regret what had just happened, only that it hadn't happened sooner and was over far too soon. She touched her fingertips to her swollen mouth and dropped her hand to her side. She straightened, shot him an undecipherable look and turned to face whoever had come into the room.

"I see the medic wasn't exaggerating your rate of recovery," the head of security said. "Glad to see he was correct." Amusement crinkled the corners of the man's eyes as he broke the uncomfortable silence. Not waiting for a reply, he stepped fully into the room to stand at the foot of Nick's bed. "I doubt you remember me, Captain Rayven, since the capture of Anto Geir and his men was fairly chaotic, so let me introduce myself. I'm Sharpe, the head of security here in Killjoy."

"Sorry, I don't remember you. I was a little preoccupied at the time," Nick answered while he raised the head of his bed to an upright position.

He didn't intend to have a discussion with this man while lying flat on his back.

Sharpe chuckled. Rocking back on his heels, he slipped his hands into his pockets. "Fair enough."

"How can I help you?" Nick asked after he settled. He reached out to clasp Tru's hand.

"I want to personally thank you and your crew mate, Siren, for the warning about Crowder and his men. They're wanted in a number of unresolved crimes spanning several of our planets and it is quite a coup they're in our custody. It is too bad we didn't know sooner so we could have avoided what happened to you."

"Unfortunately, I didn't make their acquaintance until we were trapped in that hallway," Nick said. "Until then I'd no idea they even existed and couldn't have cared less they were known criminals."

The humor slid away from Sharpe's face. "I know it doesn't feel that way right now, but you are extremely lucky. Crowder is a violent offender and never leaves witnesses to his activities. It has made him extremely difficult to capture and the fact you both are alive is nothing short of a miracle."

"Trust me, I know exactly how lucky we are," Nick replied, squeezing Tru's hand.

"This is the first break we have had, and your statements should guarantee he does a long stretch on Purgatory." Sharpe's gaze moved between Tru and Nick. He removed his hands from his pockets and let them drop to his sides. "I've been informed you will be spending at least another day in the med facility while you recover, but it has been cleared we can record your testimony for the courts when you feel up to it."

Nick was tired, the medication no longer keeping the pain away. He wanted to rub his temples to ease the headache beginning to pound behind his eyes, but stubbornly refused to show any weakness. It seemed especially important with Tru in the room and Sharpe standing at the foot of his bed exuding a disgusting amount of virility. "I don't plan to be on this rock any longer than I have to," Nick said. "Why don't I come by tomorrow, as soon as I'm released, and we can take care of it then?"

"Excellent. I promise not to take up any more of your time than necessary. In the meantime, is there anything you need?"

Nick smiled slowly, gaze locked on Tru. "Nope, I'm good. I think I've everything I need right here."

"I can see that," Sharpe replied. "If you will excuse me then, I will leave you to get some rest."

"Before you go, can you tell me what you have done with Anto Geir?" Tru asked.

"He'll be transported to Paladin Minor with a security detail when it can be arranged. There is a facility there, Harrowsgate House. It specializes in drug withdrawal and is secure enough to hold the criminally insane," he said, his voice kind. He smiled at her.

"Oh." She pushed a stray curl behind her ear and bit her bottom lip. "What will happen to him?"

Sharpe exchanged a look with Nick, who nodded almost imperceptibly. "To be honest with you," he said, with the barest hesitation, "the odds of him surviving withdrawal from this drug are minimal. It is particularly nasty, and once addicted, few are able to stop using. Harrowsgate has had some success with its patients, but those who survive are usually brain damaged."

"If he survives, what then?"

"I have no easy answer for you, I'm afraid. The authorities on Paladin Minor are coordinating with the Unified Alliance of Planets. They will try to gain as much information as they can about the cartel he worked for so they can stop this threat. I doubt they will get much information out of Geir though, but every little thing will help. They already moved to shut down his operation on Lodestone. Your grandfather has been instrumental in cutting off that avenue of shipments, from what I hear." Sharpe scratched his chin and drew his brows together in a slight frown. "My best guess is Geir will be incarcerated the rest of his life. Primarily for his own protection. You can be sure the cartel doesn't want him around in case he reveals too much. He'll be no further threat to you."

"Thank you. I just needed to be sure he's taken care of and won't be coming after me again." She let out a deep sigh.

Nodding to Tru and offering a quick salute to Nick, he turned and left the room, making sure the door panel slid shut behind him.

"I don't think Geir will be able to frighten you again," Nick said once they were alone. His shoulder throbbed unmercifully, overshadowing the aches from his earlier beating. Too weary to keep his eyes open any longer he closed them and tried to ignore it. He must have drifted off to sleep because the next thing he knew, a female medic leaned over him with a MedScan.

"I see you are awake. Good. How are you feeling?"

"I've been better."

Her smile was sympathetic, if a little distracted. She turned her attention to the MedScan readout. Nodding her satisfaction, she put it aside long enough to shoot another dose of pain medicine against the side of his neck.

"You are healing much better than expected, Captain Rayven. You are making excellent progress."

"When will I be able to leave? I'm eager to get back to my home and business," he said, his words slurring from the medication. Blinking bleary eyes, he didn't protest when the medic lowered the head of his bed so he was prone. She fluffed his pillow to make him more comfortable and pulled his rumpled blankets straight with impersonal swiftness.

"I've spoken to your partner and she's very aware of the care you will need while you travel home. If you continue as well as you have been, you may be able to leave tomorrow."

"Where's Tru?" His tongue felt thick and he fought to keep his eyes open. It worried him she was not in the room.

"I sent her to get some food. She'll return once she has had an opportunity to clean up and eat. It is important she take care of herself as well. I don't want two patients on my hands, now do I?"

He grunted and wished the medic would leave. He wanted Tru. He knew he wouldn't be able to rest until she was back with him and he knew she was safe.

"I'll arrange for a meal to be brought to you later. I'm sure you are starting to get hungry. Get some rest. I'll check in on you before I go off shift."

As quickly as she'd entered the room, she left, leaving a faint trail of antiseptic and perfume behind her.

Nick drifted on the pleasant cushion of the pain medication and allowed his mind to wander at will. Distantly, he realized he couldn't hang on to a single thought long enough to reach any conclusions, but he didn't mind. He did know he was still thirsty and once he acknowledged his thirst, it seemed to increase with every passing second.

A container of water stood on a table beside his bed, but the effort to shift enough to reach for it left him panting and irritable. Propped on one elbow Nick barely had his fingers on the container when Tru walked into the room.

"Nick! What are you doing?" she demanded and hurried to his side. "Let me get that for you."

"Damn it, Tru, I'm not helpless," he snarled in frustration. The water was just out of his reach, and no matter how it irked him, he did need her help. He flopped onto his back and bit back a groan from the sudden, unwise movement. Tight-lipped, pale and sweating, he avoided looking at her.

"Of course not," she snapped. "Anyone can see you are perfectly able to care for yourself. You don't need anyone, do you?" Grabbing the water, she shoved it at him. He could tell she was angry. She propped her hands on her hips and glared at him. "Far be it for me to interfere. I'm only a client, remember?"

* * * *

Tru's breath hitched, and she covered her mouth with her hands. She looked at Nick, appalled she would lose her temper with him after everything he'd been through for her. Until the words had left her mouth she had not realized how much being just a client truly bothered her. Her growing feelings for Nick and the kiss they'd shared earlier had made the niggling doubts resurface.

She was afraid Nick might decide the kiss they'd shared was a mistake and the reason he was in such a hurry to get back in space was to return her home now his duty was done. It was irrational, disconcerting and wholly inappropriate, given the circumstances, and she regretted the words as soon as they left her mouth.

Nick struggled to take a few swallows of water, never taking his gaze off her. His eyes looked slightly unfocused from the pain medication and twin frown lines drew his brows together. She could see he was having trouble grasping what she was upset about.

"You aren't just a client," he said, his tone weary.

"I'm sorry. I shouldn't have said that." Her fingers plucked at the bedding. "I don't know what came over me." She moved closer, removed the water cylinder from his lax fingers and placed it on the table, close enough he could reach it in future.

"S'no problem," Nick said, his words running together. "Need sleep." His eyes drifted closed only to blink back open as she moved away. "No, don't leave."

She turned back and returned to the side of his bed, unsure what to do. He barely had the energy to pat the bed to indicate he wanted her to lie down with him.

"You want me to climb into bed with you?" He scooted slowly to the opposite side, leaving enough room for her to lie down. "I don't think it's a good idea, Nick. What if I hurt you?"

"Won't."

"But—" she didn't get a chance to finish her sentence before he frowned, reached for her hand and tugged her down.

Giving in, she stretched out beside him, making sure she didn't touch any of his injuries. She laid her head on the pillow, and once she settled, he sighed.

"Better," he mumbled, looking on the edge of sleep.

Tru watched him as his breathing evened out and deepened. His dark lashes made crescent shadows against his pale cheeks, but the swelling on his eye was almost gone. Bruises had rapidly changed color from deep purple to acid yellow. All vied with the shadow of his beard and almost hid the healing cuts. Deep lines fanned out from his eyes and added to his battered look.

Her heart twisted. She was in love with him, deeply and irrevocably. Careful not to wake him, she touched a fingertip to his mouth and brushed his lips before dropping away.

"I love you, Nick Rayven," she whispered, certain he was asleep and wouldn't hear her.

Chapter 19

The wind howled outside, its eerie shriek waking Nick from his uneasy dreams. Icy snow particles rapped against the viewscreen, competing with the quiet hum of the heater keeping the cold at bay. Listening, he heard quiet footfalls outside his door as medical personnel went about their business, quiet conversations echoing in their wake.

He lay still, allowing his sleep-dulled mind to catch up and take inventory of the aches and pains gnawing at him. He felt good, considering everything that had happened and had never been more grateful for the rapid healing abilities of his people as he was now. At this rate, he would be able to leave Killjoy and head into space without too much delay.

Tru shifted in her sleep beside him, her soft sigh brushing against the side of his neck making him very aware of her warm presence. She was nestled close to his body, but even in sleep, was mindful of his injuries and careful to keep a small space between them. Disliking the distance separating them, he slipped his good arm around her shoulders and nestled her closer. She settled easily against his length, murmuring in her sleep. He rested his chin on the top of her head, taking pleasure in the softness of her hair and the tantalizing scent of her skin. Deeply content, he closed his eyes and enjoyed the peaceful moment.

I love you, Nick Rayven. The words surfaced from out of nowhere and his eyes popped open, his heartbeat thundering in his ears.

The whispered confession tantalized, making him wonder if he'd dreamed those words. Drawing brows together, he stared at the shadowed ceiling trying to remember, feeling unsettled and uncertain.

He recalled insisting Tru sleep on his bed, needing the reassurance of her presence before he'd allowed himself to give in to the medication and his body's demands. His eyelids had been too heavy to keep open, but he'd known when she'd acquiesced by the slight dip of the mattress and the instant relaxation in his battered frame.

Nick moved his head on the pillow to see Tru's sleeping face. She looked peaceful, dark lashes fanning her sleep-flushed cheeks, lips slightly parted. He turned his gaze back to the ceiling while his thoughts swirled in fruitless circles and his tension mounted.

The swoosh of the door sliding open drew him out of his mired thoughts. A medic bustled in, MedScan at the ready to record his healing progress. Tru stiffened beside him. Reluctantly, he let her slip out of his arms and sit up. She looked everywhere but at him, and his unease increased. The medic smiled at her and stood aside long enough for Tru to leave the bed and disappear into the cleanser.

Nick scowled at her retreating back, then at the door closed behind her.

"How are you feeling this morning?"

"How do you think I feel?" He was more concerned about Tru's hasty exit than talking to the man standing over him recording his vitals. Out of the corner of his eye, Nick noticed the medic's quick frown and closer look at the MedScan readout, and he sighed.

"You have astonishing recuperative abilities. Amazing, in fact," the medic murmured. "Those ribs of yours are nearly healed, the blaster wound is already knitting together and the contusions are fading." He ran another scan and whistled softly through his teeth. Raising his eyes he shifted his focus from the readout to Nick and added, "I don't think I've ever seen anything quite like this before. Do you always heal this quickly?"

"Yes," Nick replied, not interested in elaborating on the almost legendary healing abilities of his people. It just raised questions about his home world and he preferred not to discuss it. He scooted into a sitting position and shifted his pillows behind his back. "So, when can I get out of here?"

The medic regarded him with open curiosity. He waited a beat as if expecting Nick to say more then shrugged. "I'd say you should be able to leave today, if you wish. I can't see any reason to keep you longer."

"Good."

"I expect you to take it easy until you are fully healed. Once you are back on your own world, I recommend following up with your personal medical provider to make sure there're no problems."

Nick nodded, knowing he wouldn't do anything suggested to him. What he thought must have showed on his face because the medic furrowed his brow and pinned him with a stern look.

"Fine. I'll check in with my own medic. I promise," Nick conceded with ill humor.

He could see the doubt on the other man's face and was relieved when he didn't push the issue. The medic tapped in a quick update and release documentation, before he said, "I've scheduled you for release after breakfast, but there is no rush." A quick flash of a smile, and he left Nick to brood and wonder why Tru had not returned.

Bits and pieces of his conversation with her the previous night came back, but they were fragmented and he wasn't sure what was real and what was imagined. He thought he remembered her complaining about being a client, but it just wouldn't jell. He rubbed his jaw, feeling the rasp of whiskers and tried to dredge up the events of the day before. He dropped his hand from his face to knead the ache in his injured shoulder before he rotated it, testing his range of motion. He felt a twinge and winced.

"Are you trying to re-injure yourself?" Tru asked. She stood in the doorway to the cleanser, frowning at him.

"What? No, of course not," he replied, startled out of his abstraction.

"Odd. I can't help but think what you are doing wouldn't be good for your shoulder. But, then what do I know." She shrugged and strolled to the viewscreen. She opened the curtains with an irritated snap to gaze outside at the snow-covered landscape. She did not look at Nick as she spoke. "I'm not the one who was shot by a blaster and is lying in a hospital bed, am I?"

"What's that supposed to mean?" he asked, his voice sharper than he'd intended.

"Nothing." Tru traced random patterns with a fingertip on the cool surface in front of her. "Your assignment is almost over, Nick. I'm sure you will be glad to get back to your own life."

"What?" Nick frowned fiercely at her, still struggling to put the jagged pieces of memory together and listen to what she said now. He didn't like the aloof smile on her face or the fact she deliberately put distance between them. "What the hell are you talking about?"

"It's time for me to go home. Your job is done and we both need to get back to our lives."

The words were curt, but he could hear the slight wobble in her voice. He didn't understand. Of all the things she could have said, this was the last thing he expected.

"If this is what you want, then of course I will get you home quickly," he replied. "After breakfast I will meet with Sharpe to give a statement and then we will be ready to board the ship. I should have you back with your family in no time at all."

"Thank you. I'm sure my grandfather will be very pleased and I know he'll reward you well for keeping me safe."

"I don't want a friggin' reward! Do you hear me?" He felt raw and vulnerable, unable to cope and he hated it.

Nick jerked upright, grabbed a pillow from behind his back and threw it forcefully against the wall. Intense pain lanced from his ribs to his shoulder, and he bit back a curse that was half groan.

Tru jumped, glanced at him and then away, color climbing into her cheeks. Nick glared at her averted face while he grappled with the fact she wanted to leave him. He couldn't believe it, didn't want to accept it.

I love you, Nick Rayven. The words were powerful, but they were obviously a lie, a figment of his imagination. Why would she love him? Shaken far more than he'd thought possible, he sank against his remaining pillows and stared bleakly at his hands clenched into fists.

"I don't want a reward," he reiterated. His face felt frozen and stiff, the only movement a muscle jumping in his cheek from clenching his jaw as he fought for a calm he was far from feeling. Even when he'd been angry in the past, he'd always been in control, unlike now.

"I'm sorry. It wasn't my intention to offend you." Surprise was clear in her voice, along with a wariness he found disturbing.

Backing away, she turned to leave but he halted her with a hand on her wrist. His grasp was loose, coaxing more than demanding she stay. The slight tremor in his fingers was the only indication his emotions weren't fully contained. He rubbed with his thumb along the inside of her wrist, feeling the erratic beat of her pulse.

"Don't leave. I didn't mean to snap at you." His tone was contrite, his anger banked and under control. "I just wasn't expecting you to be so eager to leave me."

The vulnerability in her eyes was unexpected and left him floundering. Hope stirred, mixed with longing and his desire she stay. Relief flooded him when she nodded in agreement.

Breakfast arrived, interrupting further discussion and the moment passed. He felt he had a reprieve, but knew it wasn't over, not by a long shot. There would be plenty of time to convince Tru she belonged with him once they were on *Dominion*. He released her wrist, never taking his eyes of her face. Not for the first time, he wished he could read her mind. Her feelings were now hidden by her lowered lashes.

The tantalizing smell of food arriving made his mouth water, and his stomach rumbled. He'd fallen asleep before dinner arrived the night before and couldn't remember the last meal he'd eaten. He was ravenous.

The orderly smiled at Tru and placed the tray within easy reach for Nick. He left as quickly as he'd arrived, leaving an awkward silence behind him. Tru removed the covers over the food and placed the tray on his lap. She turned to leave, and he had a moment of panic. He grabbed a sweet roll, split it in half and held part of it out to her.

"There is more here than I can eat. It would be a shame for it to go to waste."

She hesitated for a moment before turning back and taking the roll from his outstretched hand. She nodded her thanks and took a bite.

He divided the breakfast into equal portions and then dug into his part. He ate his meal with slow deliberation, assuaging his hunger, while darting quick glances at her, gauging her mood. When she reached for something she was careful their hands didn't touch and it bothered him. He'd gotten used to her touching him and felt the loss keenly.

Finally replete and feeling stronger, he picked up his mug of tayberry and sipped the brew while he watched her demolish the remainder of her breakfast. What was the subtle change he sensed in her? She was guarded, more subdued and not meeting his gaze. How could he fix whatever was troubling her if he didn't have a clue what it was? He didn't like not knowing.

The silence stretched between them becoming more uncomfortable and setting his teeth on edge. He was a man of action, used to confronting things head on, but he admitted to himself he was out of his depth when it came to women. He had a lot to lose if he didn't get this right.

The war on Tonlith had precluded any serious connections he might have had with the opposite sex and relegated his relationships to brief hookups to satisfy his physical urges, but left him emotionally untouched. Until he met Tru, he'd never experienced instant attraction that slammed him like his first g-force maneuver. It had left him scrambling to form a coherent thought. He didn't like feeling vulnerable and unsure of himself and his knee jerk reaction had been to keep her at a distance, aware it had proved impossible to do. She wouldn't be ignored and somehow she'd wrapped herself around him until he couldn't imagine his life without her in it.

Now he needed to convince her she belonged with him, but she wasn't like the women he'd known before and he didn't know how to go about it. Pretty words didn't come easily and he suspected she would appreciate and maybe even expect them.

"What? Why are you staring at me?"

"I'm trying to figure out what has made you so unhappy and why you won't look at me." The words were out before he thought, surprising him.

"I don't know what you mean. I am certainly not unhappy." Her quick reply sounded weak. She looked away from him and busied herself removing the tray from his lap.

"Tru, we've spent enough time together for me to know when you aren't being honest with me."

"There is nothing to tell, Nick. I'm fine. I'm just tired, I think."

Nick clenched his jaw so hard his back teeth ached. She was lying. He knew it and she knew it, but now was not the time to force her to talk. There would be plenty of time to get to the bottom of this when they were confined to his ship. And, maybe if he were very lucky, he would persuade her to stay.

"It is time we got back to the ship. Do you know what happened to my clothes?" he asked, dropping the subject for now. He threw off his blankets and moved with great care to sit on the edge of his bed. He ignored Tru's muted gasp of surprise at the sight of him naked except for the short hospital gown. "I'm going to get up and get dressed. You might want to turn your back or leave until I'm finished if it bothers you. Either way works for me."

She whirled around and marched to the door, stopped only to allow it to slide open before she exited. He watched her swiftly retreating back and then eased to a standing position. The room spun for a minute, and he closed his eyes, waiting for it to settle before he ventured across the room to find his clothes.

He was exhausted by the time he was dressed, the weakness in his limbs maddening. Moving slowly, he reached for his blaster and debated using the shoulder holster, before he settled for hooking it on his belt. His shoulder and ribs ached by the time he was through. He glanced in the mirror and the sight of his bruised face didn't improve his mood.

Having located his wrist cuff, he slapped it on before he contacted Siren and let her know the plans. Everything would be ready by the time they reached the ship. Nick squared his shoulders and went in search of Tru.

She waited for him in the hallway and he paused to watch her talking animatedly with the female medic from the night before. Tru's musical laughter floated to him and his heartbeat sped up at the sight of her glowing face. He knew the exact instant she realized he was there because the vibrant glow in her eyes faded, replaced with uncertainty as she turned to look at him. Her smile was welcoming but impersonal, and Nick wanted to punch something. Fighting the urge, he reined in his frustration and returned her smile with a slow one of his own. No more hiding. It was time he let her know what he thought and felt. He dropped his guard.

Tru's smile widened. Excusing herself, she left the medic and moved to his side. Unable to stop himself, he let his gaze wander over her. He relaxed as she caressed his arm before he captured her hand, squeezing lightly.

"We need to stop by Sharpe's office before we leave, sweetheart."

She started at his endearment.

"It shouldn't take too long. Siren will arrange for supplies to be restocked while we're giving a statement." He permitted himself to hope when she didn't pull her hand out of his. Feeling much better, he raised their clasped palms and brushed a kiss across the back of her hand.

Wide-eyed, she met his smile. Satisfied, he dropped her hand and pulled her unresisting to his side. An arm looped around her slender shoulders, he guided her down the hall to find the head of security's office.

She didn't say a word, but he could tell she was off balance and confused by his easy show of affection. Her gaze on the ground, she nibbled her lower lip. He wished he could read her mind, because he had no real idea what was going on in her agile brain.

Undaunted, he squeezed her shoulder and dropped a brief kiss on the top of her head. He smiled to himself, and his heart skipped a beat when she carefully slipped her arm around his waist. She glanced at him and he could see the color climbing her cheeks, but there was a twinkle in her eyes. Unable to resist, he winked at her. Her eyes widened and then she delighted him by winking back. Nick threw back his head and laughed, ignoring the pain in his ribs and shoulders.

Chapter 20

The security station was organized chaos, which was being generous, in Nick's opinion. Officer's voices battled with the noise of the crowded room. It took a few minutes to gain the attention of the officer staffing the intake desk then Nick and Tru were escorted to Chief Sharpe's office and announced without ceremony.

Sharpe motioned for them to take a seat and nodded to his officer, indicating he close the door on his way out. The sudden quiet was as much a relief as it was obviously unnerving for Tru, who perched on the edge of her seat and looked around with cautious interest. Sharpe wore his authority with an ease only many years of service and discipline would provide. Nick found it easy to relax in Sharpe's presence understanding him from his own years of service. Sharpe's piercing eyes seemed to miss nothing, sweeping over Tru with approval before he turned his attention to Nick.

"Ah, Captain Rayven. It is good to see you up and about. How are you feeling?" His interest seemed genuine.

"Ready to put this business behind us and head back to my ship," Nick replied, shifting in his chair to ease the discomfort in his healing ribs.

"Can't say I blame you in the least." Sharpe offered a commiserating smile. "This shouldn't take too long, and then you will be cleared to leave. I've arranged with the Port Authority for a transport sled to take you and your companion to your ship once we're done. You will find your outdoor gear has been cleaned and is waiting for you. Although the snow has stopped for now, it is still treacherous footing out there and it wouldn't be in either of our best interests if you were injured further."

Nick nodded, torn between relief and annoyance that unforeseen help had been offered. As much as it rankled to admit to any weakness, he hadn't been looking forward to facing the elements during the trek to his ship.

"I've spent some time listening to the recording of events supplied by your crew member, Siren. I have to admit that was some quick thinking on your part, opening a com link while alerting my team to the situation." Satisfaction was evident in his voice as he continued, "I've had the information transcribed for public record and for transmittal to the judicial governing body of the Unified Alliance of Planets once we're done. I need you both to read and verify the accuracy of this report."

Nick leaned forward to pick up the tablet, which had been moved to the edge of the desk by Sharpe. He scanned the report and applied his thumbprint to verify its accuracy. He handed it to Tru and waited for her to do the same. He watched her closely and approved her stoicism when confronted again with reliving the events. She was pale, but composed when she slid the tablet across the desk to Sharpe. Sharpe nodded once it was done and the report was back in his hands.

"What now?" Nick asked, nodding at the report. Tru was very quiet, eyes downcast and seemed deep in thought. The usual animation lighting her face was missing, and he wished them both far away from this place and its terrible memories for her. He lifted a hand and laid it over hers resting on her lap. His touch reassured them both and he was rewarded by her smile.

"Geir is being held in one of our cells under heavy guard until arrangements are made to transport him to Harrowsgate with an Interplanetary Marshall. Unfortunately, his condition seems to be deteriorating rapidly and there isn't much we can do about it. Crowder and his cohorts will remain here until their trial. As I mentioned before, I anticipate the three of them will be spending some quality time on Purgatory once this is all said and done."

Sharpe's chair creaked as he leaned back, relaxing against its padded frame.

He drummed his fingers on the chair arm. "I've been working with other agencies trying to tie up loose ends in this case. Crowder seems to have been a very busy man and it is good he'll be off the grid for a long spell, thanks to you."

"I'd tell you I was happy to oblige, but it would be a lie," Nick replied. "Personally, I hope never to land on this planet again, but I suspect you already knew that."

Sharpe barked a laugh, which sounded rusty from underuse as he stood. He rounded his desk and offered a hand when Tru rose from her chair, beating Nick to the punch. He could see the amusement glinting in Sharpe's eyes when he shook hands with him. Nick hadn't liked him touching Tru and he was annoyed with himself over the fact. Even more annoyed it had been obvious to the other man. Nick reached the door and held it open for Tru to pass through.

Alarms shrieked. Sharpe shoved him aside. Nick swore. Agony lanced across his shoulder, taking his breath with the force of it. Black dots danced before his eyes as he caught his breath and the pain began to recede. Nick reached for Tru only to find empty space where she'd stood seconds before.

"What the hell is going on here?" Sharpe roared over the screams of the alarm.

No one in the room moved and Nick slowly turned his head to see what everyone was staring at. Tru was held immobile with a knife to her throat. Her captor had his other arm across her chest, the blaster in his hand angled toward the room at large.

He registered the terror on her face, but shut off his emotions to concentrate on the man holding her.

"Geir." It was a statement of disgust and impotent rage from Sharpe. "Let her go. There is no way you are going to make it out of here alive unless you do."

Nick moved to stand beside Sharpe and prayed no one would do something stupid to get to Tru. The tension in the room was almost palatable, but an eerie calmness drop over him, leaving deadly, single-minded concentration in its wake. Sharpe flicked a look down to the blaster held against his leg and Nick understood what he was asking without words. Given the first opportunity, they were both going to find out just how fast he was with his weapon.

"As much as I appreciate the accommodations, Sharpe, I don't plan to stick around and she's going to guarantee I get off-world." Geir tightened his grip on Tru and smirked when she choked.

"How did you escape? I had you in lockdown. It shouldn't have been possible to get out."

Nick recognized it as a ploy to keep Geir's attention on Sharpe and to give his men the opportunity to move into place. He hoped Geir wouldn't figure it out and do something reckless. Nick could see the internal battle Geir waged, the desire to brag about his escape from his cell against his desperation to get away.

Geir darted glances around the room and licked his lips as a cocky smile spread across his face. "Pfft. It was almost too easy. I just faked a seizure and when your dimwitted guard came to investigate I broke his damn neck."

"That explains how you got the cell door open, but how did you make it through the guard station? Did you have help?"

"Help? You think I needed help?" Geir's laugh was maniacal and then stopped abruptly. His eyes narrowed to slits as he pointed his blaster at an officer who had been unwise enough to get caught moving closer. He froze in place, but Geir shot him anyway. The man crumpled to the floor. "Don't anyone else move. Now, where was I? Ah, yes, I admit I was a little remiss in wounding the guard at the front desk instead of killing him, but I did stop him long enough to prevent the security doors from closing on me. Unfortunately, he was able to trip the alarms. I compounded my mistake by taking a wrong turn and ending up here. It was very kind of this Creighton bitch to be just where I needed her, don't you think? Finally she'll be useful for something other than snooping where she doesn't belong."

Tru started to squirm, but stopped immediately when Geir's knife tip broke the skin of her neck. Blood trickled into her collar, leaving gooseflesh in its path. She looked like her legs could barely support her and helpless to escape, she held onto Geir's forearm trying to create enough room to breathe.

Nick growled deep in his throat, his eyes promising death to the man holding Tru. He was poised, ready to strike at the first opportunity, his singular focus on Anto Geir and the weapons he held.

"Let's not be hasty, Geir. Why don't we negotiate? You don't want to risk trying to get out of here with a hostage. She's only going to hold you back." Sharpe spoke evenly, his voice devoid of emotion.

"Do you think I'm an idiot? I don't negotiate." Geir spit out the words, darting glances between Nick and Sharpe as if he wasn't sure which one posed the greater danger.

Nick knew he was the bigger predator and Geir had just signed his own death warrant. One clear shot was all he needed to take the bastard down.

Back to the wall, Geir held Tru immobile. Her breath panted in short staccato puffs and Nick's gut clenched.

"Don't you dare faint on me, you hear me?" Movement caught Geir's eye as another one of the officers in the room moved. "Stay right there, or I will kill her." He threatened, wild-eyed. "I swear I will kill her."

"Hold." Sharpe ordered his men, never taking his eyes off Geir and Tru. "What do you want? What is it going to take for you to release the girl?" He was still delaying, trying to keep Geir's attention on him. "How about you take me as a hostage instead?"

Geir snorted. "I don't think so. I'm not an idiot. The minute I release her I'm a dead man. I've come a long way to find her, she's mine!" He tightened his forearm around Tru. "Get away from the doors. Do it now. I'm going to move real slow and you are going to let me and this little bitch leave. Got that? If any of you so much as twitch, I will kill her and then I will take out as many of you as I can before I'm done. You," he nodded at a new recruit, still raw enough the panic showed on his face, "Stop that damned alarm now! Then I want you to make sure there is a clear path for me to get to my ship. I want immediate clearance for departure, got it?"

"Do it," Sharpe ordered, when the recruit looked to him for guidance.

Nick took an almost imperceptible step forward. Dark energy swirled around him and chills raised the hair on his arms. He was preparing to strike, knew it to his very bones. Geir was going to give him the opening he needed. He held his breath.

Nick's vision tunneled to Geir and Tru, his concentration absolute and unrelenting. His sharp gaze tracked everything, every minuscule muscle move, the droplet of sweat that splashed from Geir's forehead to his forearm, the slight tremor in his fingers. Each breath was noted, and Nick's nostrils flared, catching the scent of nervous sweat. He followed Geir's crab-like walk as he backed toward the open door, watching, waiting for the one mistake he knew was coming. He'd failed Tru before; he wouldn't fail now.

Geir was almost to the door and shot a triumphant look to the room at large. He turned his head and Nick reacted. Geir was dead before he hit the ground.

* * * *

Nick raised his blaster in a fluid move too fast to follow. Tru felt the heat of the shot pass her cheek and the rough jerk when it hit Geir. Numb, too frightened to move, she barely noticed his arms fall away as he collapsed to the ground in a boneless heap.

Cold air flowed over her back and arms where his body once blocked it. Chills raced over her skin, quickly turning to deep shudders. Too terrified to cry or even make a sound, she stood there, shock keeping her glued to the spot.

Nick's face filled her vision, she heard him speak, felt him cup her shoulders with his large, warm hands then draw her carefully against his chest, but nothing made sense. She stood passive within the circle of his arms, suspended by the events, uncomprehending it was over.

His steady heartbeat under her ear penetrated the fog. The familiar smell of his skin and strength of his hands rubbing her back, silently offering comfort, returned her from the abyss one breath at a time.

"It's all right. You're safe, sweetheart, you're safe," Nick murmured over and over into her hair, holding her close. She could feel the unnatural stiffness of her body, but was incapable of doing anything about it. Nick sheltered her in his arms, absorbing the quakes wracking her muscles, holding her so close it was impossible to tell where one began and the other ended, while pandemonium reigned around them.

Several medics arrived on the scene, along with a cleanup crew. Nick kept her face buried against his chest, preventing her from seeing the blood pooling around Geir's head. She wouldn't have looked anyway, didn't think she could endure seeing Geir's body. Somewhere it registered Drones were recording the activity, taking samples and tapping into the security vids, cataloging events for further review. Everything was efficient, impersonal and over with quickly.

She heard the activity around her, but it seemed to come from a long distance and the sounds were fuzzy. She kept her mind carefully blank. She didn't want to know what was happening beyond the shelter of Nick's arms. She needed to stay shielded by the dark world behind her tightly closed eyes.

Safe.

Sharpe was in control, barking orders, demanding answers and directing the removal of Anto Geir's body. Some small part of her mind recognized he was giving her time and she was grateful he left them alone. Things could have gone very differently, the loss of life greater if Nick hadn't taken the shot offered. She could be dead. Nausea churned in her stomach and she swallowed hard.

Through it all, she didn't move and she knew Nick would hold her for as long as she needed. He motioned the medic away with a slight shake of his head. She wasn't ready yet. Couldn't bear the thought of facing what had happened. Later she would allow herself to be checked out. Later.

Breathe in, breathe out, it was all she could do and enough for the moment. The constriction in her chest eased and her breaths became less jerky. The panicked gallop of her heart calmed as she listened to the steady beat of his against her ear. It resonated through her bones and sinew giving her strength, something solid to cling to in the madness surrounding her.

Safe.

The fabric of Nick's rough jacket chafed her tear-wet face. Her breath shuddered in as she raised shaking hands to slip her arms around his lean waist. He responded by nuzzling his cheek against hers and murmured disjointed words of comfort into her ear. Time passed, holding her suspended, until she opened her eyes to slits.

He loosened his grip as she raised her head. "Is it over?" Her voice was the barest whisper. She searched his face needing reassurance.

"Yes, sweetheart, it is." He cupped the side of her face, the warmth of his palm penetrating the chill of her skin.

"Are you sure?" Hating the quiver in her voice, she cleared her throat.

Nick kissed her forehead then dropped a whisper-soft kiss on her trembling mouth.

"I'm sure," he rasped. "You're safe. Geir won't hurt you again."

"I knew you wouldn't let him take me," she murmured, lowering her head to his chest.

It had been a near thing, too horribly close for her peace of mind. What if he'd missed? Her mind skittered away from the thought and she shivered.

Nick widened his stance to draw her closer.

Love, relief, fear and so many other emotions she barely had a name for raced through her.

"Captain Rayven?" The senior medic said softly. "I would like to examine your friend to make sure she has taken no harm. Will you allow that? It won't take long."

If only to reassure Nick, she needed to be examined. His grip tightened for an instant, he nodded, released her and stepped away.

"Why don't you follow me to Chief Sharpe's office? He has made it available for us."

Their route to Sharpe's office wouldn't take them past the spot Anto Geir's body had lain moments before. Tru wouldn't have looked regardless. Men moved aside to let them pass as she followed the medic. The look of respect when they looked at Nick brought home just how incredible his actions had been.

Inside the office, the medic turned to her with a soothing, professional smile then closed the door.

Chapter 21

The sound of the airlock doors sealing behind them allowed Tru to take her first easy breath since they had landed. Too weary for words, she removed her winter gear and handed it to Nick to stow. His movements were stiff and uncoordinated, but she knew he wouldn't appreciate her offering to help. She scanned the interior of the ship, her heartbeat not settling into a steady rhythm until she'd assured herself everything was in its place and no danger lurked in the shadows.

Tru ached all over from muscles refusing to relax. She could barely stand to let Nick out of her sight. She recoiled with disgust that she was being such a coward, but she couldn't seem to help it. Not yet, anyway. Mind carefully blank so she didn't think about the events of the last couple of days, she followed him to the bridge and slid into her seat.

Chief Sharpe had been true to his word and had provided a snow skimmer for transport to their ship. The weather had cooperated and weak sunlight made the landscape glitter. Under different circumstances, she would have enjoyed the stark beauty surrounding them, but not today. Her sole focus had been getting back to the ship and the safety it represented to her.

"Welcome back, Captain Rayven." Siren's melodious voice greeted them. Dim ship's lights created a soothing cocoon after the harsh light of the snowy landscape over which they'd skimmed to reach the ship.

"Run through a preflight check, Siren," Nick responded while he settled into his chair. "Then secure lift off permission and set a course for Bretonne."

"Acknowledged."

The ship's engines came online, the vibrations jarring before settling into a familiar powerful thrum. Information flowed across the console screen and he scanned it quickly.

"All systems ready, Captain. We have been cleared to leave."

"Excellent. Take us out, Siren."

Once through the atmosphere, Tru wilted into her chair. Her breath whooshed out in a thankful sigh as Killjoy and the planet Kaydet grew smaller in the viewscreen. The blackness of space was a profound relief.

"How are you doing?"

Nick's question was a low rumble, startling her. She glanced his way, not quite meeting his eyes, before she returned her gaze to the view she'd been contemplating.

"Fine." She knew it wouldn't be enough to satisfy him, but it was all she could manage at the moment.

He gripped the arm of her chair, swinging it toward him. All his movements were controlled and slow as if he were afraid to alarm her. Although, she recognized some of it was due to his injuries, she also understood he was being too careful of her. She was beginning to get annoyed with herself, particularly when she couldn't prevent the startled squeak she uttered.

He searched her face and she knew what he was seeing. She'd seen her reflection in the viewscreen windows of the ship when she sat down. Her eyes were huge above the bruised-looking shadows under them. She was pale. And looked thinner, burned down to an ember of her normal self. Where was all the determination and excitement she usually felt? Why was she allowing herself to wallow, to let Anto Geir win?

"We have a long trip to Bretonne. Why don't you go back to the crew quarters and rest for a bit?" The words were a gentle suggestion, but he made sure there was no doubt if push came to shove he would personally escort her to her bunk and see she lie down.

"I don't want to lie down. I'm not an invalid, Nick," she replied surprised and pleased to hear the acerbic tone. The slight burst of temper felt good. She sat a little straighter in her seat.

"The medic said you should rest," Nick pointed out. "You've had a difficult time of it. You need to—"

Tru exploded from her chair. "Do not tell me what I need, Nick Rayven! I'm not a two-year-old to be ordered about," she stormed. Looming over him, she poked a finger into his chest to emphasize her words.

Anger boiled up nearly choking her with its fury. It burned through her, sweeping away all the tears she'd cried and fear which had nearly paralyzed her. It was liberating, like riding a comet, setting her on fire and then sweeping her heedlessly into its maelstrom.

"I know what you are thinking. Why you don't want me on the bridge with you! You think I brought this all on myself by going to Lodestone in the first place! You think my actions are to blame for all of this." She made a sweeping gesture and Nick leaned back in his chair, barely avoiding her flailing hand. She relished the sound of her own voice, hearing the brittle and hard-edged quality.

"What are you yelling about? I never—"

"Stop! You hear me? Just stop. I know it is true. Do you think you would have been injured like this if it weren't for me? Do you? Do you have any idea how I felt when I thought you would die? I couldn't bear it, Nick, I couldn't bear it if something happened to you. It would have been my fault. Mine!"

Appalled at the words pouring out of her mouth, Tru slapped trembling fingers across her mouth to stop the flow. The fury was gone as quickly as it had arrived leaving her awash in guilt that made her continue in a broken whisper, "Do you think others would have died if I'd minded my own business and stayed home instead of trying to prove something to my family?"

Nick lunged from his chair and pulled her roughly into his arms. "Shh, sweetheart. You can't take responsibility for Anto Geir's madness. There was no way you could have known any of this would happen."

"He hurt you, Nick. I had to watch Crowder and his men beat you unconscious and I couldn't stop it." Tru touched his face with her fingertips. She felt the stubble on his cheeks, lightly traced the healing cuts and skimmed over the multi colored bruises seeking reassurance. "How do I live with that?" Limp and defeated, she dropped her hand. "I'm sorrier than you can possibly know you were injured because of me."

Nick couldn't bear to see her like this. He knew how destructive guilt could be, how the past could weight a person down until there was no room for anything else in your life. He'd fought those demons after the war on Tonlith. He'd survived when so many others had died, had watched, helpless, as his world burned and could do nothing to stop it. But not Tru, not if he could help it.

"Listen to me, okay? Because of you, countless lives have been saved. Twist is no longer being shipped from Lodestone. You helped close down one avenue. If you hadn't gone to Lodestone, Anto Geir would still be filling the pipeline with his poison."

Nick spoke with conviction and determination, holding her gaze with his own, wanting her to understand. "You have helped expose a bigger problem than any of us suspected existed and now we know about it, we will track down the ring leaders and stop it."

He could see her struggle to accept what he told her, to believe he was right. Her sheltered upbringing hadn't prepared her for the harsh realities life could deal out and he knew she was badly shaken. What must have seemed like an exciting adventure at one time had kicked her in the teeth. Life and death happened in an instant, cruelty for its own sake thrived in the shadows and her innocent view of life was gone forever.

She lowered her eyes and looked away. "Maybe you are right," she said without much conviction. "I think I will go to my bunk and rest after all, if that's okay with you? Maybe I'm just over tired."

* * * *

Heartsick, Nick stepped back, allowing her to leave. He watched her as she walked away, wishing he could do more. He scrubbed a hand through his short hair then sat slowly in his chair. He turned it to face the bridge console, stared sightlessly at the lights and readouts before he took a deep breath, and opened a com channel to base. Time to fill in the team and compare notes.

"'Bout time you checked in again, boss," Seth greeted him with his usual cheer. "I was about ready to launch a rescue mission."

Nick snorted. "We ran into a few problems. We were delayed a bit," he replied. Rubbing his wounded shoulder to ease the ache, he settled into a more comfortable position in his chair.

"You want to fill me in or have me waste time guessing?"

"Anto Geir is dead." Nick cut right to the chase.

"I see. What happened?"

"He had a surprise party waiting for us before Tru and I could get back to the ship. I discovered something before things got really interesting I want you or Callen to check out. Geir was addicted to twist, a new drug wreaking havoc on several worlds. He was transporting it through the missing Lodestone shipments."

Seth gave a low whistle. "I thought this was only about Geotern's mineral discovery and the missing shipments from Lodestone. It never even occurred to me drugs could be involved. Is that why he was so anxious to stop you and get Tru?"

"He was looking for a way to rise in the organization and what she found out was a threat to his ambition. The mineral gave him the edge he was looking for, something to offer whoever he worked for." Nick kept his voice low—he didn't want Tru to overhear. "It looks like Tru stumbled into a very nasty business without realizing what she was getting into. My guess is, there're some powerful individuals behind the scenes and they aren't going to like knowing a lucrative pipeline for their drug has been shut down."

"This is all starting to make a weird kind of sense," Callen interjected. He'd walked into the room right after Nick and Seth had begun to speak. "Malvin Sonne died under strange circumstances right after he spoke with us. No one saw or heard anything and cause of death is still under investigation. I've heard this drug leaves very little trace in the body once ingested, but I would be willing to bet he died of an overdose, which wasn't accidental. I'll contact Maddox and let him know."

"Which leaves us with the question of who could have killed him and how did they know the business was falling apart? Get Maddox to give you a guest list as well as the names of any staff he had on site that day. We might as well start looking there," Nick replied thinking it over.

"If what you suspect is true, then Anto Geir was a dead man regardless," Seth added thoughtfully. "Too bad he left Lodestone before they got to him and he caused you further problems."

"You have no idea," Nick said with feeling. A vicious headache pulsed behind his eyes and his energy flagged. He might heal quickly, but it still took time and he'd been pushing himself hard.

"I've got a line on Aislinn Thorpe," Callen said. "She was caught on a security vid leaving Sonne's room the night he died. It looks like she's headed for Paladin Minor. It might be worth finding her and asking some questions."

Nick had heard the undercurrent of excitement in Callen's voice once before and it piqued his interest. It was out of character for any emotion to come through with the other man. Obviously, this Aislinn Thorpe had gotten to him in some way.

"Was she the lead you referred to in our last conversation? What makes you think she might be involved?"

"Just a hunch."

"Well, your hunches are usually right. Go ahead and see what you can find out. In the meantime, follow up on the guest lists, Seth. Contact me if you discover anything."

"You might be interested to know Geotern sends its thanks for a job well done and the balance of credits they owe has been transferred, along with a hefty bonus," Seth announced.

"Excellent," Nick replied with no small amount of satisfaction. "What do we hear from Wulf?"

There was a slight hesitation before Seth answered, "We received a transmission from him a few days ago and he has been off grid since then."

"What do you mean he has gone off grid?" Nick's voice was sharp.

"He didn't have much time to fill us in, boss. He said there was an assassination attempt on Ambassador D'Kir and her ship had been taken over. He didn't go into details, but you know Wulf...he'll handle whatever comes his way. He said he would contact us once he had things under control. He sounded more pissed off than anything else."

"I'll bet. Nothing he hates worse than for plans to go sideways." Nick was perturbed, but until they heard from him, there wasn't much they could do. Burke Wulfric was a force to be reckoned with all on his own, and if anyone could keep the Ambassador safe and still complete his mission, it was Wulf. "Monitor his personal frequency and let me know as soon as you hear anything."

"Already on it," Seth replied.

Satisfied he'd done all he could, Nick disconnected the link. He had a lot to think about and consider. There wasn't enough information to take to the authorities and even then, which agency would have jurisdiction? More than likely, the information would end up with the judicial branch of the Unified Alliance of Planets, since several worlds were involved.

Pinching the bridge of his nose, Nick closed his eyes and let out a deep sigh, opened them and reached for a tablet. There were too many coincidences to ignore about this whole situation and the best way to figure it out was to log what he already knew or suspected which would make it easier to coordinate with the others.

Thinking his way through events, he tried to put them in some kind of order, starting with Tru and Lodestone.

He added what he knew about Malvin Sonne, his sudden, unexplained death and the mysterious Aislinn Thorpe. Callen had the scent on her trail and Nick had absolute faith he would find the answers he was seeking before he was through. Which brought him to the situation with Wulf and Ambassador D'Kir.

What had seemed like a simple security detail had gone wrong somehow, which left Nick with more questions than answers. He knew the ambassador was outspoken about her desire to stop the devastation on her world, Paladin Minor, caused by insurgents trying to gain control of the profitable business of ice crystal mining. Obviously, she'd made some powerful enemies if they were trying to stop her before she took her seat with the Unified Alliance of Planets and the cachet belonging would give her. The assassination attempt was undeniable proof.

The only thing any of the events seemed to have in common he could see at this point was Paladin Minor, where the ambassador was from and Aislinn Thorpe seemed to be heading.

Nick put the tablet on its docking station and transmitted the data to home base. He knew Seth and Callen would fill in missing details and between all of them, he was sure a more solid picture would form.

Hunger and thirst finally drove him out of his chair and to the crew quarters. He paused to check on Tru, but didn't disturb her. She was curled on her side, facing the wall. He knew she wasn't asleep. Her posture was too stiff and her breathing too irregular, but it was clear she wanted to be left alone.

Unwilling to disturb her, he turned away to see what supplies had been restocked while they were on Killjoy. He noticed, with some gratification, Siren had tracked items they favored and had made sure there was plenty for the trip home. She was learning more rapidly than he'd anticipated.

A meal and a mug of tayberry in hand, Nick returned to the bridge. The solitude was a balm to his weary soul and he allowed some of the adrenaline to seep away. He rolled his shoulders and took a deep breath. Ignoring his aches and pains, he dug into his food.

When Nick finally crawled into his bunk it was late. He lay on his back, one arm across his chest, the other behind his head, and wished his mind would quiet down enough he could give in to his exhaustion and find some peace. He stared at the ceiling, listening to the noises of the ship and trying to keep his focus off the woman in the bunk across from him. He finally admitted to himself, it was fruitless. Every time she so much as shifted, he was aware of her. He wanted her in his bunk, wanted them skin-to-skin and damn the consequence. He ached with it, his skin hot, stretched over muscles taut with a need held in check.

He kept circling back to their time in Killjoy and he was unsure what to do next. Had he imagined her whispered words? Conjured them in his drug-induced state? He almost convinced himself he had, but he still couldn't quite let it go. Guilt riding him hard, he faced the fact he'd nearly lost her. Accepted he'd failed to protect her.

It appalled him that in one moment of inattention, she'd been jerked from his side and held at knifepoint by a mad man. He should have known better. Did know better. He'd failed one of the basic tenants of his military career, one he relentlessly drilled into his men. Never let your guard down. It was a bitter pill to swallow.

He wouldn't blame her if she never wanted to see him again once he got her home. Maybe it was a good thing she didn't know how important she'd become to him, how much he needed and wanted her. She should to be safe with her family and not with a man who still struggled with his past and all it meant. She deserved better. Determined to do the right thing, he closed his eyes and turned his head to face the wall, refusing to acknowledge the empty, aching place inside.

It was hell.

Chapter 22

Tru bit her bottom lip and considered her options. Time was running out and it wouldn't be long before she was back with her family and Nick returned to his life on Alludra. She'd spent most of the day lying on her bunk, thinking about her choices and the consequences of her actions. Whenever her thoughts drifted to Anto Geir, she shuddered, understanding with frightening certainty she was lucky to be alive. She'd given herself no quarter, gone over everything starting with her misguided trip to Lodestone. How innocent and unaware of life outside the confines of her protected home life she'd been. She cringed remembering how certain she was of herself and her place in the world. The outcome could have been very different and she was thankful to have survived. Through the adversity, the fear and her own self-condemnation, she was finally growing up. Understood herself better, felt stronger and knew her heart and mind. Nick Rayven was what she wanted. She'd known it from the beginning.

"Nick? Are you asleep?" Tru whispered.

"No." His eyes popped open and he removed his arm from behind his head. Shifting to his side, he propped himself up on his elbow and waited.

"I can't sleep, can you?"

"Why can't you sleep?" he asked quietly.

"Every time I doze off I have a nightmare. I'm almost afraid to close my eyes," she confessed in a small voice. It was a good thing he couldn't see her face or he would know she wasn't telling the truth. She shifted uncomfortably.

"I'm right here, Tru. There is nothing to be afraid of," he assured her. "You aren't alone."

"I know that, but it isn't helping. Can I sleep with you? Please, Nick, I don't want to be by myself." Her words tumbled out in a rush. Heat climbed in her cheeks. She didn't know what she would do if he said no. It had taken her a long time to get up the courage to put her plan in play.

"I'm not sure that is a good idea."

"Because of your injuries? I promise to be careful."

"Not because of my injuries. They aren't a problem."

"Then why?"

He blew out a breath and flopped onto his back. "Don't be naive, Tru. I want you. Have wanted you for quite some time now and if you get into my bunk, I'm not going to be able to keep my hands off you."

She winced at his bluntness, but was relieved he told her what he was feeling. Time hung suspended while she waited to see if he would say more. When he remained silent, she threw her covering off, crossed the small space between them and slid into bed beside him.

His breath caught and she smiled.

"I'd almost given up hope, you know. I was beginning to think I was the only one to feel this way."

"What?" he replied. He looked stunned to find her in his arms.

She moved closer and threw his words back at him. "Don't be naive, Nick. I have wanted you for a long time. I was beginning to think you would never notice."

"Whoa...what? You do understand what I said, right?" He reared back enough to see the outline of her face in the dark. He grabbed one of her hands, which had been wandering across his rib cage, and flattened it gently under his palm to stop further movement.

"Of course I do."

"Siren, low light in crew quarters." Nick ordered. Scooting into a sitting position, he hauled her up with him and held her a small distance away searching her face. "This isn't a game. Before this goes any further, you need to understand there is no going back if we do this."

"Good." Leaning forward, she brushed her mouth across his in a feather-light kiss.

"You aren't doing this out a misplaced sense of obligation or guilt, are you?" he murmured against her mouth. "Because if you are, you can haul your sweet ass back to your own bunk."

In a smooth motion, she straddled his hips and pushed his shoulders, urging him to lie down. Trailing her fingers down his chest, she reached the edge of his t-shirt and pushed it up, revealing the ridged muscles under his taut skin.

"Shut up, Nick. I know what I'm doing and what I want. Guilt has nothing to do with it." She ran her tongue over the delicious muscles she'd revealed and he sucked in a breath.

* * * *

He trembled under her touch, reveling in the warm slide of her tongue against his skin, wanting more. His hands clasped her hips, his hold gentle.

"You weren't actually having nightmares, were you?" He took one last shot, trying not to groan when she nibbled on his earlobe then ran her tongue over its outer rim.

"Nope."

A slow grin spread across his face and he saw her answering smile, devastating in its sweetness. Between one breath and the next, he flipped her onto her back, ignoring the ache of his healing ribs. Cupping her face, he brushed his thumbs along her cheekbones. His gaze wandered over her face committing it to memory. He got lost in the blue of her eyes.

"Is something wrong?" she whispered.

He looked his fill, amazed she was in his arms. He suspected more was being revealed than he wanted, but he didn't care. When she pressed her palm against his chest his heart skipped a beat.

"No. Nothing is wrong. Everything is perfect, you are perfect."

There would be time enough later to work through all that needed to be said, but right now, he just wanted to think about making love to the woman in his arms. Slowly he lowered his head, never taking his eyes off her and watched her lashes close as his mouth claimed hers in a kiss that left him breathless with need.

She arched, pressing her breasts against the hard wall of his chest and he heard her sigh. Chills raced across his skin. Desire pooled in his lower body, making him ache. A small satisfied smile curved her mouth before he captured her mouth again and wiped all coherent thought from his mind.

He broke their kiss and put a little space between them to remove their clothing, tossing it aside with careless disregard. He wasn't satisfied until they were facing each other with nothing between them but skin. His control holding on by a thread, he explored every inch of her, urging her to open for him, discovering what gave her pleasure and finding his own doubled by her responses. Anticipation fed the hunger, and hunger turned to flames licking along his nerve endings until he was consumed.

Like a starved man, he reached for her several more times during the night and each time was more satisfying than the last. Exhaustion finally claimed him and he fell asleep in a tangle of limbs and blankets with Tru nestled close to his side.

He woke hours later, realizing his sleep had been undisturbed by nightmares for the first time in longer than he could remember. He turned over and reached for Tru, only to find her gone. Heartbeat racing, he jackknifed into a sitting position, fear bringing him fully awake. He was reaching for his pants when he heard her muted giggle coming from the bridge, and he paused to listen.

"Try again, Tru. You almost have it," Siren encouraged and repeated the words for her to hear.

"I love you. I adore you. I want you," Tru mimicked in Tonlithian. He could hear the effort she put into saying the words properly.

He flopped onto the bed, overwhelmed and touched by the effort she made to speak his native tongue. The words flowed over him, slightly mangled but more precious than she could ever guess. He grinned at the ceiling while he continued to listen to Siren teach Tonlithian.

His native tongue was a challenging language, with many words sounding similar but having entirely different meanings. Even the way words were emphasized changed their meaning in some cases. The rules were fluid, but he thought she was beginning to grasp it. She'd told him once she was good with languages and whenever he spoke to Siren in Tonlithian, he'd noticed Tru would listen. He never suspected she was trying to learn his language.

Tonlithian was a musical language, pleasing to the ear. Listening to her speak his native tongue in her soft voice was a sensual feast for his ears. One he would never tire of hearing. Now their relationship had changed, she seemed determined to master more with the help of Siren. His grin widened, he would bet she wanted to understand the words he'd whispered while he'd held her in his arms.

"Much better," Siren said. "Now translate, where is the nearest space port?"

Nick stifled a laugh. Siren may have the voice of a goddess, but she was nothing if not pragmatic in her programming. Dutifully, Tru did as asked and giggled when Siren only had minor corrections. They worked far longer than Nick would have liked. He wanted her back in his bed, hoped it was where she wanted to be. He debated getting up to fetch her, but discarded the notion almost immediately.

He lay still in his bunk, feigning sleep when he heard her approach. He waited to see which bed she would go to and fought the temptation to reach out and pull her into his, but refrained. The choice had to be hers.

Relief flowed through him as she snuggled under the covers, her back to his chest. Reaching behind her, she clasped his hand, pulled his arm around her and sighed. He drew her closer and breathed in the scent of her curls as they tickled his chin. He dropped a chaste kiss on her head and listened to her sleepy murmur as she drifted to sleep.

More content than he could ever remember, he enjoyed the warmth of her small body pressed to his, relished the way she relaxed completely in sleep, trusting him to protect her. Amusement tugged at the corners of his mouth when she began to softly snore. He lost himself in contemplating taking the longer route home to give them more time together. He fell asleep while he considered the possibilities.

* * * *

"Nick, I've been thinking." Tru handed him a steaming mug of tayberry.

"Now why does that fill me with dread?" he teased, taking the mug with one hand and tugging her onto his lap with the other.

She liked the fact she could snuggle on his lap and leaned comfortably against his good shoulder. She found it amazing how quickly they had fallen into a more intimate routine. The forced intimacy of being shipboard giving them a freedom to explore each other they might not have found otherwise.

"Nothing fills you with dread," she snorted and grinned at him. She noticed the desire darkening his brown eyes and moistened suddenly dry lips. His gaze dropped instantly to her mouth, but he didn't give in to temptation. Instead, he took a sip of his drink, quirked a brow and waited.

She cleared her throat and gathered her scattered thoughts. "What if I didn't go home right away?" He opened his mouth to reply, but she rushed on without giving him a chance to say anything. "I thought I could spend some time on Alludra with you." She waited for his answer, her heart racing.

"Sweetheart, we have already discussed this. Your family is waiting for you. It is important they know you are okay and the only thing which will set their minds at rest is seeing you." He sat his mug on the bridge console and brushed a wayward curl behind her ear.

"What if I don't want to go home?" she responded, feeling her way. She knew Nick enjoyed her company, knew he desired her, but he'd never revealed if his feelings went deeper.

She craved reassurance. She was falling deeper in love with him as time passed and was afraid she would get her heart broken if the only thing he wanted was a brief fling, even though she'd known the risks going in.

She studied his face looking for clues, but he was giving nothing away. She tried to hide her disappointment, but suspected he knew when he brought her face down for a tender kiss. It didn't take long for it to turn into something carnal, which left her yearning. He was just as affected because she could see the rapid pulse beat in his neck and she was disappointed when he pulled back. Resting his forehead against hers, he waited for his breathing to return to a reasonable facsimile of normal.

"Truthfully, I would like nothing better than to have you in my home, sweetheart. This thing between us is powerful and leaves me breathless whenever I'm near you. It is difficult to keep my hands off you. Surely, you know that?" His voice was rough and he cleared the tightness from his throat. Leaning back, he met her gaze, allowing some of what he felt to show through. "I don't want to let you go, believe me."

"Then don't," she answered.

"Tru, what we have here is new. Raw. There is no doubting the sexual attraction between us. We practically catch fire whenever we touch, but our time together has been anything but normal." He spoke carefully. She could tell he wanted her to understand what he was trying to say, hoping he would say it right. "Sometimes emotions get tangled up by shared danger and forced proximity." She started to protest, but he pressed his fingers against her mouth stopping the words. "Let me finish, sweetheart." When she nodded reluctantly, he dropped his hand to slide up and down her arm and continued, "I want us to be sure of what we're feeling. You have to be sure. That is why I want you to go home for a while. Think about what you are feeling. Be absolutely sure it is me you want. I need for you to be sure. Do this for me, please."

"I know what I feel," she shot back. "It isn't going to change, no matter what you think, but I will do as you ask. I'll give you a standard moon cycle to come for me." The words were difficult to speak. Her heart already bled from the impending forced separation as worry and doubt crept in.

Taking a deep breath, she whispered the next words in Nick's language. "I'll be waiting for you. Don't disappoint me, Nick Rayven."

She rose gracefully from his lap, leaving him open-mouthed. She snagged a portable tablet and retreated to her bunk to catch up on the lesson plan Siren had given her. She hoped it would take her mind off the exasperating man at the bridge for a while. The temptation to throw the tablet at his head had been great, but she acknowledged the truth of his words and refrained.

She was in love with the infuriating man, which wasn't going to change, no matter how noble he tried to be. Sighing, she settled on her bunk and pretended to read without a great deal of success.

Chapter 23

Nick didn't miss any opportunity to touch Tru over the next days, whether it was a light caress on her shoulder, holding her hand while they talked or allowing his hands to roam freely over her body when they fell entwined on his bunk. Or hers. Or on whatever surface was convenient when the mood hit. They couldn't keep their hands off each other, which suited him just fine.

What surprised him, though, was the amount of time they also spent in conversation. He'd always found her interesting, with a curious and lively mind, but there was something different now. Their physical intimacy had given them a greater freedom to talk about things they held close. Admittedly, she was far more giving when it came to talking about her life and views, but he discovered himself opening up about his past. Something he never thought he would do.

He couldn't share most of the memories haunting him; it was hard enough to relive the torment in his sleep, never mind talk about it. He'd never be able to wipe the horror away as he'd helplessly watched the smaller of the triad moons, Antor, hit with enough power to rip away a huge chunk and send the pieces hurtling through space. He would go days not even thinking about it and then something would trigger a memory and it would stop him cold in his tracks, make him struggle to take his next breath.

When the war came on Tonlith he'd done his duty, had believed in the united government until the dogma and cruelties of its leaders had persuaded him there had to be a better way. He'd stayed to try to be a voice of reason, joined with others who had become disenfranchised within the confines of the military and tried to mitigate the madness where they could.

He'd fought against the resistance, believing their actions could only lead to further disaster, and, in so doing, pitted himself against his uncle,

Max Rayven. Nick was stunned to realize his uncle had gained a huge following, and had rapidly turned families against one another as he'd railed against the oppressions of the government. What had started out small, had gained momentum until both sides were armed to the teeth and unwilling to find a compromise.

The war raged for five years, destroying cities, killing the citizens indiscriminately and ultimately destroying the fabric of society as families became increasingly divided over who was right and who was wrong.

He tried to explain some of it to Tru, feeling better for sharing a small part of his past, but he glossed over most of it wanting to protect her. He needed her innate goodness to remind him there was a better way, to keep the dark at bay. He feared she might pull away if she knew some of the things he'd done and seen. Besides, how could he possibly explain the violence, the absolute disregard for human life he'd witnessed? Those images burned into his mind, constant companions, and had stripped away compassion and everything gentle in his nature. Until he met her, he'd feared nothing remained but the soldier doing his duty, grim-faced and unemotional.

On the final day of the war, he'd been recalled to the command ship, and was half way back with orders screaming through his earpiece, when the percussion from the mutilated moon caused his fighter to buck and roll. Nick had fought hard, riding the energy waves until a chunk of the moon hit his fighter broadside and sent him spinning away out of control. It had saved his life.

The last thing he'd seen was Tonlith alight as his command ship exploded.

The last thing he'd heard were the screams in his earpiece as life was extinguished.

The last thing he'd felt was the warmth of blood mingled with his tears, as it dripped down his face.

There had been few survivors and sensors had shown a world dangerous to land on. Grief and a rage so deep he didn't know how to contain it had swamped him. He'd screamed into the blackness of space until his voice broke. And then, he'd screamed some more. His ship crippled, he'd drifted and waited for death.

"What happened after your ship was hit?" Tru prodded.

They were lying on Nick's bunk, her head on his shoulder as he traced languid circles on her arm. He stilled for a moment, wondering if he would answer or change the subject like he did when he wasn't ready to talk about something. His chest rose and fell as he took a deep breath and he could feel the erratic thud of his heartbeat under the palm she rested on his chest.

He pulled her closer and she shifted enough she could look up at him without raising her head from its comfortable spot. His gaze fixed on the ceiling, his mind clearly in the past.

"I drifted in space for some time. One of my engines was out and a fuel cell had been destroyed." He was careful to keep all inflection out of his voice. Wanting no hint of what he felt revealed. "I was in the middle of a debris field, unable to maneuver very well. My force shield held, but was at half capacity." He cleared his throat. "The command ship, *Warrior*, was destroyed along with its companion, *Victory*. Each ship held almost one thousand soldiers and crew. Gone. Everything destroyed in a blink, a moment of madness."

"I'm so sorry, Nick." Tru cupped his cheek.

Nick turned his face and kissed her palm then resumed staring at the ceiling. "My com unit still worked, but it wasn't picking anything up. Just static. Tonlith's sky was on fire, I couldn't get a visual on the extent of the destruction. My sensors were going wild, not giving me a clear read. One of the triad moons, Antor, was a jagged ruin. The rebel base there had been blown completely away in the weapons blast. So many killed."

He shifted, his muscles rock hard with tension. Tru started to move away to give him the space she must have thought he needed, but he tugged her back immediately. Nostrils flaring, he took a deep breath, catching the scent of her skin. He reached for a calm he was far from feeling, needing her beside him to be his anchor in the present.

Swallowing the lump in his throat, he went on. "I knew I was a dead man. My ship didn't have enough fuel to get me to safety, whatever safety meant with my world on fire. Life support was failing. All it would take was for the shields to go down and for a piece of debris to hit me to finish it. I just floated, wanting it to end."

She bit her lip. He could see she was horrified by what she heard. The war on Tonlith had been a tragedy, one he knew had made the news on most of the worlds in their system. He suspected she hadn't been affected by what had happened in more than an abstract way.

"Why did it come to that, Nick?" Her voice shook. "It makes no sense to hate so much. To think destroying your world is an option."

"We'll probably never know what happened in those final moments, sweetheart. I don't know what escalated the final launch sequences. I just don't know."

"I'm so glad you survived," she whispered.

"I owe that to a passing freighter. They picked up the distress beacon from my ship. What they did was risky. Their ship could have easily been damaged in the debris field, but it didn't stop them." His voice was a little hoarse with suppressed emotion.

He understood how lucky he'd been, but it was with some surprise and a small amount of pride he realized he'd made a good life for himself since that terrible time. He'd risen above the chaos, the rage and the grief to build something he thought mattered. It brought a measure of peace as well as hope for the future.

"Then what happened?"

"I drifted around the system for a few years, raising hell and taking my anger out on anyone careless enough to get in my way. I'm not proud of my actions, but I was wrecked from the war. Bitter. I didn't believe I had anything left to lose."

"What changed?"

Nick managed a weak chuckle. "I discovered I wasn't the only survivor from Tonlith's war. I wandered into a seedy bar in a very bad neighborhood in time to dodge a fist. A fight had broken out and in the middle was this blond pretty boy cursing in both common speak and Tonlithian. He was getting pounded, but he was giving as good as he got."

Nick smiled at the memory. "I decided to even the odds a little and waded in. We managed to fight our way out of that bar and Seth and I've been friends ever since. We eventually found Callen and Burke. By then, I'd started up Rayven Security."

"Have you found other survivors?"

"No." He paused to consider her question before continuing. "But, then, I never expected to find anyone. It's possible others survived. We just haven't found them yet."

She rose up on one elbow to study his face. "I can't begin to understand all you went through, Nick. I know I couldn't have survived it and come out whole. But, you did. Against all odds, you did. I'm amazed and awed by your resilience, your strength. It grieves me you lost everything in such a way, but I'm glad you are here with me. So glad."

With her free hand, she traced the scar bisecting his eyebrow, skimmed down his cheekbone to cup his jaw. Her thumb brushed over his lower lip before she leaned forward to softly kiss his waiting mouth. His lips softened against hers, inviting her to explore, to taste, demanding nothing in return. Her hand drifted down the column of his neck in a light caress, across his shoulders and down the muscles in his arm. He loved the feel of her hands moving over his skin, warm and strong and leaving a trail of fire in their wake.

He curved his arm across her back and urged her down so she rested comfortably on his chest once again. He moved his head, giving her greater access as she trailed kisses along his jaw and down his throat before she moved back up to capture his waiting mouth.

He let her explore, enjoying her touch, allowing it to wash away the bitter memories. Desire built between them until there was nothing else but the next touch, the next scorching kiss and the slide of skin against skin. The past slipped away along with the pain of its memory, the only thing that mattered was this one moment and the woman in his arms. It was enough for now.

* * * *

Their time onboard *Dominion* passed quickly and the closer they got to Bretonne, the more Nick dreaded their parting. Tru didn't bring the subject up again, but he could see the strain in her smile. Not for the first time, he wondered if he was being foolish by insisting she go home. Already an ache was starting around his heart and it confused and frustrated him. He'd never felt it before, never needed as much as he did now. He wasn't sure what to do about all the emotions tangling him up inside. All he knew for sure was she'd gotten under his skin and it left him vulnerable in ways he hadn't been before.

On edge, he found nothing gave him peace. His moods were uncertain and he snapped at her with little provocation, only to find himself tied in knots with regret the minute the words left his mouth. She was wary and even Siren was in a snit because of something he'd said. Instead of spending their time enjoying each other, he pushed Tru away. He didn't understand himself. He knew he was doing the right thing by taking her home, so why was he driving a wedge between them?

"I'm sorry, sweetheart." He ran a hand through his hair and sank into his seat at the bridge console. "I'm an idiot. What can I say?"

Her snort was inelegant and she rolled her eyes at him. "Of course you are an idiot," she agreed in a disgusted tone, her voice only wobbling a little. "I didn't mean to leave my locker where you could trip over it. I was just trying to make sure everything was packed before I get home. How was I to know you would be walking there with your nose buried in a tablet and not paying attention to where you were going? There was no need to yell."

"I know, I know."

He ground his teeth as temper and an overwhelming feeling of impending loss warred inside him. The sight of her pink travel locker loaded and ready to go had jarred him. Logically he knew she needed to make sure everything was stored away before they touched down in the morning, but emotionally it had been a blow. He felt hollowed out and he didn't like what he was feeling, nor could he explain it to her.

Tru looked at him out of the corner of her eye. He could tell she was miserable and wished he knew what to say to give her comfort. No matter how he tried, he couldn't stay mad at her for long. He was being a grouch, but honesty impelled him to admit, if only to himself, he sometimes got a perverse sense of pleasure when tempers flared and sparks flashed between them. They invariably ended up in bed, all control gone. The heat generated between them was enough to melt his bones.

The more he studied her, the more desire pooled in his belly and he licked lips suddenly gone dry. Without giving it much thought, he unbuttoned her tunic top, revealing the creamy skin underneath an inch at a time. His hands were shaking too much to allow him to hurry. He wanted her, needed to feel the slide of their bodies moving together. They would be parting ways tomorrow because he believed she didn't know her own mind, but he desperately needed to reaffirm their bond, wanted the memories to cling to until he could return to claim her.

Nick sucked in a breath as Tru slid her tunic off her shoulders and let it drop to the ground. He couldn't look away to save his soul. Hungry to touch, he clasped her around her ribs, his thumbs brushing the undersides of her breasts. One gentle tug and he had her straddling his hips, while his seeking mouth nuzzled a rosy nipple now positioned at just the right level. From somewhere far off he heard her moan of pleasure. Her hands in his hair, urged him closer; her back arched, giving him greater access.

Nearly mindless with lust, eager to please and be pleasured, he surged to his feet, bringing her with him. One hand under her bottom, the other circling her back, he shifted her enough her legs could wrap around his waist. The few steps to his bunk seemed to take forever.

He gently placed her on the bed, and followed her down. He stretched his length against her pliant body. Her fingers tugged at his t-shirt, and he lifted enough to allow her to pull it up and over his head. He growled low in his throat as he settled down, most of his weight held on his forearms. He looked at her, getting lost in the darkening color of her eyes and the flush staining her cheeks. Lifting a hand, he brushed it through the curls clinging to her face.

"If you only knew what you did to me," he murmured as he lowered his head and took her mouth in a devouring kiss. His blood heated and his pulse pounded in his temple. Desire, molten and raw, loosened his control until it held by a thread. Tired of fighting what he was feeling, he surrendered completely. Nothing else mattered.

* * * *

Tru had convinced herself Nick was the biggest fool in the solar system by the time Bretonne's cloud covered surface came into view. Buckled into her seat beside him, she stared glumly through the viewscreen as they skimmed through the atmosphere and headed toward her home. Their conversation had been stilted since they'd awakened and she wasn't sure what to do about it.

"Captain, landing coordinates have been transmitted. A land transport will be waiting for you." Siren's voice slid over them in dulcet tones.

"Take us in, Siren," Nick responded, while he scanned readouts and secured his portable tablet in preparation. He turned his head to glance at her. "You're almost home, sweetheart. I know your family is excited to have you back safely."

She didn't bother to answer. Her only outward reaction was she tightened her hands on the chair's armrests until her knuckles were white.

Too soon, *Dominion* settled smoothly on the landing pad. Nick shut down the engines and gave final instructions to Siren. The engines hissed and popped as they cooled, sounding loud in the silence inside the ship. Neither made a move to leave their seats.

"I don't like this, Nick," Tru stated. Her heart in her throat, she felt as if there was a tight band across her chest constricting her breathing. She turned her head to look at him, her eyes huge and shadowed. "I know it is important to see my parents, but I don't want you to leave me here."

"I promise I will be back before you know it." He reassured her. "This is the right thing to do. You need to be sure what I have to offer will be enough without my presence to sway you one way or the other."

"I know my own mind, but if you are set on this, then let's get it over with." She unbuckled the shoulder harness, pushed out of her chair then moved swiftly past the crew quarters and slapped her hand against the control panel to open the outer door. The seals released and the door slid open while a ramp lowered to the ground.

Fresh air flowed over her, teasing the curls around her face and flattening her light clothing against her body. She breathed in the familiar scent of her home world and started down the ramp. Fresh air was wonderful after the time spent onboard ship with its recycled air. She stiffened at the sound of Nick's heavy footfall behind her, but didn't look back. She couldn't. If she did, she would end up in a puddle of tears at his feet begging him to take her with him. Pride and determination kept her from doing that.

Tru spotted the family land transport right away and headed toward it. Her grandfather liked to make a statement, and the vivid blue and sleek lines of the vehicle would never pass unnoticed. She nodded briskly to the driver standing beside the open door then ducked inside and slid across the leather seat.

She heard Nick and the driver speak, felt the transport dip slightly when her trunk was stowed and waited while the two men seated themselves.

They rode in silence through the busy streets, Nick's shoulder bumping hers on occasion when the transport made a turn. It wasn't until they left the city behind and found themselves in the quieter area of her home that Nick reached out and took her hand. He held it loosely, brushing his thumb back and forth against her fingers. Giving in, tired of being mad, she leaned her head on his shoulder. She felt him relax and she smiled to herself. He wasn't unaffected by this, just better at hiding it. It gave her comfort.

* * * *

Nick was awed in spite of himself when he got his first glimpse of her home. It was huge, glittering like a jewel in the evening light. Solid iron gates swung open as they approached revealing a wide graveled road bisecting landscaped gardens leading to the heavy doors of the house. He knew Tru came from a wealthy, influential family, but it hadn't dawned on him how rich and influential until they arrived and he got a good look at the house and gardens.

The transport doors opened without much sound and he exited. He squared his shoulders, standing tall and strong and held out his hand to help Tru out of the vehicle. She tucked her small hand in the crook of his arm and his free hand came up to cover hers. He matched his steps to hers as he escorted her up the front stairs to the door, which flung open, spilling golden light over them. Feminine squeals greeted them and he took an involuntary step back as several lavishly dressed women descended on them like exotic birds.

Laughter and tears surrounded him, along with disjointed questions and hugs. Tru got her smile from her mother and she and her sister looked a good deal alike.

"It is about time you got home," Maddox Creighton greeted her gruffly. "Give her room to breathe everyone."

Just like that, the clamor ceased and Nick was able to draw breath.

"Nick, my boy, glad to finally meet you in person," Maddox said. He shook Nick's hand.

"Good to see you, sir," Nick replied, impressed with the firm grip and strong presence of the man in front of him.

Maddox turned bright blue eyes to Tru and held open his arms. She wasted no time launching herself at him, her face buried against his barrel chest. "There's my girl," he crooned. "Safe and sound at last."

Nick looked away, uncomfortable with the naked relief and joy on the older man's face, only to meet the paler blue eyes of a tall, neat man coming swiftly toward them. He was a younger, thinner version of his father, Maddox. His dark hair was going gray at the temples, giving him a distinguished air. His jaw clenched tightly, the muscles bunching with emotions held tightly in check. Without a word, Maddox released Tru and stepped back. Reid cupped his hands around her shoulders, looking her over before he pulled her into his arms and rocked her gently.

"Don't ever do this to me again. I don't think my heart can stand it," he murmured into her hair, his voice breaking.

She nodded and clung to her father. Emotions running unbearably high, she reached out a shaking hand to Nick and closed her fingers over his with bruising force. Reid noticed and pulled back slightly, a questioning look on his worry-lined face. He narrowed his eyes and looked Nick over as only a father could. The easy familiarity between his daughter and Nick spoke volumes and it was obvious he didn't like it. Not one bit.

"You and I are going to talk," he informed Nick. "Tru, why don't you go with your mother and sister and get settled in. I know they're eager to spend some time with you. We'll catch up later. Nick, why don't you follow me into the office." It wasn't a request.

Nick almost groaned out loud. Maddox must have picked up on the unspoken undercurrents surrounding him because he looked from Nick to his son and then grinned. Speculation and unbridled interest were plain to see on his face as he trailed behind them into the office.

The door closed behind Nick with a forceful thud.

Chapter 24

Tru watched her father and grandfather escort Nick into the office and shut the door behind them. She glanced at the closed door and then at her mother, Katri, whose expression remained tranquil, as usual.

All her life, Tru had tried to emulate her elegant mother, with little success. Whatever she felt showed on her face and in her actions, whereas Katri dealt with the normal upheavals of the household with a serene smile and gentle voice. When Tru had been younger, she would sometime do or say something outrageous just to see how her mother would react. Katri's calm words of reproof and mild disappointment would alternately frustrate and make her ashamed of her actions. In the long run, it was just easier to do as her mother asked.

"Let's retire to the solar room while the gentlemen talk." Katri's voice soothed Tru's jangled nerves, and she meekly followed behind her mother to her favorite retreat in the huge house.

Dusk settled over the city, adding a warm red glow to the cream-colored walls. The room was elegant, inviting and imbued with Katri's personality. Tru could feel herself begin to relax and flopped with boneless abandon onto the nearest soft couch. Her mother took a seat across from her and picked up her latest tatting project. With her long, pale fingers, she worked the threads into what Tru knew would be a beautiful piece of lace when she was done.

Her sister, Amali, settled on the window seat, her movements languid and graceful like their mother's. Tru slouched a little lower on the couch and twirled one of her wayward curls around her finger. Her mother looked her way, and she straightened, dropping her hands onto her lap.

"Your father and grandfather have spoken of Captain Rayven and his business Rayven Security," Katri said, a slight smile playing about the corners of her full mouth. "He appears to be well respected by clients from what your father tells me. I met his associate, Callen Bluestone, and he spoke highly of him as well." She looked up from her work and Tru was startled by the speculation she saw in her mother's pale blue eyes. "It seems he has taken good care of you."

"That's what grandfather paid him to do," Tru answered, avoiding her mother's eye.

"Your Captain Rayven doesn't strike me as the type to do anything unless he wants to, Tru. It is obvious he cares for you. Even your father, who never notices what is under his nose, picked up on the attraction."

Amali leaned forward to get a better look at her sister. "What happened, Tru? Do tell." Her expression was mischievous as she added, "He's one fine-looking man, if you ask me."

"Well I'm not...asking you, that is," Tru replied swiftly and crossed her arms under her breasts.

"It was only an observation. There is no need to be defensive," Amali responded, doing a remarkable imitation of their mother's dignified tones.

"Enough, girls. Do not tease your sister, Amali. She has had a difficult time of it lately. Now, Tru, I would like to hear exactly what happened from the time you disappeared until you returned safely home."

There was steel under the velvet of her voice, and Tru stiffened. Her mother wouldn't be satisfied until she told her everything. It wasn't easy trying to explain why she'd gone to Lodestone. Her words got tangled up with all the guilt, determination and gut wrenching fear she'd experienced but her mother didn't interrupt or add to the jumble of emotions Tru tried to untangle as she went.

Picking at her tunic hem, she kept her head down and explained how she'd met Nick, blaming herself for his reaction to being followed and the relief she felt once they were away from Lodestone. Her story unfolded with many stops and starts.

Her voice choked up when she talked about Anto Geir, and her mother's inarticulate exclamation of anguish made her lips tightens to stop the trembling. She didn't realize she was crying until Amali pressed a soft cloth into her hands to blot the tears.

A tray of sandwiches and a pot of tayberry were brought in by a quiet housemaid, but remained untouched while Tru talked herself out. Her eyes still shimmering with moisture, she finally ground to a halt, her last words hanging heavy in the air.

Katri placed her tatting on the table beside her. Tru was surprised to see the work wasn't up to her mother's usual standards and would need redone. Katri rose from her seat and settled next to Tru on the couch. She brushed a tear from Tru's cheek and then slipped her arms around her to cradle her close.

"I owe your Nick more than I can ever repay for keeping you safe," Katri murmured against her hair, in a voice choked with emotion. "I can see why you love him so much."

"I do love him, more than I thought I would ever love anyone, but he's determined we stay apart for a while so I can be sure of my feelings. How stupid is that? My feelings won't change. He's just being stubborn and autocratic."

Tru straightened out of her mother's arms, sniffed indelicately and scrubbed her hands over the moisture leaking from her eyes.

"I know you don't see it right now, my love, but he has given you a wonderful gift. You have only known each other a brief time, a very intense time, I admit, but gratitude can easily be mistaken for love. Use this time apart to really know your heart and mind."

"None of this will matter if Father takes it in his head to kill him first," Tru muttered. "He didn't look at all pleased when he forced Nick into his study."

Amalie giggled, breaking the tension. "Your Nick doesn't look like he would go down without a fight. I don't think you have to worry. Father is a reasonable man, you'll see."

Tru snorted and prayed her sister was right.

"Now then, who would like slightly stale sandwiches and a lukewarm drink?' Katri said, her smile belying the strain around her eyes.

* * * *

Nick reluctantly followed Reid into his office, knowing Maddox was close behind. Something in Reid's eyes hinted he was on thin ice where it concerned his daughter and Nick couldn't say he blamed him for his concern. He owed a full accounting, but he didn't have to like it.

Reid settled behind his large desk, leaving Maddox and Nick to seat themselves in the chairs facing it. Elbows on the immaculate surface and hands interlaced together, he impaled Nick with his shrewd blue gaze.

"I want to know if you took advantage of my daughter while she was in your care," he said.

"I love your daughter," Nick replied, doing his best to keep his voice even and respectful.

"That isn't what I asked," Reid shot back, leaning closer.

"Tru has a mind of her own. I don't think anyone can take advantage of her unless she wants them to."

"Not my girl," Maddox said with a chuckle, refusing to wipe the grin from his face when Reid glared at him. "Son, you know it's true."

"Are you saying you condone his behavior?" Reid asked through his teeth, nodding at Nick.

"I would never hurt your daughter and did my damnedest to protect her even when she refused to listen and went out of her way to drive me crazy," Nick said. "When she wants something she goes after it, or haven't you noticed? It was damned difficult to prevent her from getting herself killed." He ran a hand through his short hair and frowned at no one in particular. "Your daughter can get herself in trouble faster than anyone I've ever seen. She doesn't even need to try."

Reid sat back and sighed deeply. "As much as I hate to admit it, you've described my daughter fairly well. Tell me what happened. All of it."

Maddox rose and went to a sideboard to pour drinks. He brought back small crystal glasses filled with the potent liquor his son favored and handed one to Nick and Reid before taking his seat again. Nick swirled the drink for a minute watching the amber liquid and then tossed his drink back in one gulp. The only sign of distress he allowed himself was the slight widening of his eyes when the liquid burned all the way down to land in a fiery ball in his stomach. Reid did the same and then slammed his glass on the desk.

"I hear this is much better if sipped," Maddox offered mildly, hiding his grin behind his glass. He ignored their glares and continued to sip his drink.

Nick pinched the bridge of his nose and sighed. "I know Callen has filled you in on some of what happened," he began, and the other two men nodded in agreement. "I went to Lodestone for a business commission. It should have been a quick in, quick out deal with plenty of credits to show for my efforts. A storm was moving in and I needed to get off-world fast or be stuck for the duration. Tru followed me."

The silence was complete by the time he finished. Few questions had interrupted the flow of words. He had to admire their composure given what he'd just told them. Unfortunately, he wasn't feeling as calm. Tru did that to him with little effort on her part.

"You killed the bastard. It was better than he deserved." Reid's voice was strained, its normal, well-modulated tones absent.

"I'd do it again, given the chance."

"Do you think this is connected to Malvin Sonne's death?" Maddox said after a moment's thought. He lifted his glass and took a sip. "We wondered about that at the time."

"Callen believes it might be, and I trust Callen's instincts implicitly." Nick leaned back in his chair and stretched his long legs out in front of him, ankles crossed. It was a deceptive pose; his insides coiled into a tight knot.

"I want Rayven Security to find out what the connection is." Reid pushed out of his chair and crossed the room to the liquor cabinet. He carried the bottle back and refilled their glasses before he eased himself into his seat behind the desk. "I informally hired Callen with the understanding he would run it by you first."

"Callen already has my instructions to follow the lead he has. There is no need for you to hire us." Nick sipped the drink and decided he could get used to the warm burn as it slid down his throat. He planned to ask Reid what the drink was called before he left. "I'm just as eager to see this through as you are. I don't want anyone else coming after Tru."

"Regardless, I feel it necessary to hire you. Creighton Mutual is well known in this system, it can open doors for you and make it easier to get into places you might have difficulty accessing otherwise."

Nick raised his eyes to meet Reid's steady gaze. Maddox might be a force of nature, but Reid was no pushover and his respect for the man rose. A grin kicked up the corner of his mouth. "You do realize Rayven Security is not a detective agency, right?"

"Could have fooled me," Maddox scoffed. "You've done a damn fine job in what you have uncovered so far. Take a chance, boy, and branch out a little. If the rest of your crew is like you and Callen, then you are missing an opportunity here."

After only a moment consideration, Nick spoke. "Fine. We'll take on the job, but we handle it our way. This is outside our normal expertise, but I guarantee we will get you results. I have a vested interest in this."

"Excellent." Reid relaxed in his chair, relief easing some of the lines from his face. "We can work out the details later." In a swift change of subject, he demanded in a hard voice, "Now, what are your intentions toward my daughter? And I'd better like them."

Nick choked on his drink.

Maddox laughed and Reid's lips twitched. Maddox rose from his chair and pounded Nick on the back until he quit gasping for breath.

"Honorable, I assure you," Nick wheezed.

"See that they are."

The three men talked until dusk had given way to full dark. By the time they rose to stretch limbs cramped from sitting too long they were in total accord with one another. Maddox tried to persuade Nick to delay his departure until morning with little success. He was already irritable and on edge just thinking about leaving Tru behind. Staying one minute longer would be torture, particularly with her sleeping in another room and knowing he couldn't touch her. It was better he left before he could change his mind and give in to her desire to go with him.

* * * *

"I wish I could leave with you," Tru murmured against his shirtfront. She was snuggled against him, her arms wrapped around his waist, his encasing her in their warmth. Her family had said their goodbyes moments earlier and then discreetly left them alone.

"I know, sweetheart, but this is the right thing to do. I'll be back before you know it." Nick swallowed a sudden lump in his throat, surprised by the emotions engulfing him now his departure was imminent. "Your father has invited me to the Solstice Ball. I'll be back then for your answer."

Before she could protest one more time, to say she'd already made up her mind, he leaned down and captured her mouth with his. He poured everything he felt into his kiss, alternately coaxing and demanding, delighting in her response. Heartbeat thundering and his breathing ragged, he finally broke away. He forced himself to loosen his hold and take a step back. Unable to resist he dropped one last quick kiss against her swollen lips.

Taking one of her hands in his, he kissed its palm. "Until then," he said and then turned away before he could change his mind. He didn't look back until he was at the transport.

Tru's fingertips rested against her mouth and then she blew him a farewell kiss. He forced a smile before he ducked into the vehicle to go back to his ship. Bereft and second-guessing himself he watched her close the door and disappear from sight. His voice was hoarse when he told his driver it was time to go.

Chapter 25

Nick was in a foul mood and had been since he left Tru. He'd expected it to be difficult, even thought he'd prepared himself for it. Wrong. How could he have anticipated the wrenching sense of loss? He'd forced himself to board his ship all the while fighting an internal battle to turn around and go back. To give in and take what he wanted. Needed. Even now, days later, he still found it hard to take a breath that didn't hurt.

The trip home was interminable.

"Captain, we are on final approach to Alludra. Do you wish for me to alert base?"

Nick jolted. Siren had not spoken beyond an initial greeting since they left Bretonne. He'd been so immersed in his own misery he hadn't noticed until now. Shaken, he cleared his throat before he spoke. "Yes. Notify Seth we will be landing shortly."

"Acknowledged."

The ship broke through the planet's atmosphere, sped through the storm clouds. Rain lashed the viewscreen. Air turbulence rocked *Dominion* as he adjusted trajectory and slowed. Lightening streaked a jagged line through the roiling clouds, followed closely by the boom of thunder.

"Perfect." Sarcasm dripped from the word.

He straightened in his chair, automatically making minor corrections to compensate for the weather. Visibility was poor, making it wiser to rely on the ship's sensors to travel the rest of the way. He landed without mishap and powered the engines down.

The quiet was broken only by the sound of the tempest raging outside, but there was still one thing left to do. One voice left to silence. Ready to send the final sequence of commands to shut Siren down, he hesitated. He curled his fingers into a fist and drew it back to rest against his thigh all the while wondering why he delayed the inevitable. She was a magnificent piece of programming, an integral part of *Dominion*. So why was he feeling guilty all of a sudden? Then it hit him. Siren was a vital part of everything that had happened. She'd started to develop a unique and distinctive personality. She was...more. And therein lay the problem. She *was* Siren.

"Damn. Double damn." He scrubbed a hand over his face.

"Captain, our journey is at an end."

"Yes."

"I have learned much."

"Yes." His throat felt tight and he swallowed heavily.

"We will journey together again. It is all right to send me to sleep." Her voice was a soft sigh.

"I know." He unclenched his fist and sent the final commands. He sat for a moment gazing out the rain-streaked viewscreen before he rose to gather his things.

He was soaked to the skin by the time he reached his front door and stepped inside. He dropped his duffel beside his feet and then ran a hand over his wet face and hair to remove some of the moisture. Water pooled at his feet.

Seth came out of the office and walked toward him, his smile broad and welcoming. "'Bout time you got home, boss man."

Nick grunted. "I'm going to get cleaned up." He hefted his duffel and headed to the stairs. "I expect a status report on Callen and Wulf when I return."

"Sure. No problem."

He ignored the puzzled expression on Seth's face, thinking only of reaching the sanctuary of his room. He needed to get his head on straight before he tackled business and faced the questions he knew were coming.

* * * *

"I had a brief transmission from Wulf several days ago," Seth said when Nick made his appearance. "The connection wasn't good, so I only picked up part of what he was saying. He asked if we knew anything about the drug twist."

Nick's eyebrows shot up. "What the hell?"

"He also mentioned Ice Crystal mining, but I couldn't figure out how it was related and we were cut off before I could ask questions. I haven't been able to reach him since."

"Where you able to find out where he is?"

"Not exactly. I got the impression he was tracking someone and it had to do with the Ambassador and the drug. It didn't make a lot of sense to me, truthfully."

"Keep monitoring. Let me know immediately if he surfaces and needs help. There isn't much we can do until he contacts us again. He's on his own." Nick sat on the nearest chair and drummed his fingers on its arm, his gaze unfocused while he considered what he'd just learned. "What about Callen?"

"He got a lead on Aislinn Thorpe and is on his way to Paladin Minor."

"Isn't that where the Ambassador is from?" Nick quit drumming his fingers. "Mighty big coincidence, don't you think?"

"I heard from Maddox that they found trace elements of twist in Malvin Sonne's body when they did the autopsy. Not enough to be conclusive, but it does raise questions and she was the last one to see him alive. Whatever is going on, Wulf and Callen will handle it."

"Tru's name hasn't come up anywhere has it?" Nick asked, his voice as neutral as he could make it.

"I think she is safe, Nick. I don't believe anyone knew about her other than Anto and Malvin and they are both dead. I'll keep an ear to the ground, but I don't think you need worry."

"Who said I was worried?"

"Look, I don't mean to pry, but what the hell happened between you and Tru? Don't try to give me some bullshit about doing your job either. It is obvious something went on."

Nick rose from his seat to pace the floor. He scrubbed a hand through his hair. "We...I...it's complicated."

"Really? Doesn't seem complicated to me at all. You two are meant for each other."

Nick stopped pacing and a slow grin spread across his face. "Yeah."

"So why are you here and she isn't?"

"Because I'm an idiot, that's why. I wanted to give her time to be sure. What the hell was I thinking?"

Seth smirked. "I guess you will just have to woo her long distance."

"Woo—woo? What the hell kind of word is that?" He scowled.

"You know it isn't as if you two can't talk to each other. Hell, you can see each other when you use the callscreen. It will work out."

"Right. The callscreen. Of course." Ruddy color tinged his cheeks, but he felt much more cheerful all of a sudden.

Seth rose from his seat and slapped Nick on the back. "Now that we have your love life back on track, I have several contracts you need to look over for jobs that came in. We've been getting a lot of inquiries lately and I am not sure how much just the two of us can handle while the others are away."

"We'll manage. I want to run some ideas by you on Siren when we get a chance. Tru had this idea we should give her a holographic image, but I am thinking more along the lines of integrating her into the house first."

"No shit." Seth started to laugh. "That should prove interesting. So, do you want to go over the business opportunities now or—"

"I have something I want to do first. Hold down the fort a little longer, will you?" He had an overwhelming urge to talk to Tru, to see her, to—oh hell, who was he kidding? He missed her.

"Say hello to Tru for me." Seth's chuckle followed him as he headed for the nearest callscreen.

Chapter 26

Maddox greeted Nick with a hearty thump on the back upon his arrival, while Reid gave a more dignified nod. He'd barely noticed, too busy trying to find Tru in the crowd of milling guests dressed in their finest for the Solstice party. He was late arriving because his last job had taken longer than anticipated. He'd pushed his ship hard to arrive before the party ended, knowing she would be waiting.

Impatient to find her, he'd given short answers to her family's questions while he scanned the room. The time apart had been torture for him. Everywhere he'd looked onboard *Dominion*, he'd been haunted by her memory. Every time he glanced at the wrist cuff she gave him, he'd thought about their journey and their time on the space station. He wore it every day. Even Siren had moped, and while part of him marveled she was capable of doing such a thing, he hadn't enjoyed her complaining. He was making progress on giving her a holographic image for no other reason than he knew it would please Tru.

Katri made her way toward them and came to stop beside Reid. She slipped her arm through his and gave Nick a welcoming smile. Some of the tension in his shoulders diminished and returned her smile, bowing politely in greeting. If Tru had decided not to see him, he knew Katri wouldn't be able to hide it. Hope and nerves tangled themselves up, adding to his impatience to find Tru.

"I apologize for my late arrival. I had business on Alludra and it delayed my departure," he said, chafing at the necessity to explain his late arrival.

"We're just glad you were able to make it," she replied.

An awkward silence descended while he searched in vain for something else to say.

Taking pity on him, Reid leaned forward to speak so only he could hear, "She's in the garden waiting for you. It's through those double doors." He indicated the direction with a slight lift of his chin.

A wide grin split Nick's face. "Thank you. If you will excuse me."

He didn't wait around for a reply. It barely registered that people moved out of his way. Heart in his throat, he stepped into the garden and looked around.

Tru sat on a bench bathed in the silvery glow of the moon and his breath caught. She was leaning back, braced by her hands on the bench, eyes closed and her face raised to the star-studded night sky. The ice crystal clips holding her curls away from her face winked in the moonlight. He swallowed and stepped out of the shadows.

* * * *

Tru was not enjoying the party at all. She'd been too busy watching the door for Nick's arrival to waste her time on idle chitchat with guests. As the evening progressed and still no sign of him, her spirits had begun to droop. Doubts and worry had crowded her, made her wonder if he was delayed, injured somehow or had simply changed his mind about his feelings for her. Too nervous to eat, too restless to stay still for long, she'd prowled the party until her mother had sent her outside to the gardens to calm down.

The tinkling sound of the fountain and the delicate scent of flowers drifted on the breeze. Moonlight washed the garden in shades of silver and gray and glistened in the water cascading over the fountain. The family often used the peaceful retreat, but Tru found little peace while pacing the garden paths. Unable to stand it any longer, she'd plopped onto a bench and turned her face to the moon. Closing her eyes, she'd tried to clear her mind and calm her racing heartbeat. He wouldn't fail her, and, if he did, she wouldn't hesitate to hunt him down. He was hers and she was determined he knew it.

A tiny sound, barely discernible over the splashing of water drew her out of her musing. Frowning, she listened harder, afraid to hope. Gravel shifted and her eyes popped open, as her head turned toward the sound.

Nick stepped out of the shadows.

She sucked in a breath then launched herself at his tall, solid form. Strong arms closed around her, lifting her off her feet as he buried his face in the curve of her neck and she breathed easily for the first time since he'd left her behind.

Her world righted itself, and she trembled with relief.

"It is about time you got here, Nick Rayven," she whispered. "I was about to commandeer a ship to come find you."

"I told you I would come back for you, sweetheart. There is nowhere you can go that I will not find you," he replied, his voice gruff. He lowered her to her feet then cupped the sides of her face between his calloused palms. He searched her face for one long moment before he bent his head and kissed her deeply. Tru could do nothing but cling to him and return his kiss with everything she had, everything she felt. Breathless, they pulled apart and he rested his forehead against hers.

"I won't let you leave me again," she said.

"I know." He straightened and then held her gaze with his own. "I don't ever want to be without you. I missed you. I don't think I could survive it a second time."

Taking her hand he led her back to the bench she'd recently vacated. Tru couldn't bear to be out of his arms for a second and nestled against his side. Her head rested on his shoulder, his arm held her close.

Neither heard the crunch of gravel as Reid and Katri entered the garden. Reid cleared his throat to gain their attention before he urged Katri forward to join the couple.

"I see you found her," he greeted them. He waved Nick back to his seat as the younger man started to rise. "No, don't get up. Katri and I are only here for a moment."

Tru knew her smile was blinding with the happiness she was feeling. Her parents drew closer together, a solid unit, and Tru's heart clutched with love for them both. Holding each other's hands, they returned her smile.

"I can only assume congratulations are in order," Reid said. "It seems we will have a wonderful announcement to cap the party. This will certainly set tongues to wagging as word spreads. Nick, my boy, if I know my girls, you are going to be up to your ears in wedding preparations before too long." He raised his brows at Nick before he continued in a warning tone, "There is going to be a wedding, right?"

"Yes, sir." Nick replied without hesitation and grinned at Tru.

"Excellent. Now, before my wife dissolves into a puddle of joyous maternal tears, we will return to the party and leave you two alone. I expect we will make the announcement just before midnight, what do you think, my love?" He patted Katri's hand.

"A wise decision, as always," she replied, taking her eyes off her daughter long enough to smile at her husband.

Reid cleared the tightness from his throat and turned to lead Katri back to the party. "I expect you two to make an appearance long before we reach midnight."

"Of course. Wouldn't miss it," Nick replied, but his gaze locked on Tru. He reached out and caught one of her curls between his fingers.

"See that you don't," Reid warned before he and Katri disappeared around a corner.

Nick had a look in his eyes she recognized and all her thoughts centered on getting him alone.

His voice tender, he said, "I love you, you know. Have I mentioned it yet? I love you."

"I love you, too," she whispered against his mouth in his native language. "I love you, now and always."

He repeated her words, first in Tonlithian then using the language of her world.

Meet the Author

Kylie Wolfe has had a love affair with outer space since she saw the first episode of Star Trek as a kid. It is no surprise that planet hopping and space travel became the landscape for her debut novel.

She is owned by two cats, well fed and cuddly, and as of this printing, she has painted nearly every room in the house some shade of green. She jokes, "Clearly, I am not opposed to living in a leaf."

Secret vice - she feels compelled to sing "On the Road Again" whenever she hits the highway for any road trip that even remotely sounds like fun.

With loving family and good friends to support her, Kylie is ready to see where writing can take her. She invites you to join her in traveling the stars in search of intrigue, adventure, and love.